T0114712

# B-4: SPECIAL AGENT
## "ROOKIE"

# BOOKS BY AUTHORS

Jack McLaughlin

mR. bERZERKELEY: The Naked Mayor
mR. bERZERKELEY II: Big Games, Big Lies, Big Decisions
mR. bERZERKELEY III: Gators, Guns, Goodbyes
NAIVETE: A Parent's Trust Betrayed


Harold Lea brown

Deadly Invisible Enemies: Evil in the Air (Book 1)
Deadly Invisible Enemies: Hunt for Evil (Book 2)
Deadly Invisible Enemies: Evil Resurrection (Book 3)
Destiny of Tar and Feathers: A Harold L. Brown Screenplay

# B-4: SPECIAL AGENT

## "ROOKIE"

JACK MCLAUGHLIN AND
HAROLD LEA BROWN

iUniverse®

**B-4: SPECIAL AGENT**
**"ROOKIE"**

*iUniverse books may be ordered through booksellers or by contacting:*

*iUniverse*
*1663 Liberty Drive*
*Bloomington, IN 47403*
*www.iuniverse.com*
*844-349-9409*

*ISBN: 978-1-6632-5414-6 (sc)*
*ISBN: 978-1-6632-5412-2 (hc)*
*ISBN: 978-1-6632-5415-3 (e)*

*Library of Congress Control Number: 2023911528*

*Print information available on the last page.*

*iUniverse rev. date: 07/20/2023*

# DEDICATION

*To all the mothers and daughters who never say die in the face of adversity, but choose to take action to make our world a better place.*

# ACKNOWLEDGMENT

*Special thanks to Sheryl and Jane for their ongoing support of our creative passion as storytellers, and to Mary Jo McLaughlin for cover artwork.*

# AUTHOR'S BIO

Jack W. McLaughlin
Screenwriter, Author, Executive Producer

After a successful, distinguished, award-winning career as a California School District Superintendent and Nevada State Superintendent, Jack McLaughlin's desire to use his creativity and write stories about mythical characters and fabled stereotypes in the form of books and screenplays was energized by winning film festival recognition and acclaim.

Awards and honors include many official selections at several film festivals, first places including Makeup Man, Best Thriller; King Alphonse, Winner Sci-fi/fantasy; Moonlight Bandit, Best Family/Faith; Three times nominated Best Writer; Double Play and Remembering Sullivan nominated Best Scripts; Sins of Lily Liu Lu, Best Feature; Hog Heaven and Naivete Best Teleplays; Triple Destiny, Best Drama; B-4: Special Agent, Best Teleplay; Please, Santa, Best Teleplay; The King's Crown, Best Screenplay NOVA. Details of Jack's honors and awards are on IMDB.

Jack also wrote the mR. bERZERKELEY Trilogy and Naivete, A Parent's Trust Betrayed.

Jack McLaughlin's stories are unending as is his desire to entertain and provide an enjoyable experience for all those looking for an escape, at least for a few moments.

Jack and Harold were named Co-Writers of the Year at the 2019 Action on Film MegaFest in Las Vegas, and teamed up to write B-4: Special Agent as a novel.

# AUTHOR'S BIO

Harold Lea Brown
Screenwriter, Author, Producer, Publisher

Harold believes that story is life well told and a way to explore the human condition. It has always been a part of who he is—it is in his blood. His family roots are Norwegian and Finnish, where story is core to passing on history to future generations. In his teens, he told story through music when he played in a rock band. Later he told story through award winning poetry and used story as a way of communicating corporate history and vision as a chief business strategist.

After a distinguished thirty-five year career serving in a number of government portfolios in professional, management and executive roles, he refocused his talents on storytelling, evolving into an international award winning screenwriter and author. His story library catalog includes screenplays, miniseries, limited and ongoing series, teleplays and novels which have garnered recognition at more than one hundred film festivals and competitions around the world, including Canada, the United States, Mexico, Spain, Australia, Germany, Sweden, Ireland, The Netherlands,

Indonesia, Italy, India, Romania, United Arab Emirates, United Kingdom, China and Hong Kong. His screenplays/teleplays have received more than seventy awards and a further seventy-nine nominations, and his techno-thriller book series, Deadly Invisible Enemies, has received seven awards.

Harold has also received festival Writer of the Year honors three times, the Aristotle Award For Excellence in Writing and the Melissa Goodman Caregiver Award. He is featured in the "The Top 100 Indie Writers in the World Part 1" by Del Weston and Theresa Weston, and is a recipient of the Mico Award for Innovation, Courage and Excellence in Film Arts and the Producer Emergence Program Gerri Cook Memorial Award for Most Promising Producer and is a producer of television, feature and new media projects.

He gives back to the storytelling community, regularly contributing articles as a senior staff writer, co-sponsoring the annual Young Storyteller Awards at the Action on Film MegaFest, and sponsoring the Harold L. Brown Award of Excellence – 1st Time Writer Award at The Northern Virginia International Film & Music Festival.

Harold teamed up with fellow writer and friend, Jack W. McLaughlin, to write B-4: Special Agent.

For more information about Jack W. McLaughlin and his creative endeavors go to:

http://drjacksscreenplays.com

For more information about Harold Lea Brown and his creative endeavors go to:

www.storychaser.com

# ROOKIE

# CHAPTER 1

Searing heat waves danced across the Nevada desert sand. An oversized off-road Blazer leaped over the top of a sand dune at full speed, sending a blizzard of sand particles into the air before hitting the desert floor with a thump. Its huge tires dug in deep, launching the vehicle forward. It sped straight at two old camouflage-covered military vehicles that were pointing back at the dune. A pair of American flags waved furiously in the sweltering wind.

Almost at the same time, a four-wheel-drive Jeep leaped from the dune's cap at top speed, chasing the Blazer. As the Jeep hit the desert floor and bounced, its driver immediately slammed on the brakes to face off with the two vehicles that were now shielding the Blazer, which had spun around behind them.

Bullets filled the air as eight men in militia garb hiding behind the military vehicles fired automatic weapons relentlessly at the Jeep. In the back seat of the Jeep, ATF Special Agent Bonnie Brown—an athletic, rugged brunette in her twenties nicknamed B-4—held on tightly. The shoulder belt strapping her in caused her large breasts to bulge against her thin blue windbreaker.

B-4 had always loved the chase—the feeling of the wind blowing through her hair, the anticipation of that moment she would draw Johnnson, her large handgun, take aim, and pull the trigger.

Special Agent Suzanne Schietz—a shapely African American and Hispanic mixed woman with black hair in her thirties—sat beside B-4, holding on for dear life. As bullets flew, careening off the Jeep and breaking the windows, they ripped off their seat belts.

"You ready for this, rookie?" Schietz yelled over the deadly, ear-splitting noise.

"Just like back home in Battle Mountain."

In the front of the Jeep, Special Agents Martin and Garcia—men in their fifties and forties, respectively—ducked low as bullets shattered the windshield and sprayed them with splintering glass.

In the distance, two men watched the fierce battle through binoculars. Jose and Manuel stood in silence as they listened to the torrent of bullets strike the Jeep.

"This is what they wanted," Jose said.

Suddenly, through the rapid fire, a constant and sharp *boom* was heard and repeated.

"What?" Manuel said. "Impossible!"

The ATF special agents were out of their Jeep, crouching behind the open doors and returning fire.

Through the hail of bullets, B-4 had begun picking off the shooters one by one. In rapid order, she took down eight men.

The last two scrambled back inside the Blazer, attempting to escape.

Bullets ceased flying as the agents watched the Blazer begin to move. B-4 stood, took aim, and fired. Johnnson's bullets shattered the windshield, striking both men in the head. The Blazer, still running, edged forward slightly. Martin ran to it, pushed the dead driver over, reached in, and removed the keys. Then he stood with his hands on his hips, looking back at B-4.

"That's that! Ten for ten!" B-4 said. She reloaded her revolver.

Weapons raised, the ATF special agents moved cautiously toward the Blazer. Schietz walked up next to B-4 while Martin and Garcia studied the weapons and grenade launchers in the back of the vehicle.

"Nice shooting, rookie. Where did you ever learn ..." Schietz started.

B-4 feigned blowing smoke from the end of her large revolver. "Just like shooting jacks!"


Nevada's Battle Mountain, the self-declared "Armpit of America," off Highway 80 heading east from Reno, was home to the weather-beaten Roadkill Saloon with Lilly's Bordello out the back door. Once inhabited by the Paiute and Shoshone Indians and later by fur trappers, Battle

Mountain's growth spurt had come from gold and copper mines that had long since dried up. Legalized gambling, Lilly's, and the old saloon were reminders of the town's former life.

A battered pickup truck parked in front of the Roadkill backed up and headed down a crumbling asphalt road.

A man named Curley—forty, rugged, and unshaven—drove while the Battle Mountain Boys armed with shotguns rode in the back, along with B-4. Kevin, Karlos, Kermit, Kareem, and Kenny—ages seventeen, eighteen, nineteen, twenty, and twenty-one, respectively—were all sons of the prolific Lilly. Their mother had suffered an untimely death at the hands of several housewives. Their fathers were all unknown.

B-4 polished her shotgun while swaying back and forth as the truck rumbled down the road and bounced over potholes. Except for B-4, everyone wore Stetsons, boots, jeans, and long brown trail coats.

The pickup left the asphalt road and headed through the sage on a dirt road. After a few minutes, the pickup swerved into and over the sage.

B-4 and Kevin stood, leaned over the cab, and rested their elbows on its roof as they held shotguns.

"There!" yelled B-4.

As the pickup sped up and bounced through the sage, throwing up sand and dirt behind it, B-4 aimed her shotgun at a jackrabbit that was bobbing and weaving at full throttle thirty yards away. Her shotgun blast struck the jackrabbit, stopping it dead in its tracks. The pickup threw more sand into the air as it sped toward the fallen creature.

"Great shooting, B-4," Kevin said.

"I never miss. Look!" She pointed at another rabbit. "Your turn."

Kevin struggled to steady his shotgun as the truck bounced across the rough desert. He fired. The blast knocked him back as it launched a spray of lead, missing the jackrabbit, which bobbed and weaved out of sight.

"You gotta know when they are gonna bob and weave!" B-4 yelled.

"You cheat!" Kevin yelled back.

"Ha! It's all in the eyes connecting to my trigger finger. Mama said my father never missed … and neither do I."

# CHAPTER 2

The colorful, lively, entertaining Las Vegas Strip bustled with traffic and tourists. The heat, bright unrelenting sun, and crowds didn't take away from the magnetic draw of the desert of southern Nevada. The Bureau of Alcohol, Tobacco, Firearms, and Explosives was located off the strip on a heavily traveled boulevard.

Inside the ATF western headquarters, forty-year-old Special Agent Silva stared at the outline of a large revolver in the back of B-4's waistband as she entered his office. He stood, brushed a piece of lint off his tailored suit pants, and adjusted his tie knot. He took a deep breath, glanced down at the front of his tie, and pressed it flat against his white shirt.

B-4 made herself comfortable in a chair at a small table as Silva closed the door. He sat on the corner of his desk in front of her. She crossed her arms prepared to defend herself.

"Great shooting on your first assignment, Miss Brown. Better than anyone has ever seen around here, according to the others who were there. In fact, I think Special Agent Martin's exact words were 'almost embarrassing.'"

B-4 took a deep breath and relaxed. "Just doing my job, sir."

"You did stop them." Silva stood and paced the room. "We catch and contain, not kill. You need to see the big picture, Miss Brown. We got the cache of assault rifles and grenade launchers. We are gonna trace them, but we would have liked the chance to interrogate the bad guys."

B-4 started to speak, but Silva was not finished.

"But we can't because they all had their heads blown off by—"

"Me." B-4 straightened up in her chair. "Sorry, sir."

"Yes. You and that cannon." Silva nodded toward her handgun. "That's not standard issue."

"No, sir, but I do have an exemption. It belonged to my … a friend of mine and his father, a former agent."

"Former?" Silva stopped and stood face-to-face with her.

"Yes, sir." B-4 looked into Silva's eyes. "My friend was preparing to be an agent before he died in an explosion. And his father disappeared a while back. It's named after them, Johnnson."

"Agent Johnnson, the Swede. I remember." Silva started to pace again. "Sorry about that, Miss Brown. However, we have good reason to believe two of the men you killed were part of the Castillo Cartel."

"I heard about them in my training."

"Yeah. In addition to his casino and drug empire, he's been supplying weapons to several White supremacist and militia groups and many of our enemies worldwide. Now we have to continue working intel to find more leads, more of his badass guys. It's our job to stop the madness."

"Sorry, sir. Guess I was a little aggressive my first time out. A little different from training."

"Why did you want to become an agent in the first place? To go around killing people or to do what you can do intelligently, bring the bad guys to justice?"

"I guess I just always wanted to be in law enforcement."

B-4 looked off into space as she tried to remember.

The old, battered pickup stopped in front of the Roadkill, sending dirt and dust swirling up toward the sweltering sun. Curley jumped out of the pickup, followed by the Battle Mountain Boys and B-4. She carried a stringer with five dead jackrabbits dangling from it.

They walked inside the Roadkill through a pair of swinging doors. In front of a wall—and several shelves of booze bottles—former San Francisco detective Bobby Brown, B-4's father, wiped down the bar top. He was a rugged man in his seventies. Behind him on the wall hung a gold-framed plague with the inscription "Detective Bobby Brown, Award of Bravery, San Francisco Police Department." His legacy was topped only by that of Harry Callahan—Dirty Harry—and his reputation with the opposite sex had no equal, as his testosterone level overflowed, especially after taking down bad guys.

Bobby's fling with an oversexed streetwalker after a deadly Mafia battle had resulted in B-4, unbeknownst to Bobby at the time, and a trip to be in her life in Battle Mountain almost twenty years later. Also unknown to Bobby, a young girl had been born a couple years earlier whose parentless life had taken a different turn, a turn that led to her becoming the young widowed billionaire JJ Wellington. Bobby had been blessed with both, calling it blind luck many times over, or was he just a lucky drunk? Bonnie had no idea she had a sister.

Playing at an island of colorful slots across the room was thirty-year-old Joseph Benneschott. He was disguised as an old man with a gray beard, a ruffled dark hat, and a loose gray coat. He had quite a story himself. He was born to B-4's mother a couple years before her. After being raised in an orphanage and then trained as an assassin, he eventually found his mother and B-4 and swore to himself to keep B-4 safe after their mother's murder. No one, including Bobby, knew who he was, and he wasn't about to broadcast it. He was B-4's unknown brother, and it had become his mission to protect her when he had found out she was in mortal danger.

Red, white, and blue paper stringers crisscrossed the saloon ceiling. The Battle Mountain Boys walked across the old, slightly warped wooden floor, heading for the slot machines. Curley plopped down on a stool in front of his favorite bar top slot.

B-4 approached Bobby and swung the dead rabbits on top of the bar.

"Don't mess with the customer, boys. Goddammit!" Bobby yelled. "I told the old man he only has ten minutes before the party starts, and he decided to stay, and now I got to clean rabbit shit off the bar."

"Sorry, Daddy."

"Kermit. Time to set up the projector!" Bobby yelled.

"This enough jacks for the party, Daddy?"

"Should be plenty with the others you got yesterday."

Bobby picked up the stringer with one hand and wiped their remains off the bar with the other. "Glad to see you didn't use your friend's revolver this time."

"Yeah, it's not as messy with the heads still attached."

"Yeah. No need to be mopping blood off the floor and delay the celebration. It's just shit, and I can handle that since I get a lot of practice around here."

"I woulda used it and showed off if Scott were here instead of out trying to qualify for special agent training. He said he was gonna show up."

"Scott Johnnson? I want to meet this guy. If he doesn't show, I'll go out, find him, hogtie him, and—"

"Like your old Frisco days when you hogtied Mama?"

"Hogtied her? I think it was the other way around."

Kermit walked up with a Super 8 projector. "Where do you want it, Mr. Brown?"

"Right here. Where I'm wiping." Bobby finished cleaning the bar. "Kevin. Get a white sheet from Lilly's and drape it over the machines, and don't disturb the customer while I clean these jacks."

"You aren't gonna show that old home movie again?" B-4 said.

"It's your official send-off. In a few days, you'll be heading to college to become a cop just like your old man."

"Daddy! You are impossible!"

"That's just what Mama said when I met her at the Gold Spike in North Beach twenty-some years ago."

Kermit slid the projector back and forth on the bar top and finally got it aimed at a spot on the wall large enough to hang a bedsheet.

"You know the drill, Kermit. Set that goddamn thing up right!" Bobby yelled. "We gotta give the future arm of the law a proper send-off. It's what you always wanted to be, isn't it, Bonnie?"

Bobby chuckled as he disappeared into the kitchen.

# CHAPTER 3

I nside Silva's office, B-4 reached behind her back, pulled out the large pistol, and laid it on top of the small table. Silva stopped pacing, reached down to pick it up, and moved it around to different positions until he found one that seemed comfortable.

"Impressive. Very heavy." Silva pointed it at a picture of the president hanging on his office wall. He laid it back down on the table.

The office door opened, and Ruben—a tall, dark, and very handsome young man—entered, followed by Special Agent Salisbury. Salisbury's comb-over could not hide the fact that he was middle-aged, but it provided a bit of a distraction from his ruddy complexion.

"Agent Silva. Good to see you again," Ruben said. As he held out his hand to greet Silva, he spotted B-4. "My God, B-4!" He leaned over and hugged her. "I can't believe it!"

"Special Agents Ruben and Salisbury, I guess you already know Miss Brown?"

"Are you kidding?" Ruben said. "Know her? She's a legend. We were together at the academy. The Canada Border Services Agency was invited to train with ATF. They sent me."

"We're glad you're here to help with the Las Vegas-Canadian connection," Silva said. "We even seem to have some hockey players in Sin City now."

"I see you still have Johnnson," Ruben said.

"Unfortunately, she knows how to use it. Eight dead militia and two dead Castillo cartel thugs later," Silva said.

"Use it? No one ever had a perfect score on the range until she stepped up and *boom, boom, boom!*"

"Luck, just luck," B-4 said.

Agent Schietz walked into the office. "Looks like I'm just in time for the party."

"Agents, this is Special Agent Suzanne Schietz from the San Francisco office," Silva said.

Ruben, Salisbury, and Schietz exchanged handshakes.

"She'll be joining the task force, along with Miss Brown here, or is it …?" Silva asked.

"B-4 is the name we called her at the academy, something we heard she was called back home in the Nevada outback," Ruben said.

Inside the Roadkill, the Battle Mountain Boys sat at the bar with Curley. Benneschott, still disguised as an old man, played slots and watched the activity out of the corner of his eye. Bobby was behind the bar. B-4 was near Bobby, her elbows resting on the bar top. Their eyes were glued to a sound Super 8 film being projected on a soiled white sheet draped over a bank of slot machines.

As the film began to run, there was B-4's mama, a dishwater blond with a large build, huge breasts, and the mouth of a truck driver, as well as Petey, who was in his sixties at the time, unshaven, and wiry. Petey was adjusting a young B-4's white blouse as she hiked her blue slacks up.

"Look! There's Mama, Petey, and B-4!" Kermit yelled.

"I know," Curley said. "I was holding the camera then."

"Yeah, B-4's mama!" Kareem yelled.

"And my dearly departed wife for the night." Bobby groaned. "At least you coulda brought a clean sheet from Lilly's."

"They were all used, what with the Rotary convention in town," Kevin said.

As the film rolled and B-4's figure moved slightly left and right, her mama's voice boomed: "Goddammit, Petey. Hold the fucking camera steady. One of you sonsabitches go and get him a shot of Beam to settle his twitchin'."

9

A few moments later, a man's hand holding a shot glass appeared in the frame. They heard, "Thanks. I needed that." The screen then settled into a steady shot of B-4.

"Curley! Get yer sorry ass off the stool and hold the fucking sticks," Mama's voice shouted from the screen. "Her father's money may have marooned me in this shithole, but this talent show video will be my baby's ticket out."

"Yes, Mama," Curley said. "Can I have one of those shots too?"

"You are all motherfuckers! Bring the goddamn bottle!"

Curley walked up in front of B-4 and downed a shot. "Thanks, Mama. Now, what do I say?"

"Hold the fucking sticks out and say, 'take one,' goddammit! 'Take one!'"

Curley stood in front of the camera and held two sticks out. "Take one. This is take one!'"

"You do not have to repeat it, you fucking imbecile. Come on, honey. At least you know what to say."

Young B-4 wiggled slightly, holding a play pistol by her side. "Hey, all you out there. This is Bonnie, special ... special ... What am I supposed to say?"

"Cut! Cut!" Mama yelled. "Bonnie Brown, special agent."

From the bar, watching the film as it continued to run, Curley leaned toward Bobby. "Special agent. That's what you were going to be, wasn't it, Mr. Brown?"

"Yeah, but the Mafia got in the way."

In the film, Curley held the two sticks in front of a young B-4. "Take two! Take two!"

"Goddammit!" Mama yelled. "Don't repeat!"

"Hey all of you out there. This is Bonnie Brown, secret agent," young B-4 said. She stopped. "Damn, Mama. This is Bonnie Brown ...'"

"Jesus fucking Christ! How many times have we gone over your lines? How can you be a child star and get out of this fucking place if you can't remember your fucking lines? It's special agent. You know, like those bastard ATFers who keep bugging the shit out of me. This is Bonnie Brown, special agent. Try standing a little off-kilter like the sexy pose I showed you, like your worthless father, the goddamn Frisco dick."

The camera frame moved slightly as young B-4 held a play pistol, trying several sexy stances. A hand reached in with another shot of Beam.

"I needed that," Petey said.

The film frame steadied.

"This fucking film is gonna break my liquor budget."

"Mama, can I make a suggestion? It's a little one," Petey said.

"You want another bottle?"

"No, no. It's about her name. I mean, if you want her to be in the movies, she needs something a little more catchy."

"Bonnie Brown is her name, my name. If it's not good enough for those Hollywood pricks—"

"Sorry," Petey said. "But if you want them to even look at this, you need to do something about her name. I mean, Bonnie Brown is a sweet name, like her. But for a movie star, I mean, Bonnie Brown sounds like a Goody Two-shoes, dime a dozen."

"Maybe you're right. Do you have any good suggestions, you piece of shit?"

"Well, if I might be so humble. Knowing she is your daughter, she should take after you."

The camera frame suddenly turned, catching a glimpse of old Benneschott playing the slots, to Mama, zooming in on her voluminous breasts.

Those watching the film, except B-4 and Bobby, yelled in unison, "Mama! There's Mama!"

"The one and only. And just like I remember them," Bobby said.

"And there's that same guy, you know, that customer," Curley said.

Everyone looked over at the slots. Benneschott had disappeared.

"Very strange," Bobby said.

Their eyes returned to the film. A young B-4 stood slightly off-kilter, holding the pistol.

"I think something like Big Boobs Bonnie Brown or B-something or other. Maybe Special Agent Boobs Brown."

Both in the background of the film and live inside the Roadkill, except for B-4 and Bobby, everyone yelled, "Big Boobs Bonnie Brown ... B-4, special agent ... B-4!"

"OK, guys," B-4 said. "You've all seen this damn movie too many times."

As the film continued to roll, they heard Mama say, "There's only one problem, boys. She doesn't have any yet."

The film showed Curley walking to the young B-4, stuffing a red bandanna inside her blouse, and walking away. She shuffled it around slightly.

They heard Mama yell, "You are real pricks! All of you!"

A confident, sexy young Bonnie Brown looked straight into the camera. "This is take three. Hey, all you out there. This is B-4, special agent, telling you to behave or you'll have to deal with me. I can shoot, I can fight, I can drink, and I can swear, and there's no one alive I can't whip."

She pointed the play pistol at the camera and then returned it to her side, standing slightly off-kilter. "You be kind to the young, help the old, and be thankful you don't break any laws and have to deal with me. You don't want any part of what I can do to you. Remember, B-4 loves all good folks and the good old United States of America."

Offscreen, they heard a frustrated Mama say, "My God, boys. We've created a fucking monster."

# CHAPTER 4

A few miles east of the Las Vegas strip, in the direction of Lake Mead and the Hoover Dam, a Spanish-themed compound stood, surrounded by a tall block wall and enclosed by tall ornamental metal gates. The nearest building was a mile away, and the desert's unrelenting heat bounced off the sage and sand.

Inside, floor-to-ceiling windows opened onto a courtyard with a large swimming pool in the middle; on one side of the courtyard was a four-door garage. The backside of the garage had a single garage door that opened onto the desert.

At a round table beside the pool, forty-year-old Castillo, a polished, well-groomed, handsome underworld boss, sat and ate with Manuel and Jose, the men who witnessed B-4's skill as she killed ten men.

"The agents were waiting outside Pioche when Raul and Luis drove by," Jose said.

"We lost a hundred grand and a wealthy customer," Castillo said as he ate a steak.

"We were off-road and spotted them," Manuel said.

"And you didn't warn them?" Castillo asked.

"We did," Jose said. "Raul called the militia, and they decided to lead the agents into an ambush."

"Might have worked except for some chick and her cannon," Manuel said. "Her shooting was badass."

"Never seen anything like it, boss," Jose said. "Our man on the inside said she's fresh out of the academy."

"Any idea how they knew about the delivery in the first place?" Manuel asked.

"I have no idea," Castillo said. "Spread the word to anyone we think might have been told. Time to set a trap. No one betrays me. And call our Canadian suppliers."

"Yes, boss," Jose said.

"I lost two good men." Castillo wiped his face with a napkin. "We take care of whoever ratted me out, and then we take care of that rookie and her cannon."

"*Si!*" Manuel said.

In the middle of the warm day, an unmarked ATF sedan weaved through traffic on the crowded Las Vegas Boulevard. Schietz drove, while B-4 rode along in the passenger seat.

"Been here long?" B-4 asked.

"Long enough to learn I only go inside one of these glittering palaces for dinner and drinks, unless I have a well-heeled sugar daddy in tow. They don't pay me enough to do it alone."

"You learn fast. You discovered where they get the money to build the palaces."

"Well, Bonnie—or should I call you B-4?"

"Call me for one of those drinks you just talked about. Whatever suits you."

"Well, B-4, right now I'm going to find the informant who told me about the cache we found a couple of days ago and see if he has anything new. Promise not to blow this one away?"

"I only use Johnnson on special occasions. Don't worry."

"Certainly adds character to your backside."

"Bad guys usually don't look at that side."

"Well said, B-4, well said."

Schietz looked out the window. "There. The Bellagio. That's where I found him. Let's take a stroll and see if he's there."

"Sounds good. Haven't been here since I left for the academy. Where'd Ruben and Salisbury go?"

"Men's clubs. That one agent, Ruben. You and he …?"

"No chance. Still in shock after watching my friend get destroyed in front of me. Ruben's not bad, though."

"O Canada, he can stand on guard with me!" Schietz sang.

They both laughed.

Schietz waited for the light to change and then turned the sedan into the Bellagio's porte-cochere and headed toward valet. Schietz took a ticket and walked with B-4 to the entrance. Once inside, they walked through the crowded lobby toward the gaming tables. Bells rang. Red lights flashed on the slots, and eager gamblers headed in all directions.

"Who are we looking for?" B-4 asked.

"He was in this area last time. There he is."

Louis, an expensively dressed sixty-year-old African American man with a well-groomed gray goatee, sat at a blackjack table. A barely clad female dealer shuffled a deck of cards. Schietz and B-4 walked to the table and took seats on both sides of him.

"Well, well. Look who came to visit Louis again. The African Queen. And who are you, sweet thing?"

"This is my partner, Bonnie."

The only other player at the table folded and left.

"Welcome, welcome. She with you on the recent raid? Castillo lost two men. Blown to hell, I heard."

"We did confiscate a decent stash of weapons thanks to you," Schietz said.

"Well, that was my one and only contribution. I heard Castillo's very angry and looking for the one who tipped you off. I've got a few years left and more chips to play."

Joseph, a large balding man wearing a dark suit and an earpiece, walked up behind Louis. "You girls bothering our favorite customer?"

"No bother, Joseph. They're friends of mine."

"They're going to have to play or leave the table. House rules."

"Got it," Schietz said. "Need a loan, Bonnie?"

"Got my training pay," B-4 said.

Schietz and B-4 put money on the table. The dealer grabbed the cash and passed them chips.

Louis passed a chip to the large man. "Thank you, Joseph."

"No problem, Louis. Good luck, ladies."

They were dealt in. As they all peeked at their cards, they spoke in low voices.

"Castillo is always up to something," Schietz said. "Anything else coming down we should know about?"

"I told you. No more. It's too dangerous right now."

"Partner, maybe we should get the word out on how we found out about the shipment we busted," Schietz said.

"Now, you wouldn't do that to an old friend, would you? Especially an old friend who helped you?" Louis said.

"An old friend who loves the money we slip him so he can wear expensive suits, visit the best coiffeur on the strip, and drink the finest wines?" Schietz scoffed.

"An old friend who suggests you take your partner to Nellis around eight o'clock tonight and visit the old north hangar." Louis looked around to make sure no one had heard what he said.

"The one where they keep those World War II bombers for the air show?" Schietz asked.

"Sounds like a great night out. Maybe bring a couple of friends along," B-4 said.

"Those planes bring back memories of past glory, don't you think?" Louis said. "And don't forget a bottle of Dom Perignon. Look! Blackjack! You two brought me good luck."

"All you can get, Louis, all you can get," Schietz passed him her chips. B-4 followed Schietz's lead.

Louis stacked the chips. "Bye, ladies."

Schietz and B-4 left the blackjack table and walked through the Bellagio. "I love casinos, don't you?" Schietz asked.

"I was raised in one."

B-4 sat on a barstool at the Roadkill. Bobby stood behind the bar, wiping glasses and putting them on a shelf. Judging by their shouts and banging on the machines, the Battle Mountain Boys were losing at the slots.

"Where's Curley?" B-4 asked.

"He's at Lilly's, sampling the new merchandise from Reno. He'll wear himself out again."

"I sure miss Mama," B-4 said.

"Can't say I do. But there are days I do miss the one night we had together. If she hadn't been murdered by the Angel's son and was still here, I would never have come to the good ol' Roadkill and met you. I do miss Frisco, though."

"I know, Daddy. Back here to raise me. Aren't you worried about the Angel taking revenge on you and the boys for killing Junior and his men?"

"The Angel? I took care of him at the Gold Spike the night I met your mother. He and a few of his thugs."

"Someday you're gonna have to tell me more of your detective stories."

"Maybe when you get a break from college or when I'm passing through Reno on my way back to Frisco." Bobby put the glass he was cleaning on a shelf.

"You're not gonna leave Battle Mountain, are you?"

"The place does grow on you, sorta like a hairy wart or a mole."

The Battle Mountain Boys erupted with yells and screams, pushed one another, and began fighting.

"Dammit. Wish Lilly hadn't been so prolific." Bobby groaned as he reached under the bar and took out a shotgun. He fired it into the ceiling, sending chunks of plaster to the floor. "Knock that shit off! And, boys …"

"We know. Fix the ceiling. Again!" Kevin said.

The back door opened, and Curley slowly walked in. He stopped and looked at everyone. "Did I miss a quake or something?"

"God, I'm going to miss this place! And I'm going to miss the Roadkill." B-4 groaned.

# CHAPTER 5

At a men's club off the strip, erotic music blasted over the speakers, enticing visitors to enter and rousing the customers inside. Ruben and Salisbury sat at a table in front of two naked women making love to glistening bronze poles highlighted by bright, flashing lights.

"There he is," Ruben said.

He motioned toward Enrique, a slight young man standing at the entrance. Enrique grabbed a cold beer and walked toward the dancers. He stopped near their table to watch the girls and appeared to ignore the agents.

"Enrique, my man, how's it hanging?" Ruben asked.

"I see nothing, hear nothing, know nothing," Enrique said.

"Like a monkey," Ruben said. "I get it."

"If I had known you agents were here, I wouldn't be. Anyone sees me with you, I'm history."

"We just thought you might want to earn a little more cash," Ruben said.

"And be unable to spend it because I'd be looking up from the sage with a bullet in my brain. You guys have really pissed off the big man, and I don't want to be seen with you ... ever."

"That bad, eh?" Ruben asked.

"That bad. See you never." Enrique chugged his beer and walked out in a hurry.

Inside ATF headquarters, Schietz and B-4 sat at a table in Silva's office. Ruben and Salisbury entered and slumped into chairs. Silva paced the room.

"Guys. No luck finding any information, I guess," Silva said.

"Our guy is scared to death. Literally," Ruben said.

"The girls had a little better luck," Silva said.

Ruben cupped both hands where his breasts would be if he were a woman. "B-4 use her influencers?"

"Secrets," Schietz said.

"There's something going down at Nellis tonight at eight in the old B-27 hangar, according to their informant," Silva said.

"Wait a minute!" Ruben said. "A drugs and weapons delivery on an air force base? You got to be kidding."

"That's what the informant indicated," B-4 said.

"He was spot-on about the weapons drop, wasn't he?" Silva said.

"I just don't know," Ruben said. "Sounds a little suspicious to me."

"How about Bonnie and I take a little visit inside Nellis, snoop around, and check out the flight logs?" Schietz asked. "See if we can find out if this whole thing is on or not."

"Good plan," Silva said. "If they won't give you any information, we'll have Fireball find out."

"Fireball?" B-4 asked.

"The resident techie geek, little red flair in his black hair," Schietz said. "I'm told he's the best there is."

"Keep us in the loop," Silva said. "If this is real, we need to be there. You boys see what else you can find walking through a casino or two. Maybe we'll get lucky this time. If we don't …"

"Blow them away, I know," B-4 interrupted. "I was taught when I shoot at something to make sure it doesn't shoot back."

"Who taught you that?" Silva asked.

"A San Francisco detective, my good ol' daddy, Bobby Brown." B-4 stood and patted Johnnson, tucked in her backside.

On a blistering hot afternoon, B-4 and Bobby sat in rocking chairs in the shade outside the Roadkill Saloon's back door. It was only a few yards from a pink double-wide that housed Lilly's. B-4 held Johnnson, and Bobby held a Magnum.

"Daddy, thanks for the going-away party." B-4 moved the revolver around in different shooting positions. "I'll miss you."

"You're only in Reno. Not far away."

Bobby reached for a cleaning kit.

"Your friend's Johnnson reminds me a lot of my baby here. Same size, same weight, same power. Only difference is yours holds twice the shells and is a heck of a lot more colorful with that carved handle."

"He called it a Nighthawk. It holds thirteen .40 cartridges and is very valuable. Browning Hi Power, I think."

"I assume your boyfriend knows what it is and how and when to use it."

"Actually, not yet. He needs to do the physical stuff to qualify for training. Then he'll want it back for the range."

"You certainly know how to use it. Blew a few jacks clean apart."

"Did practice with it a few times. Guess shooting is in my blood. Do you remember the last time you fired your Magnum?"

"Actually, I do." Bobby wiped his large revolver with a rag. "It was the night I met your dearly departed mother."

"Mama was there?"

"Oh yes, at the Gold Spike in North Beach, a turn-of-the-century bar and restaurant that was once also a bordello."

Bobby leaned back and looked into the late afternoon sky. "I knew the Angel—Angelo Martinelli, the San Francisco underworld boss known as Mr. Mafia—was pissed. I had just killed several of his men on a big drug bust and shot up a bunch of others. He came looking for me. I visited the Gold Spike every night. It was a well-known fact. I sat at the bar, drinking Patron, while Mama sat at the other end. Two large Italian thugs carrying weapons walked in, followed closely behind by fifty-year-old, balding Angelo Martinelli wearing a tuxedo.

"'I hear you killed four of my best men, Bobby Brown,' an angry Angelo said to me with a dripping Sicilian accent. 'Now it's my turn.' I opened fire from under my right arm through my favorite tweed coat, killing the two thugs. Angelo was stunned. 'Taking turns isn't my style,' I said. Angelo turned and began to run toward the front door. I jumped off my stool, stood, pointed my baby here, and fired, striking him in the back.

"The Angel, blood dripping from his mouth, staggered outside toward a long black stretch limousine parked at the curb. I fired again, and a bullet passed through him and a closed limo window, leaving a spider-web mark. It struck the Angel's wife, killing her instantly. Angelo leaned on the limo and put his hands on a window. His young daughter, Angelanne, was screaming on the other side. She watched in horror as he slid down the side of the car, dead, blood streaking across the splintered glass."

"Whew, Daddy. That's quite a story."

"The look on that young girl's face spoke tons. I never fired it again. That young girl's innocent mother died because I only shoot to kill. That did it to me."

"You quit right there, didn't you?"

"I resigned the next day after spending the night with your mother. She came right to my side after the shooting stopped. I didn't know you were already inside when I put her on the bus to Nevada the next morning. Gave her all the money I had to get her out of town in case others came looking for me and any witnesses."

"I know. Heard it many times. She ran out of bus money right here in good old Battle Mountain, and the rest is history."

"I hope the same thing doesn't happen to you with that big gun." Bobby inserted a cleaning brush into the Magnum's barrel.

"Only jackrabbits, Daddy, and maybe a rattler or two." She reached for his cleaning rag.

"Dang, Bonnie! How could I forget? Now that I think about it, I did use it on that dirty snake in the grass, Junior. You mentioning rattlers jarred my memory."

"He earned it after killing Mama."

"More like deserved. Say, when do I get to meet this Johnnson fellow anyway?"

"One of these days. Soon I hope." B-4 wiped her revolver and then pointed it to the heavens. "Until then … *boom*! And I never miss."

# *CHAPTER 6*

Schietz drove along a two-lane highway north from Las Vegas, while B-4 studied her cell phone.

"I hear the commanding officer is a real hard-ass," Schietz said as she turned the car toward Nellis Air Force Base entrance.

"I'm liking this job more all the time. I've been dealing with buttholes all my life."

Their unmarked ATF sedan pulled up to a gate, where a handsome, buffed, and armed uniformed airman stepped up to the car. The Las Vegas skyline was visible in the distance, shimmering like a mirage in the searing afternoon heat.

"We're here to see the colonel," Schietz said.

"And you are?"

"Special Agents Schietz and Brown."

The airman took their badges and then spoke into a walkie-talkie on his left shoulder. "ATF Special Agents Brown and Schietz here to see the colonel."

They heard a female's voice: "Send them over."

The airman passed the badges back to Schietz. "Straight ahead. Take the second right and then it will be on your right. He may not be available, but you can leave a message."

"Got it," Schietz said.

The sedan moved slowly through the gate.

"B-4, that stud is one for my calendar."

"Ditto!"

They drove inside down a street, turned right, and then stopped. Schietz and B-4 stepped out of the car, walked toward the barracks office, and entered. They stood in front of a counter, behind which a young uniformed African American lady sat. "I'll see if Colonel Jacobs is available." She disappeared around a corner and then returned moments later. "Right this way."

Schietz and B-4 stepped around the counter and walked past the young lady into the office, where the graying, fifty-year-old Colonel Jacobs did not get up from his desk.

"Yes?"

"Can we?" Schietz motioned toward two wooden chairs.

"Sit."

"Agent Brown and I heard from an informant that there may be a shipment tied to a cartel landing here around eight tonight."

"A cartel ... as in drugs? Weapons? Impossible on my base."

"The informant has never led us astray, and he assured us it is going to happen out at the B-27 hangar," Schietz said.

"Impossible!" The disturbed colonel reached for a landline. "Lieutenant. Here. Now."

After a brief moment, thirty-year-old uniformed Lieutenant Jones, sporting a crew cut and an athletic build, hustled into the colonel's office.

"Yes, sir?"

"Lieutenant, these ATF agents say they've been told a cartel is landing an airplane here at eight tonight and heading to the old north hangar. That's not possible ... is it?"

"Well, I will ... My God. B-4, is that you?" the lieutenant asked.

"Lieutenant?" B-4 said. "From Fallon?"

"You two know each other?" the colonel asked, surprised.

"When I was assigned to the Top Gun School in Fallon, once in a while the boys and I would visit Battle Mountain and the Roadkill. We met this young lady there ... She was much younger then. Everyone called her B-4 for reasons we never asked."

"You know what they say, Lieutenant." B-4 smiled. "What happens at the Roadkill stays at the Roadkill."

"Now that you've found an old acquaintance who will remain in the past, what about a civilian airplane at eight tonight?"

"Let me go to my office and check. B-4—"

"And Agent Schietz," Schietz interrupted.

"Right," the lieutenant said as he left.

Once he was out of the room, Colonel Jacobs's voice was no longer commanding. He now sounded almost submissive. "The lieutenant isn't the only one who's visited the Roadkill. In my younger days, a long time ago, I remember there was this foul-mouthed, ruggedly attractive woman who ran the place in between stints inside the pink buildings in back. She didn't have any children, as I recall."

"Mama was her name," B-4 said. "And the whorehouse out back was Lilly's. It's still there."

"I didn't know she had a daughter."

"No worries. I know who my father is."

"I didn't mean …"

"Like I said, what happens there stays where it happened, Colonel. Mama was murdered awhile back."

"My God! I am so sorry."

The lieutenant entered carrying a piece of paper. "Colonel, sir, there's an old prop from the Mexican government landing tonight at eight." He laid a piece of paper in front of Jacobs. "We gave them permission to tie up in the old hangar."

"For what purpose?"

"All it says is 'supplies.'" The lieutenant pointed at the paper. "It was approved by the secretary of defense."

"Our guy was right," Schietz said. "We'll have a few agents greet them, with your permission, of course, Colonel."

"Thank you, Lieutenant," the colonel said.

"Yes, Colonel. B-4, Miss Schietz." The lieutenant saluted and then turned, winked at B-4 out of the colonel's sight, and left the office.

"Thank you for alerting me to this." The colonel pushed back and stood. "And thank you, Miss Brown, for bringing back fond old memories."

"The pleasure was all mine, Colonel."

As Schietz and B-4 exited the barracks office, Schietz shook her head. "You are full of surprises, rookie."

"Oh yeah!"

In the middle of another hot summer day, twenty-year-old Scott Johnnson, his buff frame bulging against his fatigues, walked into the Roadkill and up to the bar where Bobby was wiping up spilled beer.

"You want a drink or just directions to Lilly's out back, soldier?" Bobby asked.

"No, sir," Scott said. "I'm looking for a young lady, Bonnie Brown. She said to come over when I had a day off."

"Well, she doesn't work at Lilly's." Bobby continued wiping the bar top. "Actually, I have been doing my best to keep guys like you away from her."

"Nothing like that, sir. She wanted some information about becoming a special agent. We chat online."

"If you're one of those online predators, you'd better get out of here before I reach under the bar for my shotgun."

"We did meet once, briefly. I gave her my father's weapon for safekeeping."

"That's all? Nothing physical?"

"No, no. I was on my way to the qualifying run and didn't have much time to even have a conversation."

B-4 walked in with the remains of a dead rattler dangling from her right hand.

"Bonnie, you know this guy?"

"He's my friend from Top Gun," B-4 said. "You wanted to meet him."

"You're the Johnnson she talks about? Nice to finally meet you."

They shook hands.

"Want a drink before I take B-4's tasty hors d'oeuvre into the kitchen?"

"Found him hiding in the shade under the truck," B-4 said.

The back door opened, and Curley and the Battle Mountain Boys walked in.

"B-4, is lunch about to served?" Kevin asked as he spotted the rattler.

"That's a snack for me, boys," Bobby said. "Any luck finding a few jacks for the stew?"

"Naw, just a couple of skunks." Kareem held his nose.

B-4 handed the rattler to Bobby and stepped next to Scott. "Guys, this is the pilot I was telling you about."

Bobby walked toward the kitchen, swinging the snake.

"The special agent wannabe?" Kermit asked.

"You're the guy with the big … pistol?" Curley asked.

"Guilty." Scott shrugged.

Bobby stopped swinging the rattlesnake. "And I'm hoping that's all you're guilty of."

"We gonna get to show him B-4's special agent movie?" Kermit asked.

"Oh, hell no." B-4 grabbed Scott's hand. "Let's get out of here."

"Remember what I said about the shotgun, young man," Bobby said.

"Yes, sir. No surprises from me. What film?"

"Come on. Hurry." B-4 dragged Scott toward the saloon door. "That'd be one surprise too many."

# CHAPTER 7

A full moon shone down on Nellis Air Force Base. B-4, Schietz, Ruben, Salisbury, Silva, Martin, and Garcia waited in the shadows cast by the large old hangar that currently stored two B27s for air shows. In the distance, they saw a four-engine prop plane land and begin to approach the hangar.

"Here it comes," Silva said into a walkie-talkie.

B-4 stood next to Ruben and Schietz, holding Johnnson by her side and watching intently.

"There's something wrong," she said.

"What?" Ruben asked.

"If this is some kind of drop, where's the bad guys?" she said loud enough for the others to hear. "There's no one to pick it up."

"Hang tough," Silva said. "Maybe they're just a bit slow showing up."

The cargo plane taxied slowly toward the old hangar and came to a stop thirty yards away. The propellers appeared to spin in reverse as they slowed to a stop.

"Look! Here come the trucks," Silva said, pointing.

In the distance and closing fast were several trucks with no identification on the sides. They approached the rear of the airplane as a backdoor cargo platform lowered from it. The trucks abruptly screeched to a halt. A string of men jumped out and walked directly toward the plane.

"None of them are carrying," B-4 said from the shadows.

"Let's go!" Silva said into his walkie-talkie.

The ATF agents appeared seemingly from nowhere, their weapons poised for kill shots as they surrounded the men. Immediately the men raised their arms high into the air.

"Ruben, Salisbury, get in there and see what they have," Silva yelled.

The two agents ran up the ramp into the plane. They surveyed the cargo with their flashlights.

B-4, Schietz, Martin, Garcia, and Silva held the pick-up men at bay as the search continued. After a few moments, Ruben stepped to the cargo door. "They've got hospital supplies … all hospital supplies."

One of the pick-up men, still with his hands raised, stepped toward Silva. "They are for the Las Vegas hospitals from the president of Mexico, sir."

"Check all the crates," Silva yelled to Ruben and Salisbury. "They've got to be a front."

The pilot, a handsome Mexican wearing a flight suit, waved papers as he appeared and began walking down the cargo platform toward Silva. "Sir, there must be a mistake. It's all in this manifesto."

He showed Silva several pages listing hospital supplies.

Ruben stepped from inside the plane. "We've ripped open several crates, and it appears to be ventilators, masks, gloves … thousands of them."

"Shit! We've been had," an angry Silva said as he slapped one of his legs.

"Guess the informant had it wrong," Schietz said, standing near Silva.

Salisbury walked down the cargo platform. "I guess whoever gave us the information didn't know what he was talking about. Who was it?"

"Louis didn't lead us astray on the weapons," Schietz said. "This is very strange."

"You never know, do you?" Salisbury said.

"I apologize, everyone," Silva said. "Let's go!"

The agents lowered their weapons and walked away.

Looking down upon the old hangar from somewhere far out of sight, Jose and Manuel watched the activity with night vision binoculars and listened through earpieces.

"Guess we know who the informant is," Jose said.

"That fucking Louis," Manuel said.

"There she is," Jose said as he zoomed in on B-4. "Look at the size of that fucking pistol. I think we need to meet her up close and personal."

"Yup. Without that fucking cannon in our faces."

As the agents walked back to their vehicles, Schietz talked to B-4. "I think we should pay a visit to Louis, don't you?

"That and a drink sounds really good right now."

An unmarked ATF sedan pulled into the Bellagio valet. Schietz and B-4 exited and walked toward the entrance. They pushed through a crowded Bellagio and approached the blackjack table where Louis normally sat. They stopped and surveyed the area.

Joseph from security walked up behind them. "Ladies, are you looking to do some gambling tonight?"

"Actually, we're looking for our old friend, Louis ... You remember us?" Schietz said.

"He was here earlier. He left with two men ... And yes, I do."

"Any idea where he went?" B-4 asked.

"Nope. I don't ask questions. I just keep the party going."

"Great," Schietz said. "Thanks."

On their way back to the valet, B-4 and Schietz picked drinks off a barely clad lady's tray as they walked through a row of slot machines.

B-4 slugged back her drink. "Guess we'll have to get an address from the Fireball person."

Schietz downed her drink and looked at a glass wall. "Ever have the feeling you're being watched?" she asked.

"All my life."

In an open Jeep, B-4 and Scott pulled away from the Roadkill, leaving a cloud of dust behind them. The Jeep flew over the cracks and humps of a once-paved road and up onto a highway. A black SUV appeared and pulled behind them a hundred yards away.

Scott looked in the rearview mirror and floored the gas pedal. "Shit!" he said.

"My father and the guys aren't that bad, are they?" B-4 said.

"It's not them." Scott took periodic nervous looks in the mirror. "I've been tailed since I left the base."

B-4 cranked her head around. "The black SUV?"

"Yep. You bring Johnnson?"

"Didn't think we'd need it."

"I have no idea who they are."

"You busted for leaving?"

"I got permission. Could have something to do with my father. He was undercover for years. He got the goods on a major trafficker before he disappeared. These guys are probably after me since they can't find him."

"Is that why he gave you his weapon?"

"Yeah. He wanted no evidence that he still existed and for it to appear that he retired."

"He's not ... dead ... is he?"

"I have no idea. I haven't heard from him in a couple of years."

"I have an idea. Take the next off-ramp and head for the hills. I know a place where we can ditch them."

"Let's do it!"

He turned the Jeep onto an off-ramp and sped down a side road.

"Turn into the sage and go!"

The Jeep four-wheeled, bounced, and twisted through the desert at top speed in the direction of a mountain range, throwing up a cloud of dust and sand at the black SUV, which was in hot pursuit. They reached a canyon.

"Keep going!"

The Jeep raced ahead, moving rapidly between the steep canyon walls. The farther they drove, the narrower the walls became. The Jeep slowed and finally came to a stop, unable to go any farther.

"They won't be able to get through the opening. SUV's too big!" B-4 yelled. "Let's go!"

B-4 jumped over the windshield, and Scott quickly followed.

"The boys and I used to hide here from Mama and smoke joints." She ran through the opening toward a small cave a few yards up on one side of the canyon.

Unable to go any farther, the SUV pulled up behind the Jeep. Two men wearing dark suits climbed out, one carrying a grenade launcher and the other toting a rifle with a scope. They were squeezed between their SUV and the canyon walls as they took aim.

B-4 was a few yards ahead of Scott when she looked back at the men. She spotted the grenade launcher. "Quick! Scott!"

The grenade launcher fired, and the steep walls exploded.

B-4 was thrown into the cave and knocked unconscious.

Hours later, she woke to darkness. She rubbed her sore spots and then peered out from the cave.

"Scott!" she yelled.

He was nowhere to be seen. The SUV was gone, and the Jeep was covered in rocks.

# CHAPTER 8

A n unmarked ATF sedan pulled into the headquarters parking lot. Schietz and B-4 climbed out, and walked inside, and went directly to Fireball's cubicle, where he sat in front of several monitors. B-4 noticed the tiny red flare in his black hair and feigned reaching out to touch it. He was a young Asian man, slight of build and wearing thick horn-rimmed glasses. His fingers flew feverishly across a keyboard, faster than the ladies could think.

"Fireball … we need your help," Schietz said.

"I'm busy at the moment. Trying to trace the weapons you captured the other night."

"Park that."

Fireball swung around to see B-4 for the first time. "Who's this?"

"A rookie agent, B-4."

"I see why the others were talking …" Fireball adjusted his glasses.

"We need to find out where our informant lives," Schietz said. "Name's Louis. No last name."

"This Louis, you sure that's his name?"

"That's what he called himself," Schietz said as she spun his swivel chair so he faced the monitors. "We gave him a pile of money for information last month."

"Probably cash, like always, and untraceable," he said.

"Can you get inside the Bellagio's security system?" Schietz asked. "We saw him at a blackjack table this morning around nine."

"That I can do." His fingers danced across the keyboard, bringing up a video image on one of his screens. "There you are, Schietz, and there's B-4 … I can call you that?"

"Whatever." B-4 leaned forward, her breasts almost touching his shoulder.

"That the guy you're talking to? Let me take a good look."

Fireball punched a few keys, and a facial recognition program flashed up on another monitor. "I'll run a scan against our records database."

Faces flipped up on the screen at high speed and then stopped. "Aha! Julius Washington."

"Text me his address. Come on, B-4. Let's see what he does after midnight."

As they drove to the address Fireball sent them, a full moon shone down on the crowded Las Vegas strip. People were busy talking about their winnings and the live shows they had seen, unaware of the show being delivered by the starry night sky.

"This place never sleeps, does it?" Schietz observed.

"Never," B-4 said. "And neither do I!"


A ragged B-4, clothes torn, staggered into the Roadkill and slumped on a stool at the bar. Bobby appeared from the kitchen. He wiped his hands on his apron. Curley, head down, was snoring on top of his favorite slot at the bar.

"What happened to you? The pilot do this to you? Where's my shotgun?" Bobby demanded. "Curley, wake up!"

"What? Who?" a groggy Curley groaned.

"We were blown up in the canyon by two men chasing him."

"What?" Bobby said.

"We were followed from here. I took Scott to the cave where we used to hide from Mama, and they blew us up. I tried to warn him … but … he's gone. Where's Johnnson? I'm going to go find those bastards."

"Whoa! You're in no condition to do anything."

"I have too. He's … he could be dead or dying."

"It's midnight. Have a couple of Jager shots and get some sleep. We'll go and see what happened in the morning."

"No time to sleep. Those guys need to be dead!"

"There will be another day," Bobby said. "Those guys will be long gone back to wherever they came from."

"I'll never sleep until their heads feel Johnnson's wrath!"

Bobby reached under the counter and took out a box. He opened it to show her Johnnson and four fully loaded clips. "It'll be right here when you're ready. Guess it's yours now."

The unmarked ATF sedan stopped in front of a duplex in a Las Vegas neighborhood. It was the middle of the night. A dark van, lights off, stopped at the curb a hundred yards behind them. Schietz approached the front door and knocked. No answer. She knocked again. She checked the knob. It was unlocked. With flashlights and weapons drawn, she and B-4 walked slowly inside. They moved from room-to-room and stopped in the kitchen. Blood covered the floor, with a trail leading to a side door. Schietz opened the door and looked outside onto an empty driveway.

"He's been taken."

She closed the door, and they put their weapons away. Then they explored the house.

Jose and Manuel, weapons drawn, appeared suddenly.

"You take the rookie back to the boss, and I'll kill the other one," Jose said.

"Not in your lifetime," B-4 said angrily before she coldcocked Manuel, who knocked Schietz down as he fell.

B-4 quickly drew Johnnson from her backside and shot Manuel. The sound of Johnnson's shot rattled the duplex.

Jose, knocked slightly off-balance, turned and ran at full speed out the open front door. B-4 picked Schietz off the floor and then ran after Jose, Schietz following close behind. They looked all around. Jose had disappeared.

"No no no! Jesus, Bonnie. Not another dead one!"

"Some habits are harder to break."

"Where'd you learn to fight like that?"

"Like I said. Mama raised me."

Young B-4 ran into a bedroom and shook a sleeping Mama.

"Mama, Mama, wake up. Bikers are beating up Curley and wrecking the Roadkill."

"Worse than that. Now they woke me up after editing your fucking film all night," Mama grumbled.

She threw back the covers and got out of bed. She put on a robe over her pajamas, grabbed a baseball bat from behind the door, and charged out of the bedroom. Young B-4 followed close behind. Mama burst through the Roadkill's back door. Inside, four bikers were rocking the slots. Two more were slugging Curley behind the bar. They stopped for a moment and looked at bat-wielding Mama. The Battle Mountain Boys all lay on the floor, groaning from their injuries.

"Well, lookie here, boys," one biker said as he stopped slugging Curley. "We've woken a little old lady with a club."

"You woke a grizzly, you fucking pricks," Mama said.

"Boys, show her how we treat a grizzly who threatens us," another biker said.

The four bikers rocking the slots stopped and surrounded Mama. As they stepped forward, ready to strike, she lashed out with vicious swings of the bat, knocking them out one by one. She had a strong right hand and a lethal left leg. As they fell to the wood floor in pain, the two who had been beating Curley dropped him and walked toward her.

"Come to Mama, assholes. I got plenty left for you. And with whatever's left after I deal with you, I'm going to get my shotgun and blow you full of fucking holes."

"No need to dirty up the place anymore, Mama," Curley said from behind the bar. He held up Mama's shotgun. "Your double-barrel's loaded ... one for each."

The two bikers backed off and raised their hands slightly.

Mama glanced around. The Battle Mountain Boys were still shaking off their injuries. Some got to their knees. She turned her attention back to the two bikers still standing.

"You pricks got any money?" she asked. She nodded at the tipped-over slot machines. "Looks like I gotta a few slots needing repair."

"We were just on a fun ride from California and—"

"And decided to tear up my place of business, ruin my saloon. Boys, get up and clean out their pockets. And if we don't find enough money, go out and confiscate their Harleys. They can walk back to fucking California."

"Yes, Mama." Kevin groaned.

"Mama. You going to teach me to fight like you?" B-4 asked.

In the middle of the desert, inside his isolated compound, Castillo sipped a margarita and talked into a speakerphone lying on a glass table. "Jose, let's turn what's left of the informant over to the feds. Christmas will come a little early."

"Right boss," Jose said from behind the wheel of a van. He glanced at the dead informant lying on the floor in back.

"Too bad about Manuel." Castillo took another drink of his margarita.

"I'll be there after I deliver the present, boss."

"You are reading my mind. Leave a little note for the rookie. Then get back here. We'll figure out how to eliminate her." Castillo ended the fall, looked at the margarita, chugged it, and then broke the glass goblet on the table.

Across the desert and on the other side of the city, the van pulled up to the curb in front of ATF headquarters. Jose opened the back doors and pushed Louis's mutilated body out onto the street. He bent down and laid a piece of paper on top of the body. Then he sped away.

In the darkness, in a Jeep a few yards away, Benneschott—now disguised as a woman—watched. After a few minutes, he drove off slowly.

# CHAPTER 9

In the morning, the ATF parking lot was half-full. B-4 parked the unmarked ATF sedan she had been assigned near the entrance. She walked to Silva's open office door, stopped, and sized up the two suits sitting at a table inside.

Silva sat with them. He motioned B-4 in. The two suits politely stood as she entered.

"Miss Brown, thanks for coming in early," Silva said. "These are agents from internal affairs, Agents Smith and Gerard. Have a seat."

Smith and Gerard waited for B-4 to sit and then returned to their seats.

"Heard about your recent actions, Agent Brown," Smith said. "We've been sent by the bureau to clarify matters, especially the complaint filed by a Nevada congressman."

"Complaint? About what?"

"It seems you shot and killed several men without properly identifying yourself as an ATF agent," Smith said. "You also shot and killed three Nevada residents, again without identifying yourself."

"You mean those gunrunners in the desert and the thug who tried to kill me and my partner!"

"You didn't follow proper procedures, Agent Brown," Smith said. "You were taught that at the academy, weren't you?"

"Yes, sir. But let me get this straight. We chase the bad guys through the desert, come to a bunch shooting at us, and we're supposed to identify ourselves before we start shooting back?"

"Did they know who you were?" Smith said. "You hold up your badge or just start shooting?"

"What about the rest of the team? You talk to them?"

"They were here earlier and confirmed no notification was made … by anyone," Silva said. "Agent Schietz is on her way back to San Francisco. Martin and Garcia have been reprimanded."

"Suzanne is gone?"

"Yes," Silva said. "I asked the bureau to keep you here for the moment since you are a rookie and I'm assuming you thought someone else provided the proper identification. Also …"

"With the congressman's complaint …" Smith said.

"Which we take very seriously because he's on the committee who funds the bureau," Gerard said.

"As I started to say, we need to do a full investigation of you and your weapon," Smith continued. "Can we see it, please?"

B-4 reached behind her back, pulled out Johnnson, and handed it butt end first to Gerard.

"The complaint was correct," Gerard said as he held Johnnson. "This certainly isn't standard issue. It's an old Browning Hi Power Nighthawk, a collector's dream."

"Loaded with thirteen .40 S&Ws, ready for bad guys. I was given permission by the academy brass to use it as my field weapon."

"You have that in writing?" Smith asked.

"Nope."

"We'll have to check on that," Gerard said. "In the meantime, stay in touch."

"What? I am suspended?"

The door opened, and Ruben peeked his head in. Salisbury was right behind him.

"Sorry to interrupt, boss," Ruben said.

"I think we're done here," Smith said. He held up Johnnson. "We'll take this with us."

"Agents."

They shook hands.

Ruben and Salisbury stepped aside to let Smith and Gerard pass. B-4 stood and started to follow them out.

"Hold it, Brown," Ruben said. "Take a seat. You'd better stay."

B-4 looked at Silva, who nodded.

Ruben and Salisbury walked into the office and closed the door. Everyone sat down.

"What's up?" Silva said.

"The guy who was dumped last night, the informant? Well, he had this note on his jacket." Ruben passed a plastic bag containing the note to Silva.

"You can take it out. It's been processed," Ruben said. "No prints."

Silva took the bloody piece of paper out and read it aloud: "To the rookie with the big gun. We have a bigger one. Bang. You're dead."

"We need to get B-4 some protection," Ruben said. "Where's Schietz?"

"Gone," B-4 said.

"What?" Ruben said.

"I moved her and the two others involved in the desert shootout. Miss Brown is being suspended, pending an investigation into a congressman's complaint."

"Jeepers, boss. It's Agent Brown, or do you want me out too?" B-4 said sarcastically.

Silva nodded.

"What?" Ruben said. "This is crazy. She just did her job."

"Apparently too much for a certain elected official." Silva took a deep breath.

"My God. Politics!" Ruben said, exasperated. "Whose pocket is he in? Gotta be Castillo."

"Where are you staying?" Silva asked B-4.

"Terrible's for the moment."

"Stay there while we arrange a safe house," Silva said. "I'll have our agents come by regularly to make sure you're OK.

"Just give me back Johnnson, and I'll take care of myself."

"The higher powers already took it with them," Silva replied.

"Politics," B-4 said, scratching her head. "I remember politics. I wonder how whoever wrote that note knows I am a rookie?"


Curley came through the Roadkill's back door, carrying a piece of paper. He strolled up to Mama. She glanced up from polishing the bar top slots.

"Mama, what's this stapled to Lilly's front door?"

"Give me that!" Mama ripped the piece of paper from Curley's outstretched hand. Her eyes scanned the page. "It's a fucking cease and desist order from the goddamn Lander County judge, the do-gooder. What the shit?"

"Which one of the girls has VD this time."

"They were all checked yesterday. They're cleaner than Her Honor, that pissant judge, that's for sure." Mama looked over the order again.

Young B-4 walked through the front door. "What's the matter, Mama?"

"That damn female judge," Mama said angrily. "She's been after me to shut down Lilly's since she was appointed. Still trying to keep her husband home at night. Maybe I should give her a few sex pointers."

"Or maybe one of the girls could give her a private lesson," Curley suggested.

"Politics. It's all politics," Mama said. "I'll show her politics. Where does her husband hang out?"

"He owns Moose's Meat Shop," Curley answered.

"That's right," Mama said as if a lightbulb had suddenly lit up. "Go over there and tell him we'll tell his fucking wife he got one of the girl's pregnant if he can't get her to pull the order."

"You sure that'll work?" Curley said. "He might be happy as hell he's still got it."

"If that doesn't work, tell him I'll neuter him with a pitchfork and ream him with some Vaseline and a cattle prod if he doesn't promise to stay away from Lilly's so she'll let it reopen." Mama jammed a finger into Curley's chest while she ranted.

"Got it."

"Is that how politics works, Mama?" young B-4 asked.

"Bet your sweet behind." Mama went back to polishing the bar top slots.

# CHAPTER 10

Ruben and Salisbury pulled up next to B-4 in the Terrible's parking lot, just as she stepped out of her ATF sedan. Ruben lowered the driver's side window. "Stay in your room. We'll be back later to take you to a safe house."

"I'll be OK." B-4 slammed the side of the car with her fist. "See ya."

Ruben and Salisbury drove off.

B-4 surveyed her surroundings as she walked into the hotel-casino. Once inside, she walked down a long hallway, stopped, and quickly glanced back. She instinctively reached for Johnson. Her trusty gun was not there, something she had always depended on when a hallway door closed behind her.

She refocused and inserted her key card into her room's lock. *Click.* She entered, double-checked the hallway, and closed the door. After a quick scan of the room, she took off her short coat and tossed it onto a chair. She pulled out her cell, hit autodial, and plopped onto the bed.

Bobby answered his phone from his place behind the Roadkill bar.

"Daddy?"

"You haven't forgotten us."

"Never, Daddy."

Curley yelled, "Come to Curley, baby." He was playing his favorite bar top slot. He glanced back at the Battle Mountain Boys. They were stationed at the bank of slot machines.

"Sounds like Curley's on a roll," B-4 said.

"He's always on a roll. Say, we've been trying to follow the Vegas news. What was that editorial about the ATF and a bogus raid? You OK?"

"We were led into a trap. The informant was left dead on our doorstep late last night."

"You're learning," Bobby said. "Some of the bad guys are very smart. They also have allies."

"Tell me about it. I've been suspended in the process of being investigated after a local congressman complained about me for killing a few men in another incident."

"Sounds like good ol' Frisco … me and the Angel. He owned city hall."

"The badasses left a note on the informant's body. They're after 'the rookie,' as in me."

"You blow away a few with Johnnson?"

"Guess I'm just like you and your Magnum, Daddy."

"Yeah, the good old days."

"You are gonna tell me more of those stories, aren't you?"

"In time, in time."

Frustrated, Curley pounded on the bar top slot. "Damn. Guess it's a good time to drain the lizard." He jumped up and headed out the back door.

In B-4's room, there was a loud crash as the door was knocked open and three men wearing hoods rushed inside, pointing automatic weapons.

"Daddy, I guess I have to talk later." She jumped to her feet to defend herself and tossed her cell onto the bed. It bounced to the floor.

"What?" said Bobby, worried.

A hooded assailant threw a rope around B-4, wrapped it around her several times, and threw her to the carpet, dazing her. The assailant searched her for a gun.

"She doesn't have that big gun," he yelled.

"Bonnie … Bonnie, what's happening?" Bobby called out.

A second hooded assailant crushed her cell with his boot heel.

B-4 struggled to get free but was hit hard over the head by a third assailant. She went limp.

"Get her out of here now!" the second assailant yelled.

Outside Terrible's, an unconscious B-4 was tossed into the back of a white van. One of the assailants climbed into the driver's seat. He pulled off his hood and hit autodial on his cell as he started the engine. The others jumped into the van and pulled off their hoods.

"Well …?" Castillo voice said over the van's Bluetooth.

The van's tires squealed on the pavement as they sped out of the parking lot and pulled on to a highway.

"We got her!" the driver said. "She didn't have that fucking big gun."

Castillo sat in a soft chair in front of a floor-to-ceiling window overlooking the Las Vegas Strip, a cell phone pressed to his ear. Jose craned his neck to hear the conversation.

"That's only part of the bargain," Castillo said. "Do what you want to her for killing your comrades, but leave her alive for me. I want the pleasure of witnessing her last breath."

"We're taking her out to the camp," the driver said. "We'll tell you where to bring the money and weapons in exchange."

"Will two days be enough for you to take out your frustrations, so to speak?"

"That'll be enough, but the eight lives she took, our comrades … She deserves to die a horrible death," the driver yelled.

The van sped down the highway.

"Kill her and you won't get the second installment or the weapons."

"Two days. You'd better come through."

"You can threaten the government all you want, but never threaten me. Two days."

Castillo laid the cell phone on a glass table. Jose stepped back, pretending he did not hear the conversation. Castillo turned to him. "When we pick her up, you and the men need to kill them all. No loose ends."

"Yes, boss."

Curley walked through the back door and heard Bobby pounding the bar top in anger.

"What's wrong, boss?"

"Something's happened to Bonnie. She just called and told me she has been suspended, her gun's been taken away, and she's being investigated. Then *boom*, there was a scuffle and her phone went dead."

"Maybe having a wild party in Vegas?" Curley sat and made sure his favorite bar top slot was still intact.

"No, she's in trouble."

"When she got in trouble on that field trip, Mama took care of business. I remember."

"I heard about that. Bank robbers in Elko?"

"Yeah! Lucky B-4 wasn't the one thrown in jail."

A yellow Lander County school bus stopped on Elko's Main Street in front of a museum. Several high school boys and girls got out, including B-4, Kevin, Karlos, and Kermit. Miss Gertrude, a young bone-thin social studies teacher with thick glasses, followed the students off the bus. Before she hit the last step, she started to lecture the group in her high-pitched voice.

"Inside you'll see artifacts from before Nevada became a state." She stopped to survey the group. "Since we have all grade levels here, find the artifacts that might have come from the materials you have been studying."

Several students mimicked her shrill tone and laughed.

Miss Gertrude ignored them. "Bring your sack lunches, and we'll reconvene in the park across the street at noon. And please, you boys and Bonnie, don't wander. Your final grade will be based on the reports you write, not on how well you can imitate your teacher."

Everyone went quiet.

"OK, let's get on with the field trip," Miss Gertrude said.

B-4 raised her hand. "Miss Gertrude?"

Miss Gertrude crossed her arms. "What now, Miss Brown?"

"If I didn't bring a lunch, can I buy something next door at the café?" She rubbed her stomach. "Please?"

"The sign in the window says they only take cash. Mama give you money?" Miss Gertrude asked.

"Yes. The tip you left last night at the Roadkill."

"I thought it was at Lilly's," Kevin said.

A quiet laugh emerged from the rest of the students.

"*Shhh!*" B-4 said.

"Yes, you may. Students, twelve noon sharp!"

The rest of the students rushed to enter the museum. Bonnie, Kevin, Karlos, and Kermit trailed behind.

"I don't have any lunch or money," Kevin said.

"Neither do I," Karlos said.

"Me neither," added Kermit.

"That's OK." B-4 held up an ATM card. "I'll go next door to the bank."

"What are we supposed to find in this smelly shithole?" Kevin asked.

"Thought Mama said to only use the ATM in case of an emergency," Kermit said.

"We got to eat," Karlos said.

"Karlos is right. Besides, we already have the reports written by Kenny and Kareem when they were in high school," B-4 said. "Miss Gertrude won't know the difference."

"All right," the boys said in unison.


Inside the museum, the digital clock on the wall showed 11:30 a.m. B-4 and the boys stood in front of a display portraying an Indian slaying a mountain lion with a spear.

"Guys, it's time." B-4 walked toward the exit. "I'll go next door and get some money, Then let's hit the café."

B-4 danced around sidewalk cracks as she approached the old bank and stopped at an ATM. She inserted her card. It was immediately declined and spit out. She tried again to the same result.

"Shit, Mama."

She walked inside the bank and up to the only teller, an older male with glasses perched on the end of his nose. No one else was in the bank.

"Mama's card was rejected." B-4 slipped the card under the teller's cage window "She let me use it in case I needed money on our field trip."

"Let me look at it, honey." He pulled it close to his spectacles. "You Bonnie Brown?"

"Yes, I am."

"Do you have any identification?"

"Well, no, but I'm seventeen. I have a driver's license."

"That will do." The teller laid the card down.

B-4 pretended to search her pockets and come up empty.

"It's at home."

"Sorry, honey. Can't let you use this." The teller pushed the card back under the window.

"Call Mama. She'll authorize me over the phone."

"I'm sorry, honey. How would I know it's her I'm talking to?"

B-4 and the teller hadn't noticed a young man wearing a bandanna over his face walk in brandishing a pistol. He stepped in behind B-4 and said, "I'd say give her all the money. Now!"

"But …" said a surprised B-4.

"You just set me up." The teller glared at B-4. "You took my attention away from the front door. You must be with—"

"No, I don't even know him."

"All the money!" the robber said emphatically. "And give it to my friend."

The teller began handing over stacks of bills to B-4. With full hands, she turned to the young man. "Here, mister, it's all yours."

"Hang on to it, honey."

"But—"

"Time to get out of here. Let's go!"

The young man ushered B-4 from the bank, down the sidewalk, and past the museum and forced her into a sedan.

The boys were in the museum doorway and watched her pass by. "We'd better call Mama," Kevin said. "That guy had a gun on B-4."

"She certainly was holding a lot of cash … more than we need for lunch," Karlos said.

Moments later inside the Roadkill, Mama answered the telephone. "She did what? You're fucking kidding me, Sheriff. Put one of the boys on."

Outside the bank, the sheriff, a paunchy man in his fifties, handed a cell phone to Kevin. "Mama, this robber took B-4. The bank guy said she was part of the robbery and carried the money for man."

"That motherfucker," Mama yelled angrily.

"The sheriff wants to arrest B-4 and the robber," Kevin said.

"They're all motherfuckers. She would do no such thing. Where is she now?"

"The robber took her away in a car, headed toward Battle Mountain," Kevin said.

"What kinda goddamn car?"

"A blue one."

"Put the fucking sheriff back on, you imbecile."

Trembling, Kevin handed the cell phone to the sheriff.

"Yes?"

"You cocksucker. What kind of car is the prick driving?"

"The kids all say it was a blue sedan, California plates. Probably headed your way."

"Next time you come to Lilly's, I'm gonna cut something off, you bastard, if you lay a hand on my baby."

"Mama, just doing my job. I'm going after him, and her, now."

"Why you mother—"

The line went dead.

Curley, playing his favorite slot, jumped as the bar phone bounced off the wall.

"Curley, get the boys. We're going to the highway to wait for a blue sedan with California plates."

"The robber's got Bonnie?"

"Yep." Mama grabbed her shotgun from beneath the bar. "Gonna show the son of a bitch some fucking Battle Mountain hospitality."

As the old pickup moved onto the highway, Mama sat in the passenger seat, loading shells into her shotgun.

"Can't you drive faster?"

"The speedometer's been broken since you hit it year's back," Curley said. "Don't want to get a speeding ticket."

"The county sheriff couldn't catch a turtle. Floor it!"

Curley punched the pedal to the floor.

Kareem and Kenny sat in the back, each holding on to the truck box with one hand and a shotgun in the other. As the truck raced east on the freeway, everyone watched for signs of B-4. A blue sedan approached.

"Look!" Curley pointed at a sedan flying by.

The blue sedan's brake lights appeared as it quickly slowed and took the off-ramp into Battle Mountain.

"That's the car," Curley said. "It's turning into town."

"Don't just ogle, you asshole. Let's go!" Mama propped her shotgun out the open window.

Curley locked the emergency brakes and spun the truck around.

A cloud of burning rubber washed over them. As it cleared, Momma yelled, "Drive!"

Curley pointed at an oncoming car. Momma banged the dash with her fist. Curley gripped the steering wheel and waited until the car passed. Then he punched the pedal to the floor and sent the truck fishtailing west into Battle Mountain.

They followed the blue sedan through town and stayed back as it slowed and pulled into the Roadkill. Curley pulled the truck up behind the sedan, and the boys jumped out of the truck box, leveling their shotguns at the robber. Mama stepped out and walked up to the sedan. She pointed her shotgun at the robber's head.

"Get your fucking ass out of the car now."

"Mama, his pistol is plastic!" B-4 yelled.

"I don't care. Get your fucking ass out now!"

Curley leaned on the bar top, watching Bobby top off a foamy beer. "That prick was lucky Mama didn't blow his head off first and ask questions later."

"How did they end up at the Roadkill in the first place?"

"B-4 had convinced him to stop for something to eat. She just forgot to tell him it was her home."

"I can see Bonnie doing that."

"There wasn't much of him left when the sheriff arrived."

Bobby shook his head. "Mama … a real piece of work!"

"You going to Vegas?" Curley asked.

Bobby reached under the bar counter and pulled out his Magnum. "And pull a big Mama?"

"The boys and I are up for a road trip."

"Guess we'll have to see." Bobby moved his Magnum around.

# CHAPTER 11

A shapely African American secretary walked into agent Silva's office. "Sir, there's some crazy guy on the phone for you. Said he's Agent Brown's father ... from Battle Mountain."

"Wondered how long it would take the former detective to call."

"Shall I put him off?"

"No. He'll only drive here from Battle Mountain and barge in. He's probably heard about his daughter's suspension and investigation. Put him through."

Silva waited for the call to be connected.

Inside the Roadkill, behind the bar, Bobby waited impatiently on the phone. He glanced at Curley, who was playing his favorite slot machine a few feet away. He started to say something to Curley, but Silva came on the line.

"Hello?" Silva said.

"What has happened to my daughter?"

"Retired Detective Bobby Brown, is it?"

"Retired? I resigned. Where's Bonnie?"

"Well ..."

"What happened? Do I have to come down there and find out myself?"

"She left here this morning after we met with internal affairs. She has been suspended—"

"I know, I know, pending an investigation into the shooting deaths of eight militia and a few others."

"We believe last night's victim was another member of the Castillo cartel. We've also had a very serious complaint from a local congressman."

49

"That's old news. I was talking with her on the phone and heard a loud noise and then her phone went dead. So, like I said, what's happened to my daughter?"

"That's news to me, Mr. Brown. I'll have agents check and get back to you."

"I could—"

"No need to make a special trip from Battle Mountain."

"Right." Bobby looked at his Magnum. "So I'll just wait for your call."

"FYI, Mr. Brown, I was in the Frisco unit a few years back and know about your infamous activities."

"Trying to change the subject, Silva? Forget it. You know I will follow up if anything happens to my daughter, don't you!"

"We're perfectly capable when it comes to protecting our agents, even brand-new ones."

"I sure hope to hell you are right. Call me! Soon!"

Silva walked out of his office into a large open floor of cubicles and went directly to Fireball. "Stop working on locating the weapon's supplier. I need you to locate Agent Brown. She said she was staying at Terrible's."

Ruben walked up as Fireball's fingers danced across a keyboard. "Something happen to B-4?"

"We're checking." Silva's hands rested on the back of Fireball's tall swivel gaming chair. "I just got a call from her father. He said it sounded like something happened while he was on the phone with her."

"Want me and Salisbury to go and make sure she's OK?"

"Wait a minute," a suddenly excited Fireball said. "I'm inside Terrible's security system cameras. Look!"

They huddled behind Fireball as they watched a video of the hallway outside B-4's room. B-4's body was limp as she was carried out with a blanket over her head and her hands tied.

"Fuck!" Silva slapped the top of Fireball's chair. "Keep this information between us. If her father finds out, there'll be another problem."

"Look at the clothes those guys are wearing. Militia, if you ask me," Fireball said.

They all moved closer and studied the replay on the monitor.

"You're right," Ruben said. "I'll bet they're related to the—"

"Eight thugs she killed in the chase," Silva interrupted. "Know where they hang out?"

"Deep desert, I hear," Ruben said. "Very deep. Always on the move."

"You and Salisbury get out there and find them, Agent Brown, now!"

"The militia's probably on someone's land we've already been ordered to stay off, sir," Ruben said.

"I don't care. Find her! They sure as hell found out where she was at and did it quick."

Dust hung in the air as the van carrying B-4 pulled off a single-lane road onto a dirt trail that headed through the desert sage toward a forested grove. The van suddenly veered directly into the desert. Bouncing over tumbleweed bushes and sand hills, it twisted, turned, and spun before stopping in the middle of a grove of scrub trees. After a moment, it moved ahead slowly and parked under a camouflaged covering that hid a large tent containing trucks and Jeeps, all flying American flags.

The van was greeted by Simon, a long gray-bearded sixty-year-old dressed in camouflage. A belt of large shells was draped from his right shoulder across his body.

The assailants jumped out of the van. One threw its back doors open and another pushed B-4's limp body onto the sand.

"There's the little lady. Not much without her big gun," Simon said.

One assailant rolled B-4 over onto her back. "That's not all she has that's big. Maybe we can have a little fun later when she wakes up."

"Why wait 'til then?" another assailant said.

"Tie her to a chair and set her by the fire," Simon commanded. "When she wakes, we'll have a little chat about the men we lost, our comrades and relatives that she murdered."

Two of the assailants dragged B-4 to a beach chair and tied her to it with wire before removing the blanket from her head. She sat limp, unaware she was in front of a glowing firepit.

"Stir the embers and throw on a few more branches," Simon said. "Grab some water. Wake the bitch."

While one assailant tossed branches onto the fire, another poured water from a ten-gallon container into a bucket. Grinning, he dumped it over B-4's head.

Startled, she struggled to open her eyes.

"Hey there, rookie," Simon said with a slight smile. "Welcome to Freedom Rings, the home of our brothers and buddies you slaughtered."

B-4 glared at him and spit in his face.

"This is gonna be real fun, boys." Simon wiped the saliva off his face. "Then we'll feed her to the coyotes and rattlers."

"Castillo said we were to leave her alive for him as part of the deal," one assailant said. "If she's dead, no money and no weapon replacements."

"Might be worth it, getting justice for those she murdered in the name of the law," Simon said.

She struggled to get free. "I'll show you the law."

"Ha!" Simon laughed. "A real spirited one, just like the man on the inside told Castillo. This is gonna be a real pleasure. Welcome to Freedom Rings."

"Been a while since I've fed your kind of prairie oysters to the coyotes."

"Prairie oysters?" Simon said.

"I used to castrate calves and fry their nuts up in butter. Good eating. Human nuts, not so much. I find them a bit dry."

"What the fuck?" Simon said.

"Just saying. The only freedom I'm looking forward to right now is cutting off your shriveled up peanuts and throwing them in that fire."

"Sir, we've got drones in the air," one of the assailants said as he ran to Simon.

"Get back under." Simon pushed the man under the large net. "They'll never find us."

"After I'm through with you motherfuckers, even the coyotes will never find you. They prefer butter on their nuts."

"How can such a young girl have such a foul mouth?" Simon walked closer to B-4.

"You should have met my mama."

Simon hit her over the back of the head and knocked her out.

Mama entered the front doors of Battle Mountain High School and stomped into the principal's office. She approached the school secretary. "I've been summoned by the principal."

"Mrs. Brown?"

"Miss Brown! I took her daddy's name after he dumped me."

"So sorry. Ah … the principal, Mr. Rheault, is waiting for you. Please step inside."

Mama walked past the counter into the office. Principal Rheault, a balding man in his fifties, sat waiting behind his desk. Four walls of glass put him on public display to the world. B-4 sat in a chair to one side.

"Miss Brown, thank you for coming in." The principal stood to greet her. "We have a problem."

"You need more money?" Mama sat down next to B-4. "I gave last month for that fundraiser, and we have a collection jar at Lilly's."

"It's not about that. It's your daughter's choice of words," the principal said as he rubbed his hands together on top of his desk.

"What words?"

"With ladies present, I won't repeat what she called the coach after he called her out at home plate." Beads of sweat appeared on the principal's bald head.

"He's blind, blind as a bat," B-4 said.

"Bat is a bad word?" Mama asked. "I mean, should she have said rodent or worm … insect?"

"He is fucking blind, Mama! I was safe by a mile."

"That was the word she used, the f- word," Principal Rheault said. Sweat was now raining down into his eyes.

"Really? The fuck-word? The word *fuck*. Really?" Mama put her hands together in her lap. "In this day and age, you're worried about the fuck-word?"

"I am going to suspend her for two weeks. We can't have our students using such vulgar language or disrespecting our teachers, or anyone for that matter. You do understand, don't you?"

"What I understand is you're a prick trying to wash my baby's mouth out with soap while you justify a blind motherfucker ruining a perfectly good game of softball."

She motioned to B-4. "Come on, baby. Let's get out of this shithole school. This is going to cost you. She'll be back in two fucking weeks. Lilly's, you … never again. Keep that tiny pecker in your pants, you cocksucking asshole."

# CHAPTER 12

Silva, Ruben, and Salisbury leaned in toward Fireball's computer monitor. "Our drones have covered most of the land declared by the militants as 'their independent state' and come up empty, except for one spot," Fireball said.

They studied the footage. As the drone hovered over a camouflaged area, thermal imaging showed four moving figures and a stationary one. Fireball pointed at the stationary figure. "That's gotta be B-4. It's the only shot I've come up with. I'm thinking it could be her being held captive by four badasses."

"Badasses?" Silva said.

"Sorry, boss. Maybe I'm picking up a few too many bad habits."

"Stop worrying about bad habits. How fucking far?" Silva said.

"I estimate sixty miles, give or take another ten. Deep into the desert. Passed Caliente."

"Give us the coordinates." Silva stepped back to address Ruben and Salisbury. "You boys take off. I'll send Martin and Garcia in the chopper. It'll be dark soon. Fucking find her!"

"Will do," Ruben said.

He and Salisbury started to move toward their cubicles.

"I'll meet you in the car," Salisbury said. "Gotta take a piss."

Castillo picked up a DVD case labeled *Fly Tying Stress Reliever*. He sat on a white couch as he talked on his cell phone. "They think they found the girl?"

He tossed the DVD case back onto the table and shook his head. "Isn't that just great." He continued listening and then said, "Now we got a helicopter problem?"

He ended the call, punched in another number, and picked up the DVD case again while he waited for his call to be answered. Simon picked up. Before he could speak, Castillo said, "They're not fucking around. You've been spotted. Agents are on the way."

"How they coming?"

"They're fucking federal agents. What do you think? A helicopter and a car, you idiot!"

"So we—"

"Get rid of her now!"

"What about—?"

"You still get the money and the weapons."

Castillo tossed his cell phone onto the couch.

"Pricks. Real dumb shits." He took the DVD out of the case. An evil grin stretched across his face. "Nothing like a good fly to catch the big ones."

In the camouflaged area, away from B-4, Simon brought the three assailants together. "The agents are on their way to rescue their pretty 'little' girl."

"Can I have the pleasure of chopping off her head in honor of the others?" one asked.

"Go ahead. Make it quick so we can get out of here. You other two burn the fucking tent. I'm going to load the weapons in the van. Hurry, guys. Time's a-wasting."

The assailant who had spoken set aside his automatic rifle and grabbed a machete. He whacked down a few branches and chopped them up so they would burn faster and hotter. He carried the wood to the firepit in front of B-4 and threw it in, grinning as flames shot up.

Groggy but awake, B-4 watched him.

He picked up the machete and stepped in front of her.

"You know what, asshole?" she said as she looked in his eyes.

"That's your last words?" He raised the machete above his head.

"No," she said calmly. "Peanuts and beach chairs."

"Fuck peanuts," he said.

"You should never tie a hostage to a beach chair."

B-4 stood suddenly, causing the chair seat to collapse. The wire went limp and freed her hands. She stopped the assailant from swinging the machete and knocked him back into the fire. His scream alerted the others. B-4 grabbed the machete and drove it into his belly. She moved quickly and grabbed his rifle. She ran toward the trees.

Bullets whizzed past her head. She froze. Then her primeval instinct kicked in. She spun around and shot the second assailant between the eyes.

Simon grabbed a machine gun, turned it toward B-4, and started firing. The tree she hid behind splintered and turned to sawdust. B-4 scurried for more cover.

Simon and the remaining assailant jumped into the van and took off after her, kicking up a sandstorm in their wake.

B-4 sprinted through the sage and over a small knoll. She spun around and fired her rifle at the van. *Click.* The rifle was empty. Throwing it to the ground, she scrambled over a series of small sand dunes. She spotted a patch of tall bush and hid in it, keeping her eyes on the van as it searched for her.

The sun was disappearing fast. Darkness became her new best friend. The van flew by in a cloud of sand and dust and disappeared over the horizon.

As B-4 caught her breath, she surveyed the desert. A haunting silence filled the air. She was alone. She started walking west into the afterglow of the fading sunset. She had no food or water, but she had escaped.

"Freedom Rings. You bet your sweet ass."


Silva exited his car. The ATF parking lot was empty except for B-4's unmarked ATF sedan. As he walked toward front door, he checked his cell phone for new messages. There were none. Inside, he approached Fireball's cubicle. He could hear the keyboard. He entered the cubicle and saw Fireball working feverishly. Fireball glanced up and pointed at his monitor.

"Been watching that spot. There are two stationary figures. The other three have disappeared."

"Any sign of our guys?"

"The helicopter had to turn back. Instrument problems. They were literally flying in the dark."

"I already know that." Silva put his hands on the back of Fireball's gaming chair and nudged it.

"Ruben and Salisbury have been driving in circles trying to find the area."

"Goddammit!" Silva said. "I hope one of those stationary figures is not Agent Bonnie Brown!"

The office secretary approached Silva.

"Now what?"

"It's the guy from Battle Mountain again."

"Put him through to my office."

Silva left Fireball's cubicle and sat behind his desk. He rocked his chair back and forth in a calming fashion. He grabbed the phone. "Mr. Brown?"

Inside the Roadkill, Bobby was behind the bar, watching the usual customers. Curley hovered above his favorite bar top slot. The Battle Mountain Boys played at a bank of slots. In the corner, Benneschott—disguised as an old man—played a slot as he eavesdropped on the call.

"You got my little girl safe?"

"Not yet. Soon."

"You'd better hope so!" The tone of Bobby's voice hinted at the anger.

"The ATF looks after their own."

"Prove it. Do you or don't you have her? Do you even know where she is?"

"You know we don't normally answer questions from civilians. But, given you're a retired detective, the answer to your first question is no. The answer to your second is—"

"You guys using any technology at all?"

"Thermal imaging has picked up a spot where we think she is or was. We've got two agents searching the area right now."

"In other words, you have no fucking idea where my little girl is."

"Well, that's your opinion, Mr. Brown. I have faith—"

"Faith is a shovel away from the grave. It's not going to find my baby. I guess I'm going on a road trip." Bobby slammed the receiver into the cradle.

Curley and the Battle Mountain Boys perked up at the words *road trip*.

Benneschott stopped playing when he heard about B-4 and the potential mortal danger.

"We on, Mr. Brown?" Curley asked.

The Battle Mountain Boys immediately gathered at the bar.

Bobby reached under the bar, grabbed his Magnum, and held it up. "Grab your guns, boys, and mount up. We're going to Vegas to find Bonnie."

"B-4 here we come." Kevin raised a fist in the air.

"Who's gonna watch the Roadkill and Lilly's?" Curley asked.

Bobby looked around the bar. His eyes landed on the corner slot machine where Benneschott had been playing. He had vanished.

"I'll call JJ."

"You think she'll come?" Curley asked.

"She's from my loins." Bobby grabbed a box of shells. "She'll come or at least she'll send Rosie."

"From DC?" Curley asked.

"She might be rich and famous, but she's my daughter, in spite of me!"

"Does B-4 know she's got a sister?" Curley asked.

"I'm just getting used to having another daughter. As for Bonnie, well, that's a story for another time. Maybe after this whole thing … after we find her …"

"Two daughters you didn't know you even had," Curley said.

"Thank you, Frisco!" Bobby said fondly.


B-4 stumbled through the sage, thankful that the bright moon lit up a trail. She stopped and surveyed the area. She mumbled to herself, "No city lights. No planes. Just like back at Battle Mountain." She shook off the negative thoughts and started walking again.

A rattle sounded from a bush near her feet.

B-4 locked in on a rattler's tail. Its head was raised, ready to strike her leg. She did not flinch. "Food!"

With one swift move, she grabbed the snake behind its head with both hands and twisted it off. She looked up at the stars.

"Thank you, Mama."


Mama was at the wheel of the old, battered pickup. B-4 rode in the passenger seat.

"Where we going, Mama?" B-4 asked.

Mama stared straight ahead. She cranked the steering wheel hard right. Their pickup veered off a one-lane road and headed into the desert, bouncing and kicking up sand and dust.

"Is this some kinda shortcut?" B-4 asked.

"You are gonna have to learn to fucking survive like I did. Can't make it through the system by swearing at your teachers and the fucking principal. You do that and you'll end up in the gutter like a few Roadkill customers."

"I just want to be like you. You use 'fuck' all the time. Why can't I?"

"After your father knocked me up in good old Frisco, I spent my life trying to survive, and surviving meant kissing a few asses and playing the fucking political game." Mama wrestled with the steering wheel, trying to keep the old pickup from flipping. "Of course, that was after I realized that me living, and you being inside of me, meant doing just that."

"So?"

"Look. Once I found my fucking niche, I knew I could get back to being myself. You've got to learn to fucking survive, and there's no better way than spending a few nights in the desert … without any food, water, or whatever."

"Camp out? Is that where we are going? I don't see any sleeping bags, food … water."

"Like I said, you've got to learn on your own. Fend for yourself. I love you dearly, Bonnie, but you have to make it like I did. No money, no food, just my wits and my brains and my fucking determination to survive."

"All of this because I swore at a fucking coach?"

Mama slammed on the brakes. "There you go. This looks like a good place for you to make it on your own."

"We're miles from town. I don't know where I am. How am I going to get back home?"

"Time for you to figure things for yourself. Get out. Now! And leave your fucking backpack in the truck!"

B-4 reluctantly opened the door and climbed down. Standing in the sage, she watched Mama speed off. "She'll be back. Mama won't leave me stranded."

The truck disappeared.

"Mama!" she yelled.

# CHAPTER 13

Nearing midnight, the Las Vegas Strip was bumper-to-bumper with vehicles. Fun-seeking, alcohol-fueled tourists crowded the sidewalks and played an ongoing game of chicken, darting across the street through the heavy traffic. No one seemed worried about breaking the law, living by the motto, "What happens in Vegas, stays in Vegas."

At ATF headquarters, the parking lot was half-full, a likely sign all the night shift agents were out on a call. Inside, Silva stared out his office window at B-4's sedan. Her unmarked car had been moved into a stall marked *ATF Reserved*. Just then, Fireball walked in.

"I've checked the area for miles around with the satellite, and no B-4. The militia's disappeared too." He held up a tablet. "We've got two figures approaching the two stationary figures at the site."

Silva seemed transfixed on B-4's sedan and did not look at Fireball. His cell phone rang. He snapped back to the moment, it grabbed, and put the call on speaker.

"Ruben?" Silva asked.

Ruben was on his cell as he and Salisbury approached an assailant lying dead in a firepit with a machete stuck in his midsection. Several yards away, a second assailant lay dead. Blood oozed from a facial wound where a bullet had entered. "Sir, no B-4. Two of the militia who kidnapped her are dead."

"Fireball just picked you up on satellite."

"See any sign of her anywhere near?" Ruben asked.

Fireball shook his head.

"He can't find anything. You guys might as well come on back. Fireball will continue sweeping the area."

"Real shame," Ruben said. "She could be a very good agent, even with the body count."

"Let's stay positive," Silva said. "We'll find her."

The call ended. Silva set his cell phone down and stared out the window again. He shook his head. "*Sheez!* Two more dead bodies!"

Inside his luxurious private suite at his casino, Castillo stuffed his face with steak and potatoes. Jose entered, sat down, and patiently waited for Castillo to speak. Castillo stared through the glass tabletop at Jose's scuffed shoes.

"You need to do something about those shoes. I've got an image to maintain." He stopped and stuffed a big piece of steak into his mouth.

Jose looked at his shoes. "Occupational hazard these days, boss."

Castillo put his fork down onto his plate. "I'll let it go this time." He wiped his mouth with a napkin and then tossed it down on the table. "We've got some bigger issues. Looks like the militia evaded the feds. Well, at least two of them managed to live after the girl got loose. She escaped into the desert, and they lost her, according to their leader."

"She off another one or two?"

"Yeah! Maybe more. One in a firepit, skewered like a stuck pig."

"Doesn't sound like no rookie, boss." Jose tried to polish one of his shoes on the back of his pant leg.

"In the morning, take a few of the men, find those two militia men in the outback, and get rid of them," Castillo said calmly. "No loose ends."

"Yes, boss. What about her?"

"If she shows up again, we'll do it our way." Castillo grabbed his fork and stabbed the remaining piece of steak on his plate.

"If she isn't killed by snakes or coyotes, boss."

"She can only hope, because if I get her, I'll grind her into pulp." Castillo shoveled the last piece of steak into his mouth.

Under a bright moon, Bobby drove on a rural highway with Curley riding shotgun. The five Battle Mountain Boys sat in the truck box, preparing for some serious business as they loaded their rifles and shotguns.

"You have any idea where she is?" Curley asked.

"Deep in the desert, too many miles to walk from Vegas," Bobby said. "ATF texted me the approximate location. Best I can tell, it's in the middle of—"

Curley stared through the windshield into the desert. "Nowhere."

"'Bout describes it." Bobby yawned.

"This sort of reminds me of us visiting Junior after he murdered Mama," Curley said. "Was the first time you met B-4, wasn't it?"

"Yeah." Bobby yawned again. "The first time I knew she existed. Two unknown daughters. I'm one lucky man."

In the morning, B-4 got out of Curley's truck and walked, ragged and bruised, toward the Roadkill. Curley rushed up beside her and helped her up the steps. B-4 limped inside and up to the bar. Mama glanced up as she stacked glasses.

"You finally made it back home. Guess you won't swear at fucking school anymore."

"Mama, she's beat up, bruises all over … She's been walking all night, and her clothes are almost torn off," Curley said, sounding bothered.

"Teach her to keep her fucking filthy mouth shut, goddammit."

"I think she was …" Curley gulped as he searched for the right word. Then he blurted out, "Molested."

"Raped!" B-4 cried. "Those bastards! They fucking raped me!"

"What! Who?" Mama turned and reached for her shotgun under the bar. "Tell me who so I can blow their fucking heads off."

"I wandered into some ranch late last night, heard something about it being Angel's camp. The men, especially one little guy, tied me down and took turns. I killed one before I snuck out, knocked his dick off with a shovel. I ran like hell through the desert until Curley found me on the highway."

Mama popped the double-barrel shotgun open. Both barrels were loaded. "That's the least of what we're gonna do when we get there. Angel's camp! Tell the boys to grab their shotguns. Let's go!"

"The boys all went to Elko for some parade," Curley said.

"Mama, there's a whole lot of them at that ranch."

"I don't give a sweet fuck. No one treats my little girl like that and lives. No one."

The saloon doors swung open, and Junior, a young Italian man in his twenties, slight and short, walked in with three men. They all carried automatic weapons.

B-4 turned and pointed. "That's him, Mama. That's the little guy and the men who raped me!"

"We're here for the young lady who murdered one of my men," Junior said in a high-pitched, effeminate voice.

"You the bastards who raped my little girl?" Mama pointed her shotgun at the men.

"She's no little girl." Junior looked first at B-4's chest and then at Mama's massive breasts. "Looks like she got the best parts of her mother, assuming you're her mother."

"I am, you motherfucker." Mama aimed the shotgun squarely at Junior's head. "Get out of here now before I show you what her mother feels like doing."

"I don't think that's too wise, do you?" Junior said.

Mama moved from behind the bar, still aiming at Junior's head. She motioned to B-4. "Go! Get out the back door. Now!" She glanced at Curley. "You too, Curley."

Mama squeezed the trigger. At the last moment, she aimed high and fired over the heads of Junior and his men as Curley and B-4 ran out the back door. Once outside, they ran toward Lilly's. They heard one more shotgun blast and several rounds of automatic weapon fire inside the Roadkill ... then nothing. They stopped running.

"B-4, you get inside Lilly's saferoom. I'll wait 'til you're in and then go back to check on Mama."

B-4 rushed inside Lilly's.

Curley crept toward the Roadkill's back door, opened it slightly, and looked inside. Junior and the men had disappeared. Mama lay mortally wounded, her blood pooling on the wooden floor. Curley hurried to her side. Dying, she gasped for air. She strained to talk.

"Did Bonnie escape?"

Curley knelt down and cradled Mama's head. "Yes, Mama. She's safe."

"You gotta call that son of a bitch father of hers. Tell him what happened. He'd fucking better protect her or I'll come back from the dead and haunt the cocksucker forever."

"Take it easy, Mama. We'll get you to the hospital."

"He's a San Francisco cop, that no good motherfucker!" She held onto Curley's shirt. "Kick him once in the dick for me, will ya?"

Mama's eyes closed. Her hand released Curley's shirt and dropped into the pool of blood.

# CHAPTER 14

In the small hours of the morning, the old truck bounced along, tires humming a high-pitch tune that periodically switched to a low hum as they gripped onto repaved road patches. Bobby fought to keep his eyes open as Curley scanned the road ahead of them for wildlife. They had been traveling south on the eastern side of Nevada for hours. "Yeah, you found me in San Francisco at that home for cops they put out to pasture. I remember. I took a bus ride out to Battle Mountain after we spoke."

"You don't have to talk about it, but I thought—" Curley said.

"It's OK. Besides, it keeps me awake." Bobby's eyes seemed to momentarily drift. "I heard about what happened to Bonnie's mother more than a few times."

"What did you think of B-4 when you first met her in the old cemetery?"

Bobby yawned deeply and wiped a few tears from his eyes. "Not the best place to meet, but she was alive. She's very different from my other daughter, JJ." Bobby yawned again. "Reminded me a whole lot of her mother when I first saw her that night at the Gold Spike. Didn't take long for Bonnie and I to discover we had a lot in common."

"Like shooting bad guys? Think she's really doing that now?"

"Yeah, like taking out revenge on Junior and his men for what they did to her and her mother." Bobby cranked the steering wheel hard left and then hard right to miss an animal carcass.

"Like Angelo Martinelli's son got his," Bobby continued. "Didn't know he was related to the Mafia boss I killed a few years earlier until afterward. Coincidences sometimes catch up to you."

"You shot him right in the groin with your Magnum. His balls were never found."

"Yeah, not a good example of a father meeting a daughter for the first time." Bobby glanced over at Curley. "And thanks."

"For what?"

"Not following through on Mama's dying wish."

"You're welcome. Say, you know who that old man is who comes to the Roadkill? I remember seeing him that day at the cemetery."

"I have no idea."

"One minute he's at the Roadkill and the next he's gone. Just like a good woman, just like Mama."

"He's a paying customer. That's all I care about. And you're right about a good woman."

Bobby's cell phone rang. He snatched it up without looking at the display. "Yeah? Who's calling in the middle of the night?"

Inside ATF headquarters, a disheveled Silva sat behind his desk, talking into the speaker phone. The digital clock on the wall behind him read 3:00 a.m. In the background, Silva heard the sound of Bobby's pickup truck tires humming on the rough pavement.

"We got your cell number and figured you'd like an update."

"Yeah. Anything?"

"Our agents located the place where she was taken, and—surprise, surprise—two more dead guys. She's still on the loose somewhere in the desert."

Bobby glanced at Curley and shook his head. "On the loose! Who's the criminal in this story?"

"Sounds like you are on the road. You're not coming this way, are you?"

Bobby cranked the steering wheel hard, swerving to miss a dead rattler. "She's my daughter and I just found her. You can bet your goddamn ass I'm not going to lose her."

"That all sounds good, Mr. Brown, But she's an agent and my responsibility. That's why I'm still here and won't leave until we find her."

"Fuck responsibility. She's mine! So where would you look for her if she were yours?"

"Well …"

"Don't fuck with me."

"The militia east of Vegas took her."

Bobby locked the truck brakes, and it screeched to a stop. "East is where we're heading."

"Please, Mr. Brown, let us handle this."

"I was told that once or twice by my chief in San Francisco."

"Did you ever listen?"

"You've got to be fucking kidding!" Bobby tossed his cell onto the floor in front of Curley. "Goddamn desk jockeys!"

Curley retrieved the cell and put it on the dash.

Inside his casino suite, Castillo sat at a glass-topped table, eating steak and eggs with Jose. He struggled to swallow a big piece of steak.

"You OK, boss?"

Castillo forced the steak down. "You gonna tell me how to eat a fucking steak?"

Jose shook his head.

"Sun's gonna be up soon. Time for you to take the boys and find Simon and that other man, out in Panaca."

Jose wiped his mouth, threw the napkin down, and stood. "Yes, boss. No loose ends."

"And if you see the rookie on the way …"

"Got it. I'll bring her to you."

"If you can. If there's anything left."

"Or …"

"One way or another, bring the body, proof it's her. Something to confirm it's dealt with."

"Check, boss." Jose walked toward the elevator.

B-4 shook off the morning chill as the sky began to lighten. She dropped the rattlesnake's head into a small fire. She watched the snakeskin turn to ash and periodically wiped ashes from her eyes. Breakfast was nearly ready. As she stared into the fire, the snake cooked to medium-rare.

"Good enough." She stomped out the fire and glanced toward the sky. "Thanks, Mama, for showing me how to start a fire without a match."

The smoldering fire embers died one by one.

"Time to move on."

She began walking toward a knoll and stopped when she heard rustling behind her. "What the fuck now?"

She spun around to see a coyote following several yards back. "Great! Another fucking badass."

She kept walking and grabbed a stake that was driven into the ground. "I don't know what you're marking, but I've got a better use for you right now."

She stopped, turned, and threatened the coyote with the pointed stick. The canine seemed to realize she meant business and scurried off.

B-4 started walking again, glancing occasionally at the stick. "Someone's dream out in the middle of nowhere? Well, no time to explore."

She walked up the knoll and looked west. She spotted a glimmer off a metal rooftop as the sun peered over the desert horizon behind her.

"Well, well. Nothing like stroll after breakfast … and some good news."


At daybreak, Bobby pulled the truck to a stop and studied a bullet-hole riddled sign for Panaca and remnants of an arrow. He steered the truck onto a highway.

"What say, Curley? Time for a little breakfast? The boys still sleeping?"

Curley looked back at the truck box. The five Battle Mountain Boys were fast asleep, hugging their shotguns and rifles. "Oh yeah. They got slots out here? That'll wake 'em."

"It's fucking Nevada, isn't it?"

"Yes, it sure is."

The old pickup rolled down the worn paved road into the town of Panaca and approached a small general store.

"Might have food at that place." Curley pointed at the three pickup trucks and a white van parked in front.

Bobby pulled the truck to a stop across the street and turned off the engine. Curley jumped out and tried to remove the creases from his jeans. Bobby followed. He banged the side of the truck box.

"OK, boys. Time to rise and shine."

The boys stirred and wiped the crusty remains of sleep from their eyes.

"We're burning precious daylight," Bobby said.

The boys pushed their guns aside, stood, stretched, and then jumped out of the truck box.

Bobby and Curley walked inside the general store. They immediately spotted Simon and the remaining assailant sitting around a wood-burning stove with four other men.

A bearded man stood and greeted them. "Sorry, guys, we're closed."

"We're just looking for a little food," Bobby said. "We've been on the road all night."

Kevin entered and glanced around. "Hey, where's the slots?"

"We don't allow the sin of gambling in Panaca," the bearded man answered.

"What kind of shithole is this, anyway?" Kevin said.

The men slid their chairs back and stood. Some reached for their holstered weapons.

"Whoa, whoa!" Bobby said. "We just want something to eat."

"You have to go to Pioche. Just down the road, Mr. …?" Simon started.

"A mister you don't want to know," Bobby snarled back. "We're pretty hungry and thirsty. You do have something to drink here, don't you?"

"You know, I'm looking for a few good men to help me take down the government. They control too much of our lives." Simon stepped toward Bobby. "You and your men join me and you'll get all the food and drink you want, along with the best firearms money can buy."

"Thanks for the offer, but we're on our own mission. We'll mosey on and hit … What's the town?"

"Pioche, just down the road."

"Great. Sorry to cause you any trouble. Come on, boys. Curley. Pioche it is."

Bobby, Curley, and the Battle Mountain Boys left the general store and headed for the pickup. The boys climbed into the truck box, and Curley and Bobby got into the front seats.

"You know, Curley …" Bobby picked-up his cell phone and dialed.

"What, boss?"

"Agent Silva please," Bobby said into the phone when the call was answered.

The secretary buzzed Silva. "It's the guy from Battle Mountain again."

Silva stared out into the AFT parking lot as he rubbed his neck. "Put him through."

"Silva, that really you?" Bobby asked. "You sound tired."

"Mr. Brown. On your way back to Battle Mountain?"

"You have footage of the vehicle involved in the kidnapping of my daughter?"

"Sure do."

"Any chance you know what the vehicle looked like?"

"It was a white van. Why?"

"License plate?"

"Wait a minute." Silva turned to his computer monitor. "Give me a second." He navigated to the related file folder and opened it. He studied a photo. "FUSA."

"FUSA, got it. Makes sense." Bobby looked at the white van parked in front of the general store. "Thanks."

"Where are you? Do you see the van?"

The line went dead.

"Shit." Silva slammed the phone onto his desk.

Bobby reached for the glove box.

"What's up, Mr. Brown?" Curley asked.

"That's the van used to kidnap Bonnie."

"We gonna go back in and kill them all?"

"No." Bobby reached for his Magnum. "Suddenly, I ain't hungry no more. We're gonna wait and follow them. Tell the boys we're gonna find out where B-4 is or else."

"Like I said before, just like going after Junior!"

"Yep!"


B-4 glanced up at the midmorning sun as she walked to the large Butler building she had seen in the distance. She approached what appeared to be the front door and knocked. After a few seconds with no answer, she turned a doorknob and pulled it open. She walked inside to discover three bearded men pointing automatic weapons at her. Behind them were rows of marijuana plants with artificial lights hanging above them. Huge fans with blades the size of airplane propellers blew, rippling a large Canadian flag in the distance.

"Well, well, my Canadian brethren," one of the men said. "Lookie here. Our prayers have been answered ... again."

# CHAPTER 15

B-4 stared into the faces of the three bearded men and then looked down the barrels of the automatic weapons they had pointed at her. Suddenly, a big electric motor started and the roof peeled back, letting direct sunlight in to supplement the artificial lights.

"Welcome to heaven on Earth. Solar panels to power us and direct sun to accelerate the bounty God's blessed us with," one bearded man said.

As the sun beamed in, B-4 glanced out of the corner of her eye at the enclosed hockey-rink-sized pot factory. She refocused on the faces of the three bearded men and their rifles.

"Now, where was I? Oh, yes. You lost your way, young lady?" the spokesman for the group asked.

"By the looks of this, I'm in Canada."

"This is Canadian land, so declared by us," another man said.

"She's dropped in from heaven, brothers," the third said. "God has taken care of us again."

"I see another custom chewie coming," the third man added as he licked at his beard.

"Whoa, whoa! I'm just looking for a telephone. You got one I can borrow?" B-4 paused. She glanced at the marijuana crop again. "A chewie? Like a pot chewie?"

"Our specialty," the third man said with a smile.

"Honey, you hungry?" the first man asked. "Might as well eat first, eh?"

"Actually, I just had a little something a couple of hours ago." B-4 was getting a little suspicious of what she gotten herself into. Her eyes searched the area for any sign of a phone. "I really need to make a call."

"We can't have that," the second man said. "You see, we are humble servants of God and Canada. To the rest of the world, we don't exist."

B-4 slowly surveyed the maturing plants. "Looks like you've got quite a bit of existence in here. I see a lot of plants growing and a lot boxes over there marked 'chewies.'"

An automated watering system started dispensing water to the base of the plants.

"Flood irrigation. Impressive," B-4 remarked.

"You've seen this before?" the first man asked.

"Gets water directly to the roots, reduces mildew," B-4 said.

"We do produce a lot of things to make people happy, help them sleep, cure whatever pain they have," the third man said. "We simply use what God has given us in service to the needs of other Canadians."

"Maybe you could simply tell me where we are for starters?"

"Like I said … Canada. Just a little further south," a second man said.

"Yeah. South Canada." The third man chuckled.

"Well, I thought I was in Nevada." B-4 turned and headed for the door.

"Where do you think you're going, eh?" the first man said as he blocked her exit. "Haven't had a visitor in while."

"Especially someone who looks like you," the second man added.

"And smells like you," the third man said with a smile.

"Well, boys, this visitor doesn't want to hurt anyone." B-4 leaned on one foot, ready to walk around the man blocking the exit. "Let me go, and I will continue on my way west."

"I don't think that would be too smart, do you, brethren?" said the man blocking her exit. He looked up at the open sky in the center of the large room. "I mean, God has sent her to be with us. To be a part of the good we do for our fellow Canucks."

"Don't forget our other customers," the second man said.

"Right," the blocker said. "Besides …"

"She might tell someone about us and ruin the health foods we send to our friends and families up north," the third man said.

"Look, I'm in no mood to bust you. I just need to get back to Vegas."

"Bust us?" said the man blocking her exit.

B-4 knew she had probably revealed too much, but she had his attention. He looked concerned.

"You with the police or something, eh?" he continued.

"I'm an ATF agent. Well, a suspended ATF agent."

"You the ATF agent we heard about who escaped from that militia?" the second man asked.

"She's trying to get back to civilization. Then they'll all come after us," the third man said.

"She's not from God!" the man blocking her exit said as he raised his rifle. "She's sent by the devil!"

In one quick move, B-4 grabbed the blocker's rifle and threw him to the ground in front of her. "Like I said, I don't want to hurt you. Move away from that door and I'll be on my way."

"You're evil," the man on the ground said. "There's no way God will let you interfere with our mission. You can't hurt us."

"Get out of my way or I will do more than hurt you."

A fourth bearded man leaped out from behind the plants and clubbed B-4 on the head with a piece of pipe. Unconscious, she dropped to the dirt floor.

"Brothers, we'd better tie this devil up," first man said as he got to his knees.

"And prepare her," the third man said. "I believe her fertilizer will grow a good chewie. Better than the last couple of visitors."

"We taught those guys," the second man said. "No way they were gonna turn us in either."

"Like the good book says," the third man said, "you wicked person, you will surely die."

"And return to provide comfort to others," they all said in unison.

Silva exited a car in the ATF parking lot. He walked past B-4's unmarked car, tapping it three times as if for good look. Once inside the building, he stopped at Fireball's cubicle. As usual, Fireball's fingers were dancing across the keyboard. Periodically his monitor responded, spewing out text and images.

"You still here?"

"You know me. B-4's missing. No rest until we find her."

"So … have you found anything, anything at all?"

"No. Been monitoring the airwaves and satellites. Sent the drones up now that it's daylight. Nothing so far."

"Any more contact with her father?"

"I pinged his cell, and he's way out there in Pioche or Panaca. I lost his signal. He hasn't moved back into range."

"Why don't you go home, take a shower, eat, and then come back?" Silva feigned smelling his own armpits. "I did." He sniffed at them again. "Should've changed the shirt, but at least I'm awake."

"Maybe later. I also looked into those weapons and launchers the team captured. Another load from Canada."

"Let's let Ruben contact his Canada Border Services Agency buddies in Quebec," Silva said just as Ruben walked into the cubicle.

"Already have. I figured those weapons and launchers were more of the same. They want us to send them serial numbers and photos. They're after whoever is making them. Any news on B-4?"

"Nothing. Fireball can fill you in."

"Her father?"

"Who knows? He's out there somewhere in the desert, according to Fireball."

"Like father, like daughter."

"I sure hope not. He's a real piece of work. Some real legendary Frisco stories about him."


In broad daylight at the San Francisco wharf, a large truck stopped beside a warehouse adjacent to a docked yacht. The name "Angelanne" was clearly visible in gold lettering on its stern.

Four men appeared and walked quickly down the gangway. They greeted two men exiting the truck. After a brief exchange, the four men began unloading crates from the back of the truck and carrying them onboard the yacht.

From the shadows, several San Francisco police emerged holding automatic weapons. The captain, a graying middle-aged man, led the police team. Bobby, his Magnum at his side, stood next to him.

"San Francisco Police," the captain yelled. "You are under arrest."

The men dropped the crates, pulled out their weapons, and began firing. The police took cover and fired back. Bobby fired his Magnum and began killing men.

Men on the yacht threw the tie-downs overboard, and the yacht slowly started to move away from the dock. The men onshore who had not been killed tried to surrender as Bobby kept picking them off one by one.

"Stop firing!" the captain yelled at Bobby. "They've surrendered."

"Not all of them." Bobby switched his aim to the men on the yacht.

"Let them go!" the captain yelled.

"The yacht is getting away," Bobby said.

"We'll call the coast guard," the captain said. "They'll pick them up, along with the drugs."

"Not on my watch" Bobby fired three more booming shots.

A fiery explosion sent flames high into the air. Pieces of the expensive yacht flew in all directions.

"No! No!" the captain yelled. "There goes the evidence."

"That was one of the Mafia's yachts."

"Damn it, Bobby."

"I owe Angelo Martinelli one," Bobby said.

"You're nothing but trouble, Brown!"

"Yeah." Bobby reloaded his Magnum. "Ain't that the truth."

"He'll come after you for sure, along with his friend, the mayor."

"They know where they can find me."

# CHAPTER 16

B-4 lay on her back, unconscious and bound, near a large drain in a blood-stained cement floor just off the pot factory's grow room. A few feet away stood a woodchipper stained dark red. Empty blood-stained buckets were stacked to the ceiling off to one side.

"Think we killed her, eh?" the first man asked.

"Naw, not yet," the fourth man who had struck B-4 said as he looked down. "Those big tits keep moving up and down."

"Looks like she needs a bath, brethren," the third man said and threw water on her.

B-4 stirred and opened her eyes.

"See!" the fourth man said. "Miss Evil is not dead. She'll make the plants grow real good and make a great chewie. The best, eh?"

"How about we name the chewie, the Big Tits Special?" the first man said.

"A bestseller, eh?" the second man laughed.

B-4 glanced at the bloody machine, the bloody floor, and the stack of bloody buckets. "So what's this really all about? You guys some sort of crazy cult?" She hoped that was not the case. "This some sort of joke the ATF is putting me through, like an initiation or something?"

"You're gonna be initiated all right, into the best chewie we've made in a long time," the third man said.

"Let me get this straight. Somehow you're gonna turn me into some little piece of pot? Come on. This is some sort of macabre joke. Agent Silva's found me and is making me pay for killing all those men. Tell me the truth. I've heard about ATF rookie pranks before. I confess! I shot them all."

"Nice try, miss," the first man said. "See that machine against the wall? You ever watch that movie Fargo? We are gonna stuff you in and turn you into fertilizer. Enough for a few rows of plants. After a few months of growth, we will harvest you and make some of the best chewies on the planet. At least in Canada. It'll be a bestseller."

"It'll make you very proud to know you made a whole lot of our customers high and happy," the third man said. "You want them to sleep, be pain free, don't you? We have all the ingredients."

"You guys are sicker than I thought." B-4 tried to free herself from the wire around her wrists.

A loud knock came on the front door. All four men left the killing room and moved toward it. The first man opened it slightly.

It was Joseph Benneschott. Not wearing a disguise, he looked to be in his thirties. He was dressed in walking shorts, a short-sleeve Hawaiian shirt, and hiking boots.

"Hey, you guys see my girlfriend? We were just riding around on my ATV over there." He pointed at a chromed ATV with oversize tires and large overhead lights. "She went to take a leak while I rode around a little and then she just disappeared."

"We're always looking for young girls," the first man said. "Sorry."

"Strange. This is the only possible place she could have gone. There's nothing else around here. Can I come in and look around?"

The man opened the door all the way to reveal the second and third men holding rifles. "Come on in, son. We need more fertilizer and another special chewie anyway."

Benneschott strolled inside, not taking his eyes off the men.

"Let's throw him in with her, call the boss, and then get them ready," the second man said. "What do you think? Maybe a chewie for Hawaiian immigrants."

Benneschott held his hands up as the door closed behind him. "So you *do* have her."

"Ready to be processed and fed to our beautiful children in here to make a super chewie," first man said. "Are you her guardian angel? The Bible said a lot about you."

Benneschott studied the rows of marijuana plants. "That it does, that it does. Pot farmers, eh? Looks like pretty good stuff."

"Our Canadian brethren love it, especially our custom chewies," the third man said.

"Thought it was legal in Canada. Why hide down here?"

"Not what we're delivering," the first man said. "Besides, the government takes more than its share. And, most importantly, our custom chewies are very popular."

"Interesting. Then I suppose when I kill the three of you—"

The fourth man stepped from the rows of plants. "Don't forget me." He whacked Benneschott over the head with a pipe, knocking him to the dirt floor.

"Take her guardian angel into the killing room to be with her," the fourth man said. "Might as well do them at the same time."

"Don't we have to call the boss in Quebec?" the second man asked.

"I will while you take him," the fourth man said. He kicked Benneschott slightly in the ribs to make sure he was out.

The second and third men carried a limp Benneschott into the killing room and dropped him next to B-4. They tied his hands and feet and left.

Next to the large growing area, the fourth man was on his cell.

"Reverend Rudolph? Another heathen entered our sacred building. He's the young girl's guardian angel."

Reverend Rudolf, a man in his fifties, was working out at the gym when the call came through on his cell phone. It was the middle of the day on Saint Pierre and Miquelon, a French territory situated in the Atlantic Ocean near the Canadian provinces of Newfoundland and Labrador. The downtown streets of the capital city of Saint-Pierre were bustling.

"Two for the price of one. Who is he?" the reverend asked.

"We have no idea, sir," the fourth man said. "He just appeared looking for the young girl who came to us from heaven earlier. She said she's an ATF agent, and he lied about trying to find her. He is wearing a Hawaiian shirt and has a nice ATV parked outside."

"You don't have enough new plants to grow with these two, do you?" the reverend asked, puffing slightly from the exertion of his workout. "He might be excess."

"He is a good-looking chap. Muscular, young," the fourth man said.

"Well …"

"The chewies we made last time took a lot more to make them respectable, if you know what I mean," the fourth man said. "He might give the plants the spark they need."

"What about her? Any redeeming qualities?"  ·

"She's special," the fourth man said. "Sweet looking but strong! She'll be the unique ingredient we've been looking for. And her big tits … *bazzoom!*"

"Go ahead then. Do 'em both." The reverend puffed, visibly pushing beyond his limits. "If there's excess, there's always the coyotes."

"Yes, Reverend, and bless you," the fourth man said.

"Bless you and the brethren." The reverend ended the call and reached for a towel.

Inside the killing room, Benneschott lay on the floor next to B-4. She sat up.

"You OK?" Benneschott asked.

"You're tied up and lying on a bloody floor and you're asking if I'm OK?" B-4 tried to free herself.

"Well?"

"Again, let's see: tied up and in front of a machine that is going to shred me into fertilizer for their plants and then turn me into a special pot treat for Canadians. Other than that …"

"Relax. I have everything under control."

"That's what Mama said when we were facing a huge mountain lion in the hills outside Battle Mountain."

Mama and young B-4 sat on beach chairs in front of a blazing fire. Two trout on metal skewers cooked over the dancing flames. The night was unusually dark and cool. The flickering flames lit their faces.

"That's how you do it, Bonnie. Catch the fucking trout, descale them, pull the goddamn guts out, and shove sticks up their asses." Mama turned the skewers over. "Turn 'em a few times and then eat 'em like candy."

"I'll try, Mama. Is that what movie stars do?"

"When they see what a star you are after that fucking movie I made, you'll have a whole bunch of others catch fish and fricassee them for you. You won't have time. You'll be drinking Dom Pérignon. Even have someone else wipe your ass. Ha! My baby, the fucking star."

"I want to be a detective like you say Daddy was."

"That worthless horny fucking cop? No, honey, don't you ever be like him. Look at me. He had his way with me after building up his testosterone shooting that fucking Mafia guy and *boom*! The next day I'm out in nowhere Nevada."

"You always told me he was the bravest, strongest, nicest man you ever met."

"I must've been drinking ouzo." Mama reached for a pint of whiskey. "That Greek shit drives me fruitcakes."

"So he was the only one?"

"I was no saint." Mama took a swig of whiskey. "There were a few others, but no one gave me what I always wanted—a beautiful daughter."

"You had other … children?"

"There was one more when I was young, but he was a boy, and they took him away." Mama stared into the fire and then took another gulp of whiskey.

There was a rustling noise in the darkness. They turned and saw the burning, piercing eyes of a large mountain lion. The reflection of the fire danced in his eyes.

"Mama! A mountain lion."

"I can smell the motherfucker, Bonnie."

Logs on the fire popped, sending a few embers into the air. Mama turned to look at the fire. "Just keep doing what you are doing and pay him no attention. When the time is right, I'll take care of the bastard. Relax. I have everything under control."

"It's going to kill us."

The mountain lion crouched and licked its whiskers, ready to strike.

"Almost time, Bonnie, almost. Stay still."

"OK, Mama, but I'm afraid."

"They smell afraid."

The mountain lion opened its mouth wide and swirled its tongue around its razor-sharp teeth.

"Did it lick its chops yet?"

"Yes, Mama."

"Then it's fucking time." Mama grabbed a skewer with a fish on it, turned, and pushed it in the animal's face. "You want it, you big overgrown pussy? Eat this and get the fuck out of my sight."

The mountain lion growled, grabbed the skewer in its mouth, and darted away into the darkness.

Mama watched and then sat down. "Hungry son of a bitch. That's all he really wanted. Just like a man."

"We still have one left, Mama."

Mama rubbed some dirt off the top of the whiskey bottle. "You eat it. I'll get my fucking calories the usual way."

"Will it be back?"

"If it comes back, I'll use my knife and have a new fur coat." Mama took a big gulp of whiskey.

"Yes, Mama." Young B-4 reached for the second skewer.

"Told you I had everything under control."

# CHAPTER 17

Benneschott lay on the floor beside B-4. "What would Mama do in a situation like this?"

"She would've untied her hands."

"Like this?" Benneschott held up his free hands.

"How?"

Benneschott untied B-4's hands and feet. "Never mind. Just pretend you're still tied up when they come back."

B-4 loosely put the wire back around her feet and hands.

"And then what?"

"She'd wait until the right moment ..."

The four men walked in.

"And then ..."

B-4 leaped to her feet, followed by Benneschott. They both kicked, slugged, and threw the men to the bloody floor. They continued to kick them silly.

"... she'd kick the hell out of them until they were out cold." B-4 delivered a strong right kick.

Benneschott stood over the dazed men. "I love Mama."

"Let's get out of here!" B-4 yelled.

They hurried through the marijuana plants. Just before they exited, Benneschott stopped. He slid open the sole of one of his hiking boots and pulled out several small discs. He threw them into the plants.

"Let's get the hell out of here!" Benneschott shouted, and they ran toward the entrance.

Once outside, they sprinted to the ATV, climbed on, and sped off.

The fourth man appeared at the door, talking groggily on a cell. "They took off on the ATV!"

As the ATV flew across the desert sand, Benneschott pulled out a remote and pressed the button. Instantly, the pot factory was engulfed in an inferno. The man standing in the entrance was killed by the blast and thrown twenty yards.

"Who are you?" B-4 screamed over the sound of the ATV engine as it sped through the sage.

"Like those Bible-thumpers said: I'm your guardian angel," Benneschott yelled. "Go south to the road … the desert road … Acts 8:26."

"You a preacher?"

"Sometimes, sometimes. I'll get you to a road and then you can get back to Vegas."

"How do you know that's where I want to go?"

"Guardian angel, remember?" Benneschott glanced at B-4 and then behind the ATV. It was throwing up dirt, sand, and a cloud of dust as they sped away.

Curley and Bobby sat in their old pickup across from the general store in Panaca. The Battle Mountain Boys squirmed in the pickup truck box, nudging and poking each other.

"The boys are restless," Curley said. "They're probably starved, and I know they gotta pee because I do."

"I have no idea what those militia are doing that is taking this long," Bobby said. "Must be recruiting pretty damn hard or figuring out how to overthrow the whole planet."

Two black SUVs approached and pulled in front of the store. Six men carrying automatic weapons jumped out and walked inside.

"Holy shit," Curley said as he squirmed to sit upright. "That's pretty damn good recruiting. We don't have that kinda firepower."

In a matter of seconds, the general store exploded with gunfire. Seconds later, the men who'd walked in moments before walked out without their weapons, climbed back into their SUVs, and sped away in a cloud of dust and burning rubber.

"What are we gonna do, Mr. Brown?"

"Let's wait a bit, then go inside and see if any of those militia survived. We gotta find Bonnie."

Inside his luxurious casino suite, Castillo sat at the glass table, eating a steak sandwich and fries. His cell phone rang. He tried to swallow a piece of meat. His cell rang again. He managed to swallow and answered. "So, were we successful, Jose?"

"Done, boss," Jose said over Bluetooth as he drove an SUV with two men inside.

"Any sign of the fucking rookie?" Castillo grabbed a fry off his plate and chewed on it.

"None. Before I blew Simon away, he said she escaped and disappeared into the desert."

Silence reigned as Castillo took the last fry off his plate and ate it.

"Boss?"

"She may eventually make her way back to civilization," Castillo said. He thought about his next move. "I'll see what our guy on the inside knows."

"Let me know. Maybe we can pick her up on the way back."

Bobby opened his door and checked his Magnum for shells. "Let's go inside. You and the boys better bring your shotguns just in case."

Everyone exited the pickup and walked across the road to the small general store. They entered and saw the devastation caused by the hundreds of rounds of bullets. Simon and the other men lay in pools of blood. Automatic weapons were scattered across the floor. Embers from the potbelly stove were strewn around, ready to set the place ablaze.

"Better get our butts out of here," Bobby said.

Curley began pissing on the embers. Everyone turned to look at him.

"Why not?" Curley said. "After all, we are volunteer firemen back in Battle Mountain."

"What do you say, boys?" Bobby unzipped his fly.

All the boys unbuttoned in unison and pissed on the embers.

"Now, can we get the fuck out of here before the whole place burns to the ground?" Bobby said as he zipped up.

As they walked outside, they were confronted by the Lincoln County sheriff—a man in his forties with bulging muscles. A posse of men in uniforms stood behind their vehicles, their weapons pointed at Bobby and the boys.

"Lay down your weapons!" the sheriff yelled. "Raise your hands slowly."

Curley and the Battle Mountain Boys laid down their shotguns and raised their hands. Bobby tucked his Magnum into his belt. The sheriff and other uniformed men walked toward them with their weapons aimed, ready to shoot.

"Why are you doing this, sheriff?" Bobby asked. "We haven't done anything wrong."

"We have reports that the general store was just shot up by a bunch of armed men."

"In two black SUVs. Do we look like we have an SUV? That old piece of shit truck over there is ours."

"You all stay right here. I'm going inside."

"From what we just saw, it's getting ready to burn to the ground."

"I'm going in anyhow." The sheriff pulled out a bandanna and used it to cover his mouth. He walked into the building as smoke was just starting to pour out. A moment later, he exited carrying an AK-47. He walked up to Bobby.

"What in the hell are you cowboys doing here? This weapon is worth more than your old pickup."

"Looking for my little girl. She was kidnapped in Vegas by the militia."

"You mean Simon? The guy who owns that white van over there?"

"Most likely. Daughter's an ATF agent working out of Vegas."

"ATF? Let me give them a call. In the meantime, you all should move back before this place blows."

"Won't there be a fire brigade of some kind on the way?"

"You're looking at the fire department," the sheriff said. "This place has been an eyesore for a long time."

"What about the dead bodies in there?"

"We'll sort their ashes out later. Now if you'll excuse me."

The sheriff walked to his car and talked into a radio. After a moment, he walked back to Bobby. "Agent Silva said we are to send you guys back to Battle Mountain. He also said you are Bobby Brown, formerly of San Francisco."

"Yeah, that's me."

"I remember reading about you and that Mafia guy. That the gun you used." He nodded at the Magnum in Bobby's belt. "That the gun that killed him?"

"Yep. Only use it on special occasions."

"Like going after the people who kidnapped your daughter, Mama's daughter?"

"You've been to Battle Mountain."

"She was one of a kind. Her daughter take after her?"

"Mostly. Once in a while I see a little of me."

"Nice meeting you, Bobby Brown." The sheriff stuck out a hand to shake. "See you next time I'm up north."

After they shook, the sheriff and his men walked to their vehicles. Bobby, Curley, and the Battle Mountain Boys watched. Just as they turned back toward the general store, there was a flash. Flames licked up the side of a store wall. Then a loud explosion rocked the ground. A rush of heat whooshed over them. They seemed unfazed.

"I saw some candy bars in there," Kevin said. "Can I get 'em before they totally melt?"

"Nope. No time for s'mores now. Let's hit the road. We'll find somewhere to grab a bite."

"We didn't pass any cafés on the way here," Curley said.

Bobby walked to the pickup and then turned to Curley. "Later, Curley. There'll be plenty on the way."

"But—"

"Fuck Battle Mountain. Fuck the sheriff. I have to find Bonnie. We're going to Las Vegas."

Benneschott's ATV bounced across the desert. As they approached a two-lane road, he brought it to a stop.

"You eaten anything?" he asked.

"Nothing since a rattler a few hours back."

"Come on." Benneschott revved the engine. "There's this little shithole I know outside Caliente. We'll eat and then you can hitch a ride. Besides, I need gas."

"Yes, my guardian angel."

Out in the middle of nowhere, the ATV pulled up in front of a derelict building with a dangling sign that read, Drop Inn Gas/Café/?

"Very creative," B-4 said. "Wonder what the question mark stands for."

"You? Someone from Battle Mountain! You really have to ask that out here?" Benneschott laughed.

"You're right. Sort of sounds like the Roadkill minus the gas."

They stepped off the ATV.

"You go inside and get a table while I fill up."

B-4 entered. Her ATF training had honed her attention to detail, and she immediately noted there were ten empty tables. Gina, a waitress in her fifties with large breasts held high by a cinched-up red strap, approached. Her rippled stomach was exposed just above the tight short shorts she wore. Her high-heeled boots clomped on the wooden floor.

"At least I know what the question mark stands for," B-4 said to herself.

"What'll it be? Drink, food, me? I go both ways."

"My friend and I are famished. What's on the menu?"

"Besides me, the house special is all anyone ever wants."

"A couple specials. Food, that is," Benneschott said as he walked in.

"Sit anywhere. Gina will find you."

"Yes, ma'am," Benneschott said.

"Madame Gina, that's me." Gina swaggered off. "I shall return."

B-4 surveyed the room, which was filled with flags, banners, and pictures. She spotted a Canadian banner over a stack of round tins. "Looks like our chewie friends have been here."

Benneschott walked up behind B-4 and took a chair. "Chewies fertilized by some of her other customers, I would guess."

"Who and what are you really, guardian angel? I saw the guns you have and know you just don't carry explosive devices around when you are out for a spin on your ATV. Which side of the law are you on?"

"Somethings are better left unsaid." Benneschott reached out to touch B-4's hands. "Let's just enjoy whatever she brings us, and I will make sure you get safely to a place where you can get back to Vegas."

"And how do you know I want to go back to Vegas? I could've been kidnapped in Los Angeles, San Francisco … anywhere."

"But it was in Vegas, wasn't it?"

"Yes." B-4 pulled her hands away from his. "But how did you know?"

The front door swung open, and Jose walked in, followed by six men.

"Just a quick bathroom break while I refuel," Jose said. "No sampling Gina today."

Jose moved to a table, sat, and acknowledged B-4 and Benneschott. "Great day for a ride in the desert."

"Check," Benneschott said.

Gina walked through a door. "Jose, my old friend. You sure you don't want Gina today or something not quite as special?"

"My guys are using your facilities … if you don't mind."

"Gina never minded before. Why now?"

"We'll be on our way back to Vegas, sweet thing. Maybe next time we'll stay a little longer."

"You leave Gina a tip?"

Jose pulled out a roll of cash and handed her a bill. "Will this do?"

Gina put the bills between her breasts. "Say hi to the boss for me." She strutted away.

"He's going to Vegas," B-4 whispered. "Maybe my ride."

"Not a good idea," Benneschott whispered back.

The six men appeared from the washroom. Jose stood. They began to walk out.

"Enjoy your meal," Jose said.

"Will do," Benneschott said. "Travel safe."

Jose nodded as he walked outside. As Jose and the men piled into their SUVs, Jose's cell rang. He quickly answered. "Yes, boss?"

Castillo sat on the white couch in his luxurious suite. A large full margarita goblet was in front of him. "Our Canadian friend said one of his producers was just beaten up by a man and a woman. They left on an ATV somewhere outside Caliente. His description sounds like our favorite escaped rookie."

Jose looked at Benneschott's ATV parked nearby. "What? An ATV? A man and a woman … her?"

"I lost contact with the guy. Sounded like a big explosion. They might be near you somewhere."

Jose motioned through the SUV window to his men. "Boys, back inside and get them."

Jose and his men jumped out, handguns drawn. They walked quickly toward the front door and barged inside. It was empty. Gina entered, carrying two steaming plates of food. "Where'd my customers go? These are my specials. A little snake, some coyote, and rabbit sprinkled with fresh chewies!"

They looked out a café window and spotted Benneschott's ATV heading into the desert at top speed.

"Who's gonna pay for these?"

Jose rushed toward the door.

"You want these specials to go?"

"No time today, Gina."

# CHAPTER 18

Agent Silva sat at his desk. Dejected, he stared out at B-4's empty car in the ATF parking lot. Ruben and Salisbury walked in, sat, and waited for Silva to speak.

"No luck?" Ruben asked.

"None. Just a trail of dead bodies."

"She's still alive," Ruben said, offering hope.

"Oh, she's out there doing her thing and still alive. Five dead guys in Panaca, including two militia. The local sheriff said they found Bobby Brown and six others carrying shotguns and standing outside a burning building. Also appears that a pot factory's been blown to bits with four more dead bodies. My guess is she walked through the desert, ended up at the pot factory, did them all in, and is still on the loose. At least, I'm hoping to have it confirmed that one of those dead bodies is not hers."

Salisbury's cell rang. He walked toward the door. "Excuse me. Gotta take this." He quickly left.

"Sounds like we have to find her before the whole countryside is destroyed," Ruben said. "What about her father?"

"The Lincoln County sheriff sent them back to Battle Mountain. You two get into the helicopter and check out the pot factory. Take Fireball with you."

"OK," Ruben said. "B-4 on the loose is not a good thing."

"Shades of her father's past?" Silva took a deep breath and stared off into space.

The San Francisco police, wearing vests and with weapons drawn, approached an old building on the wharf. The captain glanced at his watch. It was noon.

"ATF intelligence said Angel's men have enough explosives in there to blow up most of the wharf and knock down a few buildings on the Embarcadero."

"Maybe we should throw in a match." Bobby held his Magnum at his side.

"That is usually your solution to everything: kill them all."

"Saves a lot in lawyers and prisons."

"Seriously, go around to the ocean side and take a look. See what we are up against."

"Any of those ATF bastards going to help?"

"They're letting us take the lead ..."

"And all the risk."

"Go!" the captain commanded.

Bobby, Magnum drawn, walked to the corner of a building and down the side toward the waterfront. Almost at the next corner, he looked through a window.

"I count ten heavily armed men and several crates marked 'Dog Food' behind them," Bobby said into a walkie-talkie.

"Don't do anything stupid," the captain said.

"I'll distract them."

"No!" The captain seemed worried that Bobby was going to do something he shouldn't. "Don't you dare, Brown."

Bobby walked around the corner and headed for an open bay. Once in the open, he stood slightly off-kilter and held his Magnum behind his right leg. The men he'd seen turned suddenly and pointed weapons at him. "You boys seen my lost dog running around here? He's a German shepherd with a red collar."

"What the fuck?" one of the men answered.

"I suggest if you do see him, give him some of that dog food you have in those crates."

"Mister, get the fuck out of here," the man said. "Now!"

"You know, maybe I should just blow a hole in one of those crates and open it for you ... maybe make it easier."

"You are stupid!" The man raised his weapon. "Maybe I should blow a hole in you."

"Now, that wouldn't be very nice to a dog owner, would it?"

Bobby raised his Magnum and shot at one of the crates that was set apart from the others. It caused a massive explosion and knocked all the men to the cement floor.

At the other side of the building, the police rushed in. Bobby approached them. "Guess the ATF intelligence was wrong about the explosion."

"Goddammit, Brown," the captain said angrily. "You could have blown up the whole wharf."

"But I didn't, did I?"

"And there's no way the ATF is gonna take your application now. They'll never make you a special agent."

"Just like life. Shit happens. Guess you're stuck with me."

# CHAPTER 19

Bobby's pickup moved on a two-lane road toward Caliente and Las Vegas. His cell phone rang, and he answered. "JJ?" JJ Wellington, a tall, blond, athletic man in his thirties, was inside the Roadkill with Rosie, an African American woman who was not to be messed with. She was six foot five and at least three hundred pounds.

"Father? I flew Rosie out here to take care of the Roadkill. What is that place next door? A bordello?"

"Hi, JJ. Thanks for helping me out. I was in a real bind. Good guess, by the way. The place out back *is* a bordello. The girls usually take care of themselves. Please have Rosie just keep the peace until we get back."

"You taking care of my half sis?"

"Trying to find her now."

"If you need any money …"

"I know, you're a—"

"A billionaire widow. So?"

"I'm still a bit overwhelmed at finding you after all these years."

"Now you have two daughters."

"Yeah, and I don't want to lose one … or both. Go back to DC and take care of that great grandson."

"Yes, Father! Rosie can handle anything anyone can throw her way, even in Battle Mountain."

"I believe it. Travel safe."

"You too, Father."

Bobby handed his cell phone to Curley.

"Must be nice … two beautiful daughters," Curley said.

"Yeah. I was lucky at one thing in my Frisco days."

Curley pointed ahead to a shack in the middle of the desert. "There's a place to eat."

"The Drop Inn. Looks like our kinda place."

"Gas/café/? Reminds me a lot of Battle Mountain, especially the question mark," Curley said.

They pulled up to the Drop Inn. The Battle Mountain Boys jumped from the truck and ran inside while Bobby and Curley watched them.

"I better go inside and control the boys," Curley said.

"I've got things covered here." Bobby surveyed the sparsely vegetated desert sand around the building.

"It really does remind me of Battle Mountain." Curley climbed from the pickup and walked inside.

Bobby slowly unfurled his legs and stepped out of the truck and up to the gas pump.

"Where in the hell are you, Bonnie Brown?"

Inside his luxurious casino suite, Castillo sat in a tall chair at a glass-topped bar, periodically glancing at his cell phone. It rang, almost startling him. He quickly snapped the cell up.

"You almost here?" Castillo sipped a margarita from a goblet as he waited for a response.

"The rookie and some young guy took off from Gina's place," Jose said.

"Are you sure it was her?"

"Had to be, from your description."

"Who was the guy?"

"Don't know ... some joyrider, from the way he looked. They took off across the desert, headed west."

"Got some news from here. Our ATF insider said he and his partner are headed toward the desert factory, the one where fertilizer is made."

"I saw a stack of chewies at Gina's."

"Bad news is the factory is destroyed, along with our Canadians partners and maybe her."

"Couldn't be her, unless the girl on the ATV wasn't the rookie."

"He'll let us know. We could be chasing our tails right now. All I know is I want her dead."

"Yes, boss. Can we stop at the compound?"

"Why not? I'll see you there, and we'll wait for a report from our man inside ATF."

The Battle Mountain Boys had spread out to two tables inside the cafe. Curley and Bobby sat at another. Gina appeared.

"You boys want the same … specials?"

"I guess," Bobby said.

"You must have rabbit on the menu," Curley said.

"Honey, I've been hopping around here for years." Gina put one of her ring-covered hands on Curley's shoulder. "You looking for a little cottontail?"

"Well … I …" Curley's cheeks turned slightly red.

"Looks like the cottontail needs to do a little cooking instead," Bobby said. "The boys are hungry."

"Hon, I can multitask like no one you've ever seen." Gina rubbed Curley's shoulder.

Kevin and Kermit fingered through a stack of chewies. "Can we have one of these?" Kevin asked.

"One comes with the special," Gina said. "Pick one out and it's yours."

"I like this one … Gorgeous George." Kermit raised a tin.

"I want Thunderballs," Kevin said.

"You can give mine to one of them," Bobby said.

"Mine too," Curley said.

"They are really good sellers. Locally made." Gina dropped her hand from Curley's shoulder and strutted away.

Curley watched her wiggle into the kitchen. "Multitasker!" Curley said.

"At least at Lilly's they get checked regularly," Bobby said.

"Thanks for letting us have the chewies," Kareem said. "Mine tasted great, almost like perfume."

"What's yours called?" Bobby asked.

"Sophia Special," Kareem said.

"God knows what's in them," Bobby said.

"Their stomachs are like iron after some of the specials Mama made," Curley whispered.

Fireball stared at the smoldering pot factory. He was on his cell phone. "Sir?"

Silva sat at his desk, speaking into his cell phone. "You find anything?"

"No. Haven't gone inside yet. But I just pinged Brown's cell. He's out near Caliente, just over the hill from here."

"Shit! Thanks. Let me know what you find inside."

"Got it!"


Bobby's cell rang. He glanced at the display. Agent Silva was calling on his office landline.

"On the road to Battle Mountain, Mr. Brown?"

"We had to make a little pit stop." Bobby watched the boys gobble up chewies. "The boys are hungry."

"Caliente is a little out of the way, isn't it?"

"You tracking my cell, Agent Silva?"

"Part of my job, Mr. Brown." Silva swiveled around to look at the ATF seal on his wall. "What can I do to get you to stay out of our way so we can do our job?"

"Find my daughter."

"Trust me, we're looking everywhere."

"Seems like you haven't done a very good job of it so far."

"We're using all the resources we have."

"This is my daughter we're talking about, a daughter I didn't know existed until her mother died. I can't lose her now, and I will use all my resources to find her."

"Please, Mr. Brown, stay out of our way. I understand you had a close one with the Lincoln County sheriff."

"Yeah, kinda like old times. He accused me of shit I didn't do."

"I seem to remember you always got out of whatever it was that you didn't do, didn't you?"

"And I will find my daughter."

"Stay in touch."

Silva's cell phone buzzed. He looked at the display.

"Wait a minute, Mr. Brown." Silva held the landline open with Bobby. "What you got, Agent?"

He listened, ended his cell call, and got back on the landline. "That was one of my agents. He is inside a burned-out building not far from where you are. He and the other agents found four dead. None of them are your daughter. My tech guy on scene found records indicating what they have done with several bodies. It seems they grind up the dead and use their remains for fertilizer to grow edible marijuana products. They use their identities or features to give the products names—"

"Like Sophia Special chewies?" Bobby watched the boys emptying the tins.

"Yeah. There's records going back a couple of years. A lot of dead people … men and women … maybe even kids."

"Jesus! We'll keep looking for Bonnie. Bye." Bobby looked at the Battle Mountain Boys still munching on chewies and shook his head.

"Everything OK, Mr. Brown?" Curley said.

"That was Agent Silva."

"He going to arrest us and send us back home?"

"No, but … those chewies … well, they are made from pot fertilized by human remains."

"The boys seem to like 'em. Want me to tell them?"

Bobby reflected for a moment. "Naw. Let's not spoil the fun."

Bobby wiped the sweat off his brow as Gina entered carrying two steaming plates piled high with her latest formulations. She stopped for a minute, admiring her food creations, and then approached Bobby and Curley.

"Today's special … snake, gopher, leftover coyote, and I did find a cottontail snooping around the garbage. Sure you don't want me to put one of the new chewies on top?"

"No!" Bobby and Curley said in unison.

Bobby studied the two steaming plates. "I think I'll pass on the special too."

"Not me." Curley reached for one of the plates. "I'm starved."

"Suit yourself, hon." Gina leaned on Bobby's shoulder. "You want Gina instead?"

Bobby took a photograph of B-4 from his wallet. "Actually, have you seen this young girl around?"

Gina leaned over, her breasts almost slapping Bobby's face. "Why, she was here a couple of hours ago with some young handsome guy on an ATV."

"Seriously?"

Gina stood up straight. "Yeah. They owe me for the specials they ordered. They disappeared when those guys showed up."

"What guys?"

"My old friend Jose. He and his boss, the big guy from Vegas, well, they both like Gina. Jose really wanted the girl in the picture bad. I could tell. She works in a bordello? She's really cute. I can do things young girls like her haven't dreamed of yet."

"She's my daughter, not a whore."

"Too bad. If she needs work, let me know." Gina wiggled off toward the Battle Mountain Boys and dropped a special off in front of Kevin. Hoping to give the boys a show, she slowly wiggled her way back into the kitchen.

"She's still being hunted. We're going Vegas."

"You sure you don't want some of this, Mr. Brown?" Curley stuffed a hunk of cottontail in his mouth. "It's pretty good."

In the afternoon heat, B-4 and Benneschott sat on two rocks on top of a small mountain, looking down over a valley. They could see Las Vegas in the distance.

"Why are those men after you?" he asked.

"I just happened to take a few of them down in a bust a few weeks ago." B-4 wiped her forehead with a wet rag and tossed it to Benneschott.

"That the chase I heard about on the news?" Benneschott wiped his face.

"Yeah. I was in my normal zone. Ten dead out of ten shots fired."

"Normal is pretty amazing." Benneschott tossed the rag onto the ATV. "Where did you learn how to shoot like that?"

"Genes, I guess, and a very special revolver." B-4 looked up at a circling vulture overhead.

"Special?"

"I call it Johnnson after its owner, a friend of mine. It belonged to his father."

"Sounds intriguing. So whoever the men are working for is after you for killing his men?"

"I guess. I certainly have no idea why I was kidnapped by the militia."

"Probably hired guns, so to speak."

"Could be." B-4 stood and tried to brush the desert dust off. "All I want is to get back to Vegas and clear my name. I was suspended for killing those men before telling them I was ATF."

"Politics and politicians, got to love 'em." Benneschott stood, glanced at the ATV, and then scanned the desert.

B-4 started to brush off the back of Benneschott's shorts and froze. It was an automatic reflex, something she did all the time with the boys. "Sorry 'bout that."

"I'll clean up later. So you're a fugitive on the run, trying to clear your name?"

"That's my story. What about you? Just a guy who magically appears and zooms in over the desert, throwing bombs and beating up bad guys?"

"No story." Benneschott started to walk to the ATV. "In the right place at the right time."

"My guardian angel." B-4 followed him. "Where do you live? And what's your name?"

"I am a resident of the world." Benneschott prepared to climb into the ATV. "You can call me Joe. You've had quite a couple of days. Any other clues, anything you've heard?"

"Why? You can't do anything about it … can you?"

"It interests me. Maybe I'll turn it into a book or a screenplay." Benneschott fumbled for the keys.

"So you're a writer?"

"Among other interests." Benneschott held up the keys.

"I did hear them talk about Castillo, a guy with underworld ties whose men I killed, and there's someone on the inside providing information to him." B-4 joined him in the ATV.

"Time to get you back to Vegas and intrigue." Benneschott scanned the desert and motioned toward the Las Vegas skyline. "Sin city if there ever was one. Ready to go? I'll get you closer."

B-4 nodded.

He started the ATV and headed down a small hill onto the desert floor. The ATV sped up, bouncing over desert sage, throwing sand and dust in the air.

"How did you know we had to escape from that shithole cafe?" B-4 yelled.

"Intuition. Gotta know when to get out!"

"Yeah, that's what Mama always said, especially about men."

"I'm really beginning to love Mama."

"She was the best!"

A look of warmth and love crossed Benneschott's face as they moved through the desert toward Las Vegas. "I will always love you too, Mama," he said a low voice so that B-4 didn't hear.

# CHAPTER 20

As the red-hot sun set, Benneschott stopped the ATV at the curb in front of the sign for the North Las Vegas Police Station. B-4 climbed out.

"Certainly was an interesting day!" she said.

"One for the books," Benneschott said.

"Write me into your next thriller?" B-4 smiled, an attempt to show Benneschott that there was a little emotion under her thick skin.

"How could I forget?"

B-4 was pretty sure he was trying to pretend he didn't feel her display of warmth.

"When will I see you again?"

"You never know about us guardian angels."

B-4 was certain Benneschott's and her paths would cross again. He said he was her guardian angel, but she sensed a stronger connection of some sort.

"See you around then ... Joe." She stepped back from the ATV.

Joe hit the gas and sped off, darting in and out of traffic. B-4 watched. She shook her head and mumbled to herself, "Mama's intuition tells me that boy is a keeper. Oh well."

She walked to a counter inside the police station. She could feel stares from the officers. It was as if she were a homeless person. What else could it be? Her clothes were ragged, torn, and dirty. An African American female officer sitting at a nearby desk stood and approached her. She was in full uniform.

"The homeless shelter is across the street, miss."

"I know I must look like I haven't slept all night, and it's true." B-4 rubbed a cut below her right ear. "Can you please dial up Agent Silva at the ATF office?"

"ATF? You mean Alcohol, Tobacco, Firearms …"

"Yep, and Explosives … ATF." B-4 leaned her elbows on the counter and rested her filthy face in her hands. "I'm an agent. Just escaped from my kidnappers in the desert."

"We don't get that kind of explanation a lot. That's a good one."

"True. It's a first for me too. I'd show you my badge if I had one on me."

"Can I get you a Band-Aid … water … something?"

B-4 wasn't sure if it was a fact that she was an ATF agent or the fact that she was kidnapped, but she appreciated that the officer had started to show a bit of concern for her situation. "Just a call to Agent Silva will do."

Inside ATF headquarters, Agent Silva was on the phone. He looked worried as he glanced out into the parking lot at B-4's unmarked car. It was lit by the setting sun. "She's there? I'll send a car immediately."

He hung up, stepped out of his office, and looked toward Ruben's cubicle. "Ruben! Agent Brown is at the North Vegas Police Station. Go get her!"

Ruben looked toward the heavens. "Thank God." He yelled to Silva, "I'm on my way!" He rushed past Salisbury's cubicle.

Salisbury caught sight of Ruben out of the corner of his eye and immediately stood. "Hey, partner, need me to go along?"

"No. I'll scoop her up and bring her back, unless she needs to go to the hospital."

"Call me if you need help?"

After Ruben left, Salisbury pulled out a cell phone and immediately started texting.

Fireball walked into Silva's office. "That's great news. Maybe you should call her father and tell him. And while you're at it, have him tell his men to stop shooting at our drone from the back of his pickup."

"What?"

"I've got a drone following them. Their shotguns don't quite reach high enough."

"Goddammit!" Silva pounded his desk. He grabbed his landline phone and dialed. "Brown?"

The old pickup moved through the desert on a four-lane highway. The Battle Mountain Boys stood in the truck box, taking turns shooting at a drone following them high above. Bobby shielded his eyes from the setting sun as he held his cell phone. It was on speaker.

"Stop shooting at the drone!"

"They're just letting off a little steam. You know boys will be boys."

"They hit our drone and it'll be several days in jail and a heavy fine."

"We know how to hunt birds with shotguns. Your bird is flying higher than geese going north. Anything else?"

"Bonnie just walked into a Vegas police station," Silva said as he took a deep breath to regain his composure. "We're picking her up."

"Is she OK?"

After a brief silence, Silva said, "She'll be coming here, unless she wants to make a stop."

"Stop?"

Silva wished he could have his last words back. "Figure she might need something to eat."

"We'll be there shortly."

"Put away those shotguns!"

"They're harmless. Now my Magnum … well, I could hit your drone."

"No!" Silva slammed his landline phone down. "Fireball! Get that fucking drone out of there now!"


Inside an isolated compound, Castillo and Jose sat by a swimming pool. Nearby, six men lounged in the churning water of a large hot tub, slugging back beer.

"Our man said she just showed in North Vegas at the police station," Castillo said.

"You want me and the crew to go and give her a special Vegas welcome?" Jose asked.

"It'd better be her last Vegas welcome."

"Last sounds good, boss. Then we can get back to real Vegas business."

"You're right." Castillo lit a cigar.

"Sure you should be smoking that?" Jose asked.

Castillo exhaled. "I'm taking up fucking fly-fishing and becoming a man of leisure. I can have one of these."

"But—"

"Look, we've got another large explosives shipment arriving." Castillo blew on the cigar tip and watched it burn red hot. "Worry about making sure it gets done right and end her life permanently."

"Yes, boss. Boom!"

Castillo's cell phone rang. He picked it up and listened. Then he said, "Thanks for the info," and ended the call.

Castillo puffed on his cigar and exhaled. He locked eyes with Jose. "We've got an old pickup with five cowboys carrying shotguns in the back." He put the cell down and savored his cigar. "Apparently the rookie's father and others are on their way to Vegas ATF headquarters to meet her when she arrives. Maybe you and the men should welcome them too?"

Jose took a gulp of his margarita.

Castillo watched Jose impatiently and motioned toward the door. "What you waiting for? Get out of here!"

"Got it, boss." Jose turned to the men in the hot tub. "Guys, time for a little fun."


Night was almost upon them as Ruben drove toward the ATF headquarters with B-4 in the passenger seat. "Thanks for picking me up."

Ruben nodded at B-4 and then noticed the cut below her right ear. "Sure you don't need to get that looked at? I mean, you look pretty ..."

"Messed up! I love you too. I need to check in with Silva and find out what's next in the investigation. I've gotta get cleared, get Johnnson back, and go after that bastard Castillo."

"Work? Castillo?"

"I heard his name mentioned by the militia. He's behind all this shit and who knows what else."

"That's not all that's been happening. Your father and his friends have been looking for you."

"Daddy, Curley, and the boys?"

"Been leaving a trail of rabbit turds, kinda like you. What's that saying, like father—"

"And his only daughter!"

"He's been on your trail. Out in Panaca, where a militia party was wiped out, an old store was burned down, at the scene where several other men were killed—"

"They killed people?"

"I don't think so," Ruben mused. "But they were certainly nearby, on their way to rescue you."

"Oh my God, Daddy and the Battle Mountain Boys on the loose. That's not gonna be nice for anybody."

"That's kinda the message I got from Silva. Is there any way you can convince them to go home?"

"Daddy's head is as hard as this dash." B-4 pounded the dashboard softly. "Maybe harder." She pounded it harder. "Made him a great detective, I guess."

"We had a couple like that in Quebec, actually in Saint Pierre. They ended up dead. They had no friends but a lot of enemies."

"Sounds like Daddy, but he's still alive and kicking. What can I do?"

"So who was this guy who saved you from the marijuana farm?"

"Did more than that. Got me out of the Drop Inn before Castillo's men 'dropped' in. Ever been there?"

"Out in Caliente? I've heard rumors. So this guy …?"

"His name is Joe. At least that's the name he gave me. Other than that, I have no idea. Referred to himself as my guardian angel."

"Where you staying tonight?"

"I'm open for suggestions. Just not a sand bed." B-4 took a deep breath and fought off the temptation to yawn in front of Ruben.

"No desert stars?"

"Not tonight."

"Well, I don't want to sound fresh or anything like that, but I have an extra room at my rental."

"Sounds like I need to find a place for eight."

"You're probably right."

As daylight faded over Pahrump, Bobby's pickup pulled to the curb in front of ATF headquarters. He looked at his cell phone and shook his head. He turned to Curley. "Gotta love technology."

"Maybe you can teach me that someday," Curley said.

"Tell the boys to get out and go inside. Better leave their shotguns in the truck."

Bobby climbed out, stretched, and moved around the pickup. Curley took the shotguns from the Battle Mountain Boys and laid them across the front seat. "You leaving your Magnum in the glove?" Curley asked.

"Naw. Give it to me. Feel kinda naked without it."

Curley reached into the glove box, pulled the Magnum out, and handed it to Bobby. Bobby immediately checked the chamber to make sure it was loaded and that the safety was on.

"Let's go," Bobby said.

Curley locked the truck.

Bobby and the Battle Mountain Boys walked along the short sidewalk to the entrance. A black SUV approached, windows down. Automatic weapons began spraying bullets at them and their old pickup truck.

"Everybody down! Now!" Bobby yelled.

Bullets hit the sides and windows of the building and the pickup truck. One shot hit the gas tank, and the truck exploded into an inferno.

As the black SUV sped off, Bobby pulled out his Magnum and aimed. He fired twice, breaking the SUV's back window. Silva and several other agents exited the building, weapons drawn. Curley and the Battle Mountain Boys got up off their knees.

Silva moved next to Bobby as they watched the SUV screech around a corner at full speed and disappear. "You've got to be Agent Brown's father. What an arrival!"

"Can't go anywhere these days," Bobby said. He reengaged the safety on his Magnum.

"Seems your reputation proceeds you."

B-4 and Ruben pulled up moments later and surveyed the pickup truck on fire, ATF agents with their weapons drawn, Bobby holding his Magnum, and Curley and the Battle Mountain Boys brushing themselves off. Their sedan stopped in the driveway, and B-4 dashed toward them.

"Daddy! What happened to you and the boys?"

Flames whooshed up from under the pickup engine hood, catching everyone's attention.

"And Mama's poor pickup!" B-4 watched the flames devour the truck.

"Nice to see you too." Bobby reloaded his Magnum.

"Come on you two, inside," Silva said, walking toward the entrance. "The fire department's on the way."

"Vegas is just like I remember from the good old days," Bobby said.

"I heard about you being here once," Silva said with a slight chuckle.

It was evening as Bobby, dressed in his tweed coat, black slacks, and black string tie, walked from the airport to a waiting taxi. A heavy-set Hispanic female driver reached over the front seat and opened the back door.

Bobby tossed his jacket onto the rear seat. "Paris and hurry." He jumped in and slammed the rear door behind him.

The taxi driver flipped the meter on. "You here for a convention, hon?"

"No."

"Gamble a little?"

"No."

"Girls, Chiquitas? You look like you need a senorita, maybe *dos*."

"No."

"Entertainment ... men's club?"

"No. And no more twenty questions either."

"OK. Paris it is. Whew!"

A short time later, the taxi pulled into the Paris Hotel and Casino. Bobby got out, grabbed his jacket off the rear seat, and put it on as the taxi driver glanced at meter.

"Thirty dollars."

Bobby pulled out a twenty and a ten and handed it to her.

"Not a big tipper either."

Bobby walked into the casino. He straightened his jacket as he moved through a packed lobby to the concierge desk. A young African American woman greeted him with a big smile.

"I am looking for Abdul," Bobby said. He pulled out a rolled twenty-dollar bill and handed it to her.

"I'll get him for you." She stuffed the twenty into her pocket.

Bobby waited, tapping his foot as he surveyed the crowd, which resembled the United Nations.

Abdul, a middle-aged Middle-Eastern man with a ribbon beard and wearing a suit and turban, emerged from behind a curtain. He locked in on Bobby and approached him. "Can I help you?"

"Detective Brown, San Francisco Police Department." Bobby flashed his badge. "I flew here because I was told you had information vital to our search for the serial killer we posted online today."

Abdul leaned closer to Bobby and whispered, "The man you are looking for is one of our guests."

"Why didn't you just tell the Vegas police?"

"They won't do anything," Abdul said in a low voice as his gaze darted around to see if anyone could see him talking. "He's a high roller, a very high roller, and friends with some very important people … like the ones who own this fine establishment. We need him out of here quietly. Can you do that for us?"

"That I can arrange. The quietly part, not usually my style."

"The owner knows all about it but will never admit it."

"Great. No harm, no foul. Not my style either. Room number?"

Abdul slid a key card across the counter. "You have no idea where that came from."

Bobby grabbed the key card and walked away, shaking his head as he mumbled, "Never did like head wraps."

He stepped into an elevator along with several partying men and women who were obviously bombed and looking for a good time. He inserted the key card and rode directly to the penthouse floor. He exited and took his next directions from the floor map and arrows. Once at the penthouse, he knocked on the door. A heavyset, balding white man wearing glasses and expensive silk pajamas opened the door. Bobby immediately locked in on the bloody knife the man was trying to conceal behind his leg.

"Yes, what can I—"

Before the man could finish, Bobby slugged him with a right cross, sending the knife flying and the man reeling back into the middle of the plush room.

"Room service, you pervert," Bobby said, gritting his teeth.

Bobby dragged the man to the balcony by his pajama top, stood him up against the railing, and held his Magnum in the man's face. "All I'm after is you confessing to killing all those young girls in San Francisco and who knows where else."

"I don't know what you are talking about." The man's tears mixed with the blood smeared across his face. "I'm just a businessman, that's all."

"How many did you kill? What about Las Vegas? How many have you murdered here?"

"None. You're mistaken."

"That bloody knife? Is that from carving a turkey, you pedophile?"

"I cut my finger. Look." The man held up a bloody finger.

"Where did you bury the bodies?" Silence. "That's not all that's going to be bloody if you don't confess."

"Please, sir, put that down gun down. Let's go inside and talk. You have the wrong man."

Bobby lowered his Magnum and shoved him back inside the penthouse. They stopped at a glass-topped bar, behind which was a shelf with several decanters and crystal glasses.

"If you're not the man I'm looking for, prove to me you're telling the truth."

"You want a drink? I need one."

"Pour and talk. You're the pervert I was sent to take back to the city."

"I have no idea what you are talking about." The man's hand shook as he poured from a decanter.

Just then, a naked young girl stumbled into the living room from the bathroom, bleeding profusely.

"Help me, help me. I'm ..." The girl fell dead onto the carpet.

"Not a pervert or a murderer, eh?" Bobby grabbed the man by his pajama top, dragged him through the open balcony door, and shoved him headfirst over the railing. He watched the man fall into the swimming pool far below.

As the lifeless body floated to the surface, Bobby said, "I think I'll have that drink now." He walked to the bar, poured himself a drink, downed it, and walked out.

Back down in the casino, Bobby approached the concierge desk. The concierge saw him coming and stepped out of sight through a curtain. Abdul appeared as Bobby slid him the key card.

"The guy in question just took a dip in your pool. You better call the police and the coroner to take care of his handiwork upstairs."

"Thank you, sir," Abdul said nervously.

"The pleasure's been all mine." As Bobby turned and walked away, he whispered to himself, "It's definitely been a pleasure."

# CHAPTER 21

A large black van drove up the long driveway into the glittering Palms Hotel and Casino on Flamingo, a mile from downtown.

"I'll get the room key," Ruben said as he jumped down from the driver's seat.

Bobby exited from the front seat while B-4, Curley, and the Battle Mountain Boys exited from a sliding side door. They watched Ruben walk through the tall glass doors into the hotel.

"Daddy, pretty nice, my boss offering the Paris penthouse to us."

"Been there, done the Paris gig. Personally, off the strip like this is better, much better. The guys after you will have a harder time locating you, unless there really is someone on the inside. I hope what you heard is wrong."

"Agent Silva and Fireball will find the rat, if one exists."

"Fireball, nice name."

"There's a little red splotch in his hair."

"Got it." Bobby watched Ruben walking toward them from inside the casino.

"They gave you the best they have ... swimming pool and all the amenities." Ruben handed keys to Bobby. "They'll bring in enough rollaways to—"

"The boys have been sleeping on the floor for years, if they sleep," Bobby interrupted. "They'll be OK. Thank Agent Silva for us."

"He emphasized *one night*. Tomorrow, B-4 goes to the range in the morning with IA. We'll find her a safe house."

"What about my dad and the others?"

"We'll be on our way back to Battle Mountain to rescue Rosie," Bobby said.

"Who's Rosie?"

"That's a story I've got to tell you one day."

"Now's a good time."

Bobby watched the boys play fighting in front of the tall glass doors. "So, Ruben, they have room service here?"

"It's the penthouse. They've got everything, and room service is expecting your call."

"Thanks, Ruben," B-4 said. "See you at the range?"

"Maybe." Ruben started to climb back into the driver's seat. He hesitated, turned, and hugged B-4. It was an awkward moment.

"Now get outta of here," B-4 said.

Ruben stepped into the van. "Be safe."

B-4 double-tapped the side of the van. Ruben started the engine, winked at B-4, and drove away.

"Nice young man," Bobby said.

"Not bad for a Canadian, eh!"

"Sounds like you've already been hanging around him too long."


Inside ATF headquarters, Silva studied a file at his desk. Salisbury walked in.

"Where'd they all go?" the agent said, scanning the office area. "Guess I missed the fun."

"The broken glass, the truck fire, the bullets. Where'd you go?"

"Had to run an errand for my mother. Her Alzheimer's getting a lot worse. Where's Ruben?"

"He had an errand too. He'll be back soon."

"OK. I'm here if you need me."

Salisbury walked out of Silva's office and sat in his cubicle. He nervously looked around and then took out a cell phone.

"Fireball. Can I see you?" Silva yelled from his office.

Fireball walked past Salisbury's cubicle as the agent was talking on his cell phone. Fireball entered Silva's office. Silva motioned to him to shut the door.

"Sir?"

Silva motioned to Fireball to keep his voice low. "Agent Brown thinks we have a leak in our organization."

"With all she went through, she could be mistaken."

"Look. Do me one. Can you just go through everyone's phone records and see if there's anything strange?"

"Like phone calls to Castillo?"

"Mine too. Go through them all."

"Yes, sir." Fireball feigned a salute.


In his isolated compound under the dark sky, Castillo sat by the pool, reading a fly-fishing manual. Jose walked up, grabbed a pool chair, and then turned it around and straddled it. Castillo reached for his latest margarita concoction and sipped it, without acknowledging Jose's presence.

"Success?" Castillo asked, not looking up.

"We scared the hell out of 'em, boss."

"They dead?"

"More than a hundred rounds. They'd better be. Their truck's destroyed. We had a couple of casualties."

Castillo looked up. He took another sip of his margarita. He waited to hear more. "Causalities?"

"Two of our men ... couple of lucky shots. I'll put 'em on ice 'til we find another way to get rid of 'em now the pot farm has been destroyed."

"Maybe a few dropped in the old mine?"

"Sounds like a plan."

Castillo took another sip of his drink. "We have room for another in that mine?"

"Her?"

Castillo sipped his margarita again and stared into space. "No. Just gotta call from our man. He thinks they're on to him."

"No problem, boss. Just say when."

"When! Fucking when? Now! Clear enough?"

"Missed the first 'when' boss. Sorry." Jose stood and left in a hurry.


Inside the Palms penthouse, B-4, Bobby, and Curley sat in a large indoor-outdoor hot tub, staring out at the Strip in the distance.

"The boys joining us?" B-4 asked.

"They're downstairs having fun," Curley said as he sipped a beer. "As soon as they saw all those slots, that was it."

"I wondered." B-4 took a drink from a water bottle.

"They said, 'Thanks for the cash,' and off they went, trail coats and all."

Bobby's cell phone rang a foot away on a deck chair. "And it was turning into such a beautiful night." He reached out and picked it up. "Bobby Brown here."

Inside the Roadkill, the Lander County sheriff leaned on the bar, cell phone to his ear. Rosie poured a whiskey straight up and slid it in front of him. He nodded. Three young men lay on the floor, groaning and nursing various injuries.

"Mr. Brown. This is Sheriff Cox. I'm inside your establishment."

"The Roadkill or Lilly's?"

"The Roadkill. I got your number from your bartender. She poured drinks for three of your customers, and they didn't like them. There was name calling and whatever. She tossed them around like paper dolls. They're threatening to sue."

"Put Rosie on, Sheriff."

The sheriff handed his cell phone to Rosie.

"Rosie, this is Mr. Brown, JJ's father. What happened?"

"These three guys came in all drunk and wanted a drink. I made them one, and they began calling me names."

"What drink?"

"They wanted a sugar drop, so I made them each one."

"What did you put in it?"

"Mrs. JJ didn't leave me a book about drinks, and I couldn't find one anywhere, so I made it up. One jigger of whiskey, one of vodka, and one of maple syrup."

"Maple syrup? No wonder. What did they call you?"

"The n-word several times, along with dumb and bitch."

"Give the phone back to the sheriff."

Rosie handed the cell phone back to the sheriff.

"Sheriff, I understand from Rosie the three men in question called her names, including one that has a bad racial connotation. Could you ask them about that, please?"

The sheriff surveyed the customers. He muffled his cell phone microphone with one hand. "What did you call this young lady here?"

"She tried to poison us, sheriff," one of the young men said.

"I said, what did you call her?"

"A nigger!" one of the young boys yelled. "That's what she is, a nigger!"

The sheriff took his hand off the cell. "Mr. Brown, sorry to bother you. I'll take it from here. There are certain things that aren't tolerated even in Battle Mountain."

"Put Rosie back on."

"Sir?" Rosie said. "You want me to call Mrs. JJ and have her come and get me?"

"We're going to try and get back there tomorrow afternoon. You can call her and tell her to pick you up then if you want. When I get there, I'll show you how to make a sugar drop."

"Rosie thanks you, Mr. Brown."

"Thank you, Rosie." Bobby put the cell phone down on the deck.

"OK, so who is Rosie?" B-4 asked as she splashed a bit of water on Bobby.

"Want me to leave? Some father and daughter time?" Curley asked.

"You know about her?" B-4 asked.

"Yes. Well, no," Curley said, trying not to get in the middle of what could be trouble.

"Stay around," Bobby said.

"Daddy?"

"You see, my days in Frisco, I did what any normal guy would do: eat, sleep, work, drink, and try to seduce any chick I could find." He sank lower in the water and leaned his head back against the side of the hot tub. "And when you stare death in the face all day every day, finding a chick becomes ... Well, it was more important than eating, sleeping, and drinking. Well, maybe not drinking. I met a few, no, a lot, and I guess I was more fertile than I thought. JJ's mother, well, who knows? JJ found me after a search of adoption agency records. Her wealthy lawyer husband had died in a tragic car crash. She has a young son—"

"And a billion dollars," Curley said.

115

"Yes, a lot of money, estates, airplanes, yachts … But she wanted to know who her parents were. Her mother died when she was born, and then there was me."

"I have a sister? I thought I was your only living relative."

"I was gonna tell you when the time was right. I guess that time has come. Her name is JJ Wellington, and she lives in Mount Vernon on the Potomac. I visited her once, for her son's, Connie's, birthday."

"Grandpa Bobby Brown?" B-4 scoffed.

"Don't go there."

"Does she look like me? Any resemblance?"

"She's blond and athletic. Was a soccer player, all-American at Vassar."

"Not a desert rat who barely got out of high school alive and eats jackrabbit?"

"You're each beautiful in your own way. I knew she had some of me in her when her friend told me stories about breaking her knee in a soccer game, stepping on her, and spitting in her face. You know, if this whole thing with the ATF doesn't work out, maybe you can team up with her back in DC. She's started a foundation to help catch child molesters."

"And Rosie?"

"I saw her once in a newspaper picture JJ sent me and missed her at the birthday party. About six foot five or so, big, very dark, African American. She and JJ got into it inside a jail cell and became best friends. Rosie helped her catch the worst kind of child molester, a pervert who almost killed both of them."

"And she's the one watching the Roadkill and Lilly's? I'll bet she's a real hit."

"According to JJ, she's one of the nicest, most gentle people you could ever meet, except when you cross her. Three boys just found out."

"Daddy, I am very disappointed you never told me any of this before. I don't want to do anything else but be the best special agent I can be. There aren't any more brothers or sisters out there, are there?"

"You never know."

"Daddy!" B-4 splashed him with both hands.

"Well, gotta be honest. I sowed a lot of oats."

"And planted a lot of seeds … maybe enough to start your own detective agency?" B-4 said sarcastically.

The penthouse telephone rang. Curley climbed out of the hot tub and plucked the phone from the wall cradle. "Yes?" He listened and started shaking his head. "They're doing what? I'll be right down." He walked back to the hot tub. "The boys are riding slot machines and causing quite a ruckus. I gotta throw on some clothes and go down to keep them from being tossed in jail. You two gonna be OK?"

"Yeah, unless he's got another relative to tell me about." B-4 laughed and reached for her water bottle. Bobby playfully splashed her.

"None that I can remember. Of course, the night is still young."

B-4 splashed back.

"Daddy! Or is that Grandpa?"

"Now that's a low blow."

"Well?"

"There are no more, OK?"

"Now you're just trying to shut me up!"

"Never." Bobby climbed out of the hot tub and went to grab another beer.

In a row of apartments off the Strip, Jose and two men walked up a flight of stairs and knocked on a door.

Salisbury answered. "Jose! Guys. What's up?"

Jose opened his jacket to expose a revolver. "The boss wants to talk to you. Let's go."

"But my mother." Salisbury realized what was happening.

"Tell her good-bye," Jose said.

"But—"

Jose pulled out the silenced revolver and shot Salisbury in the head. The agent fell over, and Jose's men picked him off the floor.

From a bedroom inside, Salisbury's mother called out, "Is that you, my darling Steven? We are going to be late for our wedding, I know. Steven." She drifted back to sleep.

At his isolated desert compound, Castillo was watching the news on a big-screen television when his cell phone rang. He listened to the person on the other end and then said, "Put him in storage like the others. Take him into the desert tomorrow after you handle the rookie at the shooting range."

Castillo pulled out a cigar, started to light it, but then stopped and listened.

"Sure. Use the casino suite and the regulars. You deserve it," he responded.

Early the next morning, the sun was already taking the desert night chill out of Las Vegas. Bobby, B-4, Curley, and the Battle Mountain Boys stood waiting outside the Palms. Their clothes, trail coats, and jeans had been washed, and they were ready for another day of adventure. A huge red four-door pickup with oversized tires sat nearby. It was hard to miss the chrome exhaust pipes that lined both sides of the cab.

"How do you like that one, boys?" Bobby motioned for the valet to bring it up. They watched the large pickup approach.

"I like it a lot, a whole lot," Kevin said.

"Well, it's ours. Gotta a name for her too." Bobby nodded toward the boys. "The JJ Posse Express."

The valet jumped out. "She's a beaut, Mr. Brown."

"Thanks, Jimmy." Bobby looked at the boys. "Well, what you waiting for? Get in. They wouldn't let me buy shotguns online. Gonna have to pick them up on the way back home."

"Your other daughter?" B-4 asked.

Bobby held up a gold credit card. "Thanks to a little seed."

"You are impossible." B-4 shrugged.

"It's so nice to be a father." Bobby took the keys from the valet. "Hop in. You have the address of the firing range, daughter?"

"Got it from the concierge. It's way out there near the hills."

Heading to the Vegas outskirts, the JJ Posse Express flew over the road leading to the hills. Bobby drove as B-4 played navigator. Curley and Kevin sat behind them in the cab.

"I dealt with internal affairs a lot," Bobby said. "You never know about them. Usually weak kiss-asses that can't make it on the street so the brass kicks them upstairs. What's this all about again?"

"Killing several guys without identifying myself."

"How many?"

"Ten, eleven? And a few others if you count the militia. I told the brethren at the chewie factory. Also for using Johnnson, not regular issue."

"I thought you had that cleared."

"They told me at the academy it would be OK, seeing as how I broke every marksman record they ever had."

"Well, if you need a good lawyer, your half sister owns a whole building full in DC."

"I gotta meet her one of these days. Maybe she'll tell me some stories about you I haven't heard. When you headed back to Battle Mountain?"

"Later today. I'd rather stay and keep you safe. But those agents seem to be in your corner. Besides, who knows what Rosie is going to get into next. You gonna miss me?"

"Maybe after. I guess I do have only one father. Maybe several siblings."

"What's she talking about, Mr. Brown?" Kevin asked.

"Nothing, Kevin. Nothing at all."

"I heard her say 'several suckers.'"

"Siblings, Kevin." Curley hit Kevin with his cowboy hat. "Dumb shit!"

Agent Silva sat at his desk inside ATF headquarters. He stared out the window at Sin City as it slowly woke, preparing to unleash its tentacles on those eager to give away their life savings and those helping them do it.

His secretary walked in and said, "Sir, Agent Salisbury's neighbor keeps calling. Something about his mother and a wedding dress."

"I have no idea where he is."

Fireball walked in past the secretary. "Sir, it's about Agent Salisbury. He has three calls on his cell from Castillo."

"From Castillo? To him?"

"Yes. But last night when I walked by him in the hall, he was on a cell. There is no record of that one."

"A burner. Guess we know where the leak is coming from."

"What should I tell the neighbor?" the secretary asked.

"Call social services. I am guessing he went for a ride with some of his newfound friends."

"Yes, sir." The secretary walked out.

"Have you pinged our favorite father?" Silva asked Fireball.

"Yes. He's on the move toward the firing range, probably taking B-4 to meet the IA guys."

"Great! Let's hope he keeps moving north."

Fireball walked out as Ruben walked in. "Sir, one of my informants, Enrique, wants to meet me at Denny's. He said he's got some information he's willing to sell."

"Take some cash."

"Sounded like a lot of cash, sir."

"Shit! Between B-4's friends, the bill from the Palms, and your informant, I'll need to call the congressman and ask for funds to keep us going."

"The congressman who filed the complaint against B-4?"

"One and the same."

"Shit!"

"Yes! You better get out to the shooting range in case Salisbury told Castillo about the IA investigation and Agent Brown."

"Got it!" Ruben headed out the door.

The Battle Mountain Boys, minus Kevin, held onto their cowboy hats as they took in the scenery from the truck box. The JJ Posse Express roared down a gravel road and pulled into the shooting range parking lot.

Bobby looked over at B-4. "Give 'em hell, Bonnie."

"Yeah. Good luck, B-4," Kevin said.

"Bye, guys. Tell the other boys I'll be thinking about them while I am putting holes in those targets. Just like shooting jacks."

"Remember, you have a sister with a whole lot of good lawyers," Bobby said.

"And I thought I was your one and only."

"Get out of here."

As soon as B-4 was out of the truck, Curley moved into the passenger seat, and Kareem jumped from the truck box to sit with Kevin in back.

"Gonna be cooler in here," Kareem said.

Bobby held up his gold card. "Come on, boys. Let's go find us some shotguns and boogie on back to Battle Mountain."

B-4 watched the big pickup roar out of the parking lot in a cloud of dust and gravel. As she walked toward the firing range, she noticed Smith and Gerard, the internal affairs agents, waiting.

Just then, Ruben drove up, stopped his car, and rolled down his window. "Where's your daddy?"

"Headed back to Battle Mountain."

"Gonna smoke a few targets like at the academy?"

"I have no idea what they want me to do." B-4 studied the waiting agents.

"Interesting news. My partner, Salisbury, has been leaking information to Castillo. For how long we don't know."

"He arrested?"

"Disappeared. We have no idea what he might have told Castillo about you and what you might be doing."

"Like going to the shooting range?"

"Exactly."

"Never a dull moment."

She walked up to the internal affairs agents as Ruben parked.

"Agent Brown, you ready?" Smith asked.

"Always, no matter what."

"Just a little test comparison between the standard issue and that cannon of yours," Gerard said.

"No problem."

B-4 followed the agents through a gate, where they flashed their badges, and then they walked toward the gun stations. They studied several targets twenty-five yards away. In the background, a mountain cliff rose several hundred feet above them. Gunfire from several shooters firing various weapons, including AK-47s, machine guns, and pistols, filled the air.

Smith and Gerard put on earmuffs and handed B-4 a pair. She put them on and studied the targets.

Smith pulled out a standard issue revolver. "Use this one on the first target."

"No problem." B-4 ejected the clip, made sure there were twelve cartridges, and reinserted it. She spun around and fired rapidly at the target.

Smith watched through binoculars. He squinted as he adjusted them. Finally, he dropped the binoculars to his side.

"Twelve for twelve in and around the bullseye! Great shooting, Agent," Smith said.

Ruben stood twenty feet behind them. He smiled as he removed his earmuffs.

Above them, three hundred yards away, Jose lay on the ground, peering over a cliff through a monocular. Jesus lay next to him, adjusting the scope on a sniper rifle that was equipped with a long silencer.

"You got her?" Jose asked.

"Clear. No problem."

"Fire when ready."

"She keeps moving. When she stops …"

"It's up to you."

On the range, B-4 handed the standard issue back to Smith.

"Now your pretty cannon." Gerard handed Johnnson to her.

"That's Johnnson, Agent."

"Whatever," Gerard said.

B-4 ejected the clip, studied it, and put it back in. She stepped up to the gun station, aimed, and fired eleven times, knocking the paper target from the post.

As it dropped, Smith reached toward her. "Stop!"

At the same time he yelled, a sniper's bullet ripped through his head.

"What the fuck?" A stunned B-4 turned and saw a flash of light reflect off the sniper's weapon above them on the hill. She turned and fired her last two shots. Chaos reigned as other shooters and Gerard ducked.

"Get down, Agent Brown!" Gerard yelled.

"Why?" B-4 stood tall and slightly off-kilter, holding Johnnson at her side. "There's no need."

Ruben, Gerard, and B-4 walked up a steep trail to the top of the cliff. The sniper lay dead with two bullet holes in his head.

"Like I said, no bother." B-4 looked at the dead man.

Ruben scanned the area. "His rifle is missing."

"I don't believe it," Gerard said. "Maybe two hundred yards …"

"More like three. Just like a jack." B-4 reached down and picked up a shell. She quickly glanced around. No one was watching as she put it into her pocket.

# CHAPTER 22

Silva sat at a small conference table in his ATF office. The door was closed. B-4 and Ruben sat across from him.

"Now an IA agent. Trouble just keeps following you. How many dead bodies is that?"

"I don't keep track, sir. By the way, did I pass? Do I get Johnnson back?"

"Gerard is putting your heroics and unbelievable marksmanship into his report. He can't explain the dead man's relationship to Agent Smith's death, though."

"Great! He was a sniper."

"No weapon was found, was there?"

"Shit!"

"Come on, sir," Ruben pleaded. "I need her in the field with me now that I'm without a partner."

"I haven't gotten the word on her status yet."

His secretary opened the door and walked in with a small FedEx package. "This just came for you, sir." She handed the package to Silva. "It's marked urgent."

"Thanks." Silva took it and watched the secretary leave the room. After she closed the door behind her, he opened the box. His eyebrows raised. He pulled out a plastic baggy. Inside was a left hand wearing a ring. There was also a note. He unzipped the baggy, took out the note, and quickly read it.

"One less agent," Silva read. "The rookie's father is next if she doesn't resign."

"That's Salisbury's hand," Ruben said, studying the baggy. "I know that ring. Like I said, I need a partner when I go to talk to my informant."

"She's still suspended." Silva looked at B-4. "Maybe with this threat you'll want to resign."

"I'll take her with me and talk to her," Ruben said, looking at B-4. He picked up the note and studied it. "I'll make sure she behaves."

"No more dead bodies," Silva said, looking at B-4.

"No more dead bodies, right?" Ruben confirmed, directing his words to B-4.

"Right. So, guess it's standard issue for now, right? And resign? The answer is no."

In his isolated compound, Castillo sat with Jose by the swimming pool, enjoying a plate of steak and eggs. He finished chewing a piece of steak and put his knife down.

"Now that's what I call a breakfast," Castillo said. "So ... Jesus?"

"Yes, boss. He was far away. Impossible with a handgun."

"My dead wife's cousin." Castillo stabbed another piece of steak and raised it to his mouth. He paused. He looked into Jose's eyes and said, "Our best sniper to boot."

"And my friend. I got his rifle to give to you."

"I'm trying to make it so difficult for her to stay here, yet she keeps killing my men."

Castillo stuffed the steak into his mouth and chewed it like a lion that had not eaten in days.

"She'll go back to Battle Mountain and shoot jackrabbits with that big gun," Jose said.

"First she's got to resign." Castillo pointed his empty fork at Jose.

"Time to really threaten her father?" Jose suggested.

"That's the plan." Castillo cut another piece of steak. "We threaten to kill him and his posse, and she'll quit like the note said."

"And if ...?"

"We'll kill them all one way or another." Castillo chewed another piece of semiraw meat.

"Her father and the rest left this morning, boss. It's a long way up north if we have to get up there."

"After our 'supposed' delivery this afternoon is set up, if she shows, be ready to use one of my jets and take a trip to Elko. You can rent an SUV and visit good old Battle Mountain. Just in case, be ready. She resigns today, we'll drink margaritas instead."

"That's why you're the boss, boss."

"Line up some men for the trip. Promise them anything and be ready to take them with you."

"You got it."

"Pass me the ketchup?"

The JJ Posse Express pickup moved slowly up a hill into the small town of Tonopah around midday. Inside the truck, Curley grimaced as he crossed his legs. Bobby noticed out of the corner of his eye and smiled.

"We gonna stop, Mr. Brown? The boys probably gotta take a piss."

"How about we get another hundred miles in?"

Curley squeezed his legs together harder. Bobby bust a gut laughing.

"Gotcha good. I think there's a gun shop in town. Maybe we'll buy some three-inch Magnum double-barrel shotguns with my new gold card."

"Those'll blow a barn door off the hinges."

"I was thinking more like turn it into sawdust."

Curley nodded as they stopped in front of Hotel Mizpah.

"Tell the boys it's a piss break."

"In the Mizpah? Are you kidding? That's the place Mama swore is full of ghosts. She and B-4 stayed there for some school thing. She was scared shitless."

"Scared? Mama scared? I didn't know her long, but she didn't seem like the type who ever got scared."

"Deathly, as I heard her tell it." Curley held his crotch. "The Red Room. She heard a voice."

It was early morning when Mama's pickup pulled into a parking spot beside the Mizpah. Mama took her sunglasses off and turned to a young B-4 in the passenger seat.

"You get our shit together, follow me inside, and register for the fucking spelling bee." Mama tossed her sunglasses onto the dash. "You better win this fucking idiotic state thing, having me drive all this way before dawn. Bring my goddamn suitcase too."

"Yes, Mama."

Mama stepped from the pickup like a seasoned trucker and walked inside. After climbing several steep steps into the lobby, she pounded the bell on the registration desk. She surveyed the faded wallpaper; some sections were fighting to cling to the wall, while others had given up and were rolling off. She pounded the bell again.

Young B-4, wearing a dress, lugged two suitcases up several steep steps and waited a few feet behind Mama.

A bespectacled female clerk appeared from a room behind the counter. "Checking in?"

"No, I'm waiting for a fucking streetcar."

"I'll take that as a yes." The woman adjusted her glasses. "You here for the state championships?"

"We're gonna win the whole goddamn thing."

"Had a lot of winners checking in. The hotel is full except for the Red Room. No one will take it."

"Why? Bedbugs? Rats? Peeping Toms?"

"Ghosts! We've had several reports and a couple of suicides."

"Sounds like the Roadkill and Lilly's on a good day. We'll take the goddamn room … at a fucking discount, of course."

The clerk took out a key and placed it on the counter. "It's—"

"Why not have one of the fucking ghosts take us up?"

The clerk started to take the key back.

"It's just a fucking joke." Mama put one big hand on the key.

"You'll have to pay now." The clerk quivered slightly. "No refunds on the Red Room. And that's no joke."

Mama pulled out a credit card. "Here you go. No jokes, but no refunds sounds pretty heavy-handed, seeing as you can't rent the room anyway."

"Sorry. Fifty bucks. Cash only." The clerk adjusted her glasses again. "No cards."

Mama reached into her pocket, hunting for cash. She pulled out a handful of bills. She crumpled them more than they already were and started counting. "Bonnie, you'd better win the fucking contest."

"It's not a f—"

"Don't you start with the fucking excuses!"

Mama almost took out a sign—"Welcome to the State Spelling Bee Championship"—as she peeled out into a full high school parking lot, throwing dirt and sand into the afternoon air.

"Get inside and fucking win!" she said to B-4.

Later that afternoon, the blazing sun danced on the horizon as it set over Tonopah and the hotel. Inside the Red Room, Mama slugged back booze straight from a half-full bottle of forty-year-old Canadian Club. Young B-4, dressed in pajamas, lay beside her in their king-size bed.

"How could you? I mean, what fucking powder do the girls at Lilly's use to keep their privates dry and smelling fresh? *T-A-L-C-U-U-M.* How could you forget that extra *U*?"

Mama glanced at the whiskey bottle. She shook her head. "Fuck! Good thing I only got the forty-year-old stuff."

"Sorry, Mama. Second place isn't bad."

"I never raised you to be second." Mama took another swig. "I wasted the entire day and now the night, leaving Curley in charge of the Roadkill and Lilly's for what? Second fucking place!"

Suddenly, out of nowhere, an eerie female voice called, *"Whoooo arrrre youuu?"*

"What did you say?"

"Nothing, Mama. I'm so sorry."

*"Whoooo arrrre youuu?"* the eerie female voice said again.

"You're teasing me, right? Mad because I'm angry you only took second goddamn place." She took another swig.

"No, Mama. I haven't said a word."

"You musta heard that fucking voice: Whoooo arrrre youuu?"

"Yeah. You just said it. What's the matter?"

"Must be the Canadian Club." Mama poured it into the toilet and flushed. She climbed into bed next to B-4.

*"You are in my room, the room where I murdered my fourth husband after he cheated on me,"* the eerie voice said out of nowhere.

"You had to hear that." Mama put one slightly shaking arm around young B-4.

"No. Is there something wrong?"

*"I cut off his dick and then his balls before I slit his throat,"* the eerie voice said. *"Were you the one he slept with?"*

Mama jumped out of bed and yelled, "Get up now! We're leaving this fucking shithole!"

"I'm sorry I disappointed you so much. I'll wash dishes for a month."

"Hurry. The bar's almost closed, and I'm grabbing a bottle, maybe two, for the ride home. We're never coming to this goddamn hotel again."

# CHAPTER 23

"**S**ure you don't want me to drive?" B-4 asked Ruben as they pulled into the heavy midday Las Vegas Boulevard traffic.

He hit the brakes. They screeched to a stop at a red light. B-4 launched forward, snapping her seat belt tight.

"Little different than Quebec," B-4 said.

"No, and not at all," Ruben said. "Seat belts take all the fun out of it."

"Where's this informant hangout? Hope it's not the Bellagio."

"Why?"

Their vehicle started to move forward.

"The last one I met there didn't live much longer."

"Sort of like everyone around you?"

"Come on. Only bad guys ..."

"And an internal affairs agent."

"I'm sure they'll hang that one on me too since the rifle wasn't found."

"This informant is scared, really scared. He doesn't want to be seen anywhere near us."

"Sounds like a smart one."

Their sedan traveled south and pulled into Denny's on Rainbow. B-4 and Ruben stepped out and walked into the crowded restaurant. Ruben surveyed the crowd. He spotted Enrique.

"He's in the corner booth over there."

They walked through the restaurant and stopped at the booth. Enrique's eyes darted around, searching for unwanted company.

"OK if we sit?" Ruben said.

"Hurry. I need to get out of here before I'm spotted with you."

B-4 and Ruben slid into the booth across from Enrique.

"Enrique, Agent Brown. Brown, Enrique," Ruben said.

"I have a couple of tips."

"They'd better be good," Ruben said.

"You're Agent Brown, the rookie, right? The one they're after?"

"They?" B-4 said after nodding.

"First things first, there's a large shipment of putty coming into Castillo's casino in a few hours."

"Putty?" Ruben said. "Not kiddy dough?"

"Explosives?" B-4 asked.

"Yep, from Canada. PE something or other. They're gonna sell it to the protesters and militia popping up everywhere. I heard it's the biggest deal Castillo's ever made."

"Gotta call my CBA guys on this. Anything about France?"

"France?" Enrique asked.

Ruben brushed it off. "This coffee … French. It's great. So?"

"You bring the cash?"

"Two big ones."

"Two hundred? More like five."

Ruben dug out some bills from a pocket. "Here, five."

"Who are 'they'?" B-4 asked.

"That's five more."

B-4 nodded toward Ruben's pocket.

"It better be good." Ruben pulled out more cash and handed it to Enrique.

"They are Castillo and his men, and they're really pissed at you. How many of his men did you kill?"

"Lost count."

"He's sending his right-hand guy and his killing team to take care of your father and those boys if you don't quit and leave him alone."

"My daddy?"

"They're bragging about it, getting the ATF rookie to resign."

"Holy shit!"

"I'm out of here and out of town." Enrique slid out of the booth. "You never saw me and won't ever again."

Enrique left as the waitress walked up. "He left? Without paying?"

B-4 pulled out a blood-stained twenty. "Here, take my last twenty."

The waitress picked it up and studied it.

"It's real," B-4 said. "It's been through a lot."

The waitress stuffed the twenty into her pocket and walked off.

"Ruben, can I borrow your cell phone?"

Ruben handed it to her, and she dialed.

A fair distance away, as the new truck moved along a two-lane road, Bobby picked up his cell, looked at the number, and answered. "Who is this?"

"Me, Daddy. Just heard there's a bunch of Castillo's men who are gonna kill you."

"If you don't resign, today, I'm guessing. I've been threatened all my life. Who's your source?"

"A fairly reliable," B-4 stopped and looked at Ruben, who nodded, "informant. Maybe we should—"

B-4 heard two shotgun blasts over the line. "Daddy! What was that?"

"We just left Tonopah, where the boys and Curley picked up new shotguns, twelve gauge. Got them chambered for three-inch shells, plus three in the magazine."

"You and the twelve gauge. Three-inch?"

"We're out in the middle of nowhere trying them out on a few rabbits, crows. Don't want to shoot the hawks."

"Stop in Fallon somewhere for the night. We'll call the FBI, DEA—everyone—and have them ready for Castillo's men."

"And have us miss all the fun? No way. We'll throw them a surprise party, maybe their last one."

"Daddy, no!"

"Come on, Bonnie. You're having all the fun down there. Let your old man have a little too."

"Daddy! I'll resign now!"

"Give the cell to the agent, will you?"

Bonnie handed the cell to Ruben.

"Yes?"

"You aren't gonna let my little girl resign from something she always wanted, are you?"

"Sir?"

"You don't work for me, but you've got my daughter's life in your hands."

"Thinking that's totally up to her." Ruben looked at B-4.

"You believe the informant?"

"And the note left in the hand of my dead partner threatening you."

"Thanks from an old codger who loves her. Got it?"

"Yes, sir. Got it!"

The line went dead.

"What Daddy say about the threat?"

"He will always love you."

# CHAPTER 24

Inside his isolated desert compound, Castillo sat with Jose by the swimming pool. Both were drinking margaritas.

"Did our man deliver the message?"

"Yeah, boss."

"And they received our little gift-wrapped package."

"Yeah, boss." Jose cracked his knuckles. "She's got the message."

"Let's see what happens at the casino." Castillo sipped his margarita. "She shows, you head for Battle Mountain."

"Got it, boss." Jose raised his goblet to toast. "Great plan."

Ruben and B-4 entered the ATF parking lot and drove past two Las Vegas Glass Company window replacement trucks. The crews were unloading sections of glass. They parked, entered ATF headquarters, and walked to Agent Silva's office.

Silva spun his chair around and motioned for B-4 to close the door. They took a seat in front of him.

"See you're still here, Agent Brown."

"I am, and I'm not resigning."

"I tried to talk to her, sir, but—"

"I come by my hard head genetically, sir. When someone threatens me, I think immediately of Mama. Threats lead to fighting words, and Mama never backed down from a good fight, no matter what."

"From what I know about your mama, it got her killed, didn't it?"

"It was to protect me and Curley."

"This threat about you … you going to protect your father and your friends and maybe save your own skin, is that it?"

"If it's for real, I'll deal with it. Could just be a smoke screen, something Mama dealt with many times."


Jessica Whitehall, an ugly bone-thin woman in her thirties, marched into the Roadkill and over to Mama behind the bar. At Jessica's side was Boris, a burly six-foot-eight man with a beard. He wore coveralls and held a baseball bat.

"Well, well, what do we have here? Mrs. Fucking Ugly and … " Mama glanced at Boris and did a double-take. "Say, didn't you used to wear those thick glasses?"

"You talking to me?" Boris grumbled.

"Oh, that's right. It was fucking hearing aids."

"Enough." Jessica Boris cut off. "You killed my Jasper. You and your evil girls."

Mama reached under the bar, pulled out a ledger, and pretended to study it. "Jasper. Let's see … One of Lilly's best customers. If he could get what he wanted at home, he wouldn't have visited so often, would he? Or maybe that part of your anatomy has a fucking lock on it."

"If you don't shut the whorehouse down, Boris is gonna beat you within an inch of your horrible life, you and that little girl who kisses all those worthless boys."

Young B-4 entered through the back door and saw angry Jessica and huge Boris. "Mama, you want me to get Curley and the boys?"

"It's OK, Bonnie. Mrs. Whitehall thinks we should shut down Lilly's for killing … let's see … her husband, Jasper."

"He the one with the funny little—"

"That's the one. Couldn't hear either."

"You having her work inside Lilly's? That's child abuse!"

"Looking at your fucking face, now, that's child and adult abuse."

"Boris, show the lady who's boss?" Jessica stepped aside to give Boris a clear path to Mama.

Boris walked forward, ready to swing the bat.

"I was half-right. He can hear. Just can't see where to swing that!" Mama reached up and grabbed his nose with one hand and his crotch with the other. She pinched tightly, and Boris dropped the bat, screaming. "You get out of here and take Mrs. Godzilla with you. Your Roadkill and Lilly's privileges have been hereby revoked."

Jessica glared at Boris. "What? You?"

"Out, both of you. Now!"

Boris left holding his crotch as Jessica pointed her finger at Mama. "You haven't heard the last of this."

"Boris has."

"Get fucked!"

"Yes, I can. By the way, Lilly's does lesbians too."

As they left, Mama grabbed the baseball bat Boris had dropped. She studied it. "Willie Mays, my favorite."

"Did she just try to threaten us, Mama?"

"Nah, just a little idle chatter." Mama feigned swinging the bat. "This bat isn't all that big."

It was late in the afternoon as the JJ Posse Express pickup pulled into Hawthorne. Curley glanced into the truck box. The boys were asleep.

"A bit too much excitement." Curley rubbed the barrel of his new shotgun. "These new shotguns … shiny gold triggers. Never had one like this."

"The best a credit card with unlimited money behind it can buy." Bobby pulled the platinum credit card from his shirt pocket and flashed it at Curley.

"Real nice. From your other daughter?"

"Apparently she has a lot, with a little to spare for the old man."

"What's B-4 gonna do? Resign?"

"If I know her, absolutely not. She takes after her mother, and you know better than I that she would never let a threat stop her from doing what she wanted to do."

"Never, and I mean *never*. So should we get ready for World War III?"

"I guess we should prepare. Find it hard to believe that someone would come all the way from Vegas thinking doing us in would stop Bonnie."

"What we gonna do?" Curley asked as he stared at his new shotgun. "These new guns are beautiful and shoot straight, but those guys, they'll have automatics, firepower. We won't have a chance."

"We've got right on our side. No matter what, right always wins over wrong."

"Not in a casino. You could gamble on right and still lose your ass."

"A roll of the dice, Curley. We'll give it our all."

"That's what I'm afraid of." Curley rubbed the gold triggers.

"That's not a genie lamp. Got two chances with that, Curley."

Curley smiled and continued rubbing.


Three men wearing dark suits exited an SUV in the ATF parking lot and walked toward the building. Inside, the secretary ushered them to Silva's office.

"Sir, three FBI agents are here to see you."

Silva nodded. "Show them in."

Shortly after, FBI agents Hall, Shannon, and Klein sat in chairs in front of Silva's desk.

"Gentlemen, to what do I owe this pleasure?" Silva stood and shook their hands.

"We've been sent here to arrest one of your agents, a Bonnie Brown," Agent Hall said.

"Arrest?" Silva returned to his chair and sat down. "What for?"

"We have information and direction from the Department of Justice to put Agent Brown in custody and investigate the murder of a citizen, apparently killed by wild shots from a shooting range," Agent Hall said. "She's also killed several other law-abiding citizens."

"And, if I can ask, where does this information come from?"

"From a Nevada Congressman and anonymous sources," Hall said. "The attorney general has demanded we look into this immediately."

"You're saying that the named agent, in defending herself from a sniper on a hill who had just killed one of our own ATF agents, is somehow breaking the law?"

"We don't have any information about there being a sniper," Agent Shannon said. "We do understand that an ATF agent was killed by an errant bullet at a shooting range that allows AK-47s, machine guns, bump stocks, and automatic handguns, many without proper supervision."

"Unbelievable!"

"Would you like to call the attorney general and verify the orders we received?" Klein said.

"I'll take your word for it after I see your identification."

"You don't believe we're with the FBI?" Hall said.

"Trust me," Silva said as he looked at Hall's badge. "We have had all kinds of people say they were all kinds of—"

"So that good enough or do you want to see the others?" Hall interrupted.

"Looks authentic." Silva handed the badge back to Hall. "You need to understand, Agent Brown has been under tremendous pressure from an underworld boss for killing his men and others in a weapons raid. Then being kidnapped! Then there's the pot factory that turned murdered people into fertilizer."

"You must be kidding," Agent Hall said.

"That's only been in the last couple of days. And she's a rookie."

"Regardless, we follow orders," Hall said. "Do you?"

"We both work for the government. What do you think?"

"Where is she?" Hall asked. "We need to arrest her ASAP and get on with it."

"One of our agents took her to pick up a cell phone and some lunch."

"Call the agent and get her back here immediately," Hall said.

Silva picked up his cell phone and dialed. He pretended it was answered. "Agent Ruben, please call me ASAP." Silva put his cell back on top of his desk. "Left him a message. He must be involved in something important."

Hall stood and handed Silva his card. "Have her here for us in an hour or we will go looking for her ourselves."

"I'll see what I can do."

The FBI agents stood and left Silva's office. Once they disappeared, Silva texted Ruben, "Call me ASAP!"

His cell phone rang almost immediately. He answered. "Agent Brown with you?"

"Yes, sir," Ruben replied, talking into a dashboard speaker. "Any more information on the drop?"

"FBI agents were just here looking for Agent Brown."

"Me?" B-4 leaned toward the dash. "What for?"

"They have orders from the attorney general to detain you while they investigate the alleged murder of that sniper on the hill and—"

"What? The sniper killed Agent Smith! Who's doing this to me?"

"My guess is the same congressman who filed a letter on you earlier."

"He's done it again? Castillo. This is all Castillo!"

"What should I do, sir?" Ruben asked.

"They said they wanted Brown here in an hour or they'd go looking for her."

"After we eat, we're on our way to pick up a new cell phone for B-4. Want me to bring her in now?"

"You didn't hear this from me, but maybe you two should check out Castillo's casino and prevent the drop. That should take precedence over a phony investigation."

"Got it," Ruben said.

"Maybe I should just resign … make everyone, including Castillo, happy."

"Hell no, Brown," Silva said angrily. "This is about all of us, not just you!"

"Sure does seem to be just about me."

"Agent Ruben, you want to do something? Don't let Brown resign."

Ruben pressed the speaker button, ending the call. "That was certainly exciting."

"You and I have different definitions." B-4 leaned back. "So the casino?"

"On our way after we eat and get you a cell phone."

Inside his isolated desert compound, Castillo sat next to the swimming pool with Jose. "Think I'll go to the casino with you."

"Isn't that taking a risk, boss?"

"I want to be there if she does show up." Castillo dipped a finger into his margarita and sucked on it. "I want to look into her eyes and see what kind of person she is."

"I saw her briefly, boss. She's hard."

"I'm harder." Castillo grabbed a slice of lemon and sucked the juice out of it. "If she does show, let me see for myself."

Castillo's cell phone rang. He listened and then said, "Thank you, Congressman Jacoby." Castillo glanced at Jose and smiled. "The FBI? Excellent." Castillo looked at an unlit cigar sitting in an ashtray while he listened. "Yes, I hope they do throw her in jail for a while. Thank you." He put the cell phone down and picked up the cigar and a lighter.

"The rookie is going to jail?"

"According to our congressman, within the hour." Castillo bit the tip off his cigar.

"Then my trip to Battle Mountain is off?"

"Only on hold." Castillo flicked the lighter. "Let's see what happens."

Ruben and B-4 walked into Castillo's casino. The slots were jammed with customers. Payout bells rang, lights flashed, and the tables were packed three deep.

"Obviously a shipment wouldn't come inside here," Ruben said.

"They all have an internal area almost as big as the whole casino where they provide services to employees. Day care, banking, whatever," B-4 said as they walked. "The receiving dock is usually around the back."

"Lead on, Agent." Ruben surveyed the crowd. People watched on as eager gamblers spent their earnings as fast as they could, only to lose. Cheers and groans were everywhere.

B-4 nodded toward the ceiling and corners. "Their security. We'll be on every screen."

"Smile, B-4. Let them know we're happy to be here."

B-4 led Ruben through the casino and then motioned toward the washrooms. "Come on. Behind the bathrooms. Strange. Don't see the usual security a casino has ... Should be everywhere."

Across the building, inside a room with multiple monitors, Jose peered over the heads of two male security techs. "Look! Near the bathrooms."

"That the couple you're looking for?" one of the techs said as he pointed at the monitor.

"That's her, probably with another agent."

"You want us to get them?" the second security tech said.

"No. Let's see where they go."

Jose stepped away and dialed his cell phone. "Boss?"

Castillo sat on a white couch inside his luxurious casino suite, thumbing through a fly-fishing manual. He paused and answered. "She here?"

"Yep. She and a guy are walking past the restrooms toward the hallway leading to the delivery tunnel."

"Let her go. I'll call our new friends at the FBI and tell them where she is."

"I thought you wanted to see her personally."

"I do. Bring her upstairs. Send the FBI to my office when they arrive."

"What about the guy?"

"If he gives you any trouble, you know what to do."

"Yes, boss."

Ruben and B-4 walked toward the receiving dock. Ruben glanced at his watch and surveyed the area. "This is very strange. The shipment should be here now. It's two o'clock."

"You think we've been set up again?"

"I trust my guy."

"Only things I trust are my daddy, the boys, and Johnnson, and none of them are here now."

They took a few more steps. Several men with automatic weapons appeared.

"Shit! No Johnnson, no chance."

Ruben and B-4 took out their badges. "ATF agents doing an inspection."

Jose stepped up from the shadows. He pointed at Ruben. "You can leave."

"Not without her."

"Walking or in a box?"

The men raised their weapons ready to fire.

"Go." B-4 nudged Ruben slightly away. "They don't want you."

"You're crazy. We stick together. Besides, they're breaking the law."

"Go! He's the guy I saw at that shithole café. He means business."

"She is very smart for a rookie. We're just holding her until the FBI gets here."

"Leave! Get out of here."

"OK, OK." Ruben stared at B-4. Then he began to walk slowly toward an opening leading to the parking lot.

"Follow him until he gets in his car and leaves," Jose yelled.

Several armed men immediately started to follow Ruben.

Jose looked at B-4. "Bring her."

Several more men with weapons forced B-4 toward a door that led to a service elevator. They pushed her inside.

Jose and three men with weapons pointed at B-4 stepped in behind her. Jose punched a VIP floor button. Moments later, B-4 was escorted inside Castillo's luxurious suite. Castillo was still sitting on the white couch but was now drinking a glass of red wine. B-4 was forced to sit in a white chair opposite Castillo. Jose and the three men pointed their weapons at her.

"Finally, I get to meet the little lady who has depleted my workforce. No need to trim my employees when you're around."

"And you're the son of a bitch who has been after me for doing my job, catching and eliminating criminals, or as you say, 'trimming your employees.'" Bullies like Castillo did not, and would never, scare her.

"Criminals … employees … I call them my customers, my brothers, even my cousins. This morning it was Jesus. My favorite relative, my dead wife's youngest brother, if you care to know."

"I don't really care about that piece of shit."

"Well, like you, he was a great shot, the best I had. I'll miss his cooking. His tamales were the best in the world. Might set my family back for generations."

"Don't care for tamales. But when I get Johnnson back, I will show you what real shooting is like. Then I'll blow off that ugly head of yours like a ripe old pumpkin."

The men clicked off their safety locks and aimed at B-4's head.

"Relax, everyone. Don't waste your bullets. Just hollow words from a reckless person about to lose her father, and maybe her friends, while she marks time in a federal jail."

"Never been much for using the safety lock when I'm about to kill someone."

"Well, we're just being responsible. But I think that time has passed."

"You want me to resign, I resign. Leave my father and the rest out of this. But agent or not, I will blast that shit-eating grin off your face before I pop your fat ass and feed it to the coyotes."

"My oh my, so much anger. I'm not sure if coyotes like pumpkins. But those big tits must store of a lot of venom."

B-4 grabbed her breasts and pointed them like dueling pistols. "These are Mama's tits, and if she were here, she'd shoot off your dick and balls before she killed you."

A male security tech walked in. "Sir, the FBI is here."

"Show them in."

Hall, Shannon, and Klein walked in. Jose and the men lowered their weapons.

Castillo stood and said, "Gentlemen, welcome. It took several of my men to detain her until you got here."

"The congressman said you set a trap for her," Hall said. "The FBI thanks you."

"Just doing my job as a law-abiding citizen."

"Who's not long for this world," B-4 said.

"She's definitely not worth one cent of my hard-earned taxpayer money." Castillo sipped his wine. "I hope she gets what she deserves."

"Thank you, Mr. Castillo." Hall reached for handcuffs. "Do we have to cuff you, Agent, or are you coming willingly?"

"We're not done." B-4 walked up to Castillo, leaned down, and went nose-to-nose with him.

"Come on, Agent." Hall grabbed her arm and put the handcuffs on her.

B-4 glared at Castillo and then turned and was escorted out by Hall. The door closed behind them. Jose and the men looked at Castillo.

"Battle Mountain, boss?"

"You read my mind." Castillo tipped the goblet back and chugged the rest of his wine.

# CHAPTER 25

B-4, handcuffed, was led by FBI agents Klein and Shannon past a county detention center sign and into a modern facility in downtown Las Vegas. Agent Hall followed. He was on his cell phone. "Had to cuff her. Booking her now."

Inside a detention center interrogation room, they sat her down and handcuffed her to the table. Hall, holding a file, and Shannon sat on the opposite side of the table. Klein sat nearby in a chair against the wall. The door opened, and Ruben and Silva walked in.

Silva immediately spotted the handcuffs. "Really, Agent Hall?"

"Her call."

Silva and Ruben sat down next to B-4, opposite the agents.

"Take the cuffs off," Silva demanded.

Hall glanced at B-4 and nodded to Shannon. Shannon pulled out a key and freed B-4's hands.

"Ruben called and told me what was happening," Silva said to B-4. "Castillo captured you?"

"Captured? More like trapped."

"Never trust an informant."

"Enough of the ATF homecoming formalities," Hall said.

"What kind of brotherhood do you have down here?" Ruben said. "We'd have her in a minute back up in Canada."

"Welcome to the good old USA." Hall laughed.

"You work for Castillo, the congressman, or the FBI?" Silva asked Hall.

"Fuck you too, ATF Silva," Hall said.

"Special Agent in Charge Silva."

"We are going to tape Agent Brown's conversation if you're finished, Silva. Or do you want me to tape the dick measuring contest?" Hall asked.

Silva leaned back in his chair and nodded to B-4 as Shannon placed a tape recorder onto the table and turned it on. "Agent … Special Agent Bonnie Brown, whatever you say may be used against you," Hall started.

"Against me? For what?"

"There are serious charges, all calling for some serious prison time," Hall said. "At your trial—"

"Are you telling me I'm being arrested for doing my job?"

"Please, Miss Brown," Hall said.

"Special Agent Brown, sir!"

"Right, well, we've been sent by the attorney general of the United States to investigate very serious allegations against you made by a local congressman on behalf of his constituents," Hall said.

"Very serious charges," Agent Shannon added.

"Who's doing the interview? You or Agent Hall?" Silva said.

"I'm the agent in charge," Hall said.

"Right, so I assume Mr. Castillo is one of his constituents," B-4 said. "Who else?"

"Let's just say, the most recent murder of a citizen this morning has been added to the charges," Hall said.

"Murder? The sniper on the hill who shot and killed Agent Smith?"

Hall picked up a file on the table as B-4 ranted.

"Smith was standing next to me. I think the bullet was meant for me. Got that in your file?"

"What I got is you took two wild shots from inside the range and just happened to kill an innocent bystander watching from a hill," Hall read the file aloud.

"I don't understand."

"That's the report we have." Hall tapped the file with his right index finger.

"And Agent Smith?" B-4 said. "Explain that!"

"There was a lot of gunfire at that range," Hall said. "Agent Ruben, you were there. A lot of fire, right?"

"Yes, but what Special Agent Brown is saying is the truth. There were no wild shots fired by her. She spotted the sniper's weapon and fired."

B-4 took an empty cartridge from her pocket and placed it on the table. "What about this? I picked it up from near the dead sniper."

"How'd you get that in here?" Agent Shannon asked.

"I'm a woman and I—"

"Too much information," Hall interrupted.

"Right then."

"How do we know it came from the alleged dead sniper?" Hall said. "You could have picked it up from anywhere. There were certainly enough casings around the firing range."

"Check it out with the bullet they dig out of Agent Smith's skull," B-4 said.

Hall picked up the shell with a tissue and studied it.

"There was no weapon found, was there? Nothing is listed in the report I have."

"Well, no," Ruben said.

"So tell me how there could be a shell?" Hall said.

"Well …"

"And have you ever seen anyone shoot like that from at least two hundred yards, maybe three? Two holes in a man's head?" Hall asked.

"Actually, I have. Agent Brown can shoot the wings off a mosquito at a hundred yards. She did it at the academy."

"Look! Castillo threatened to kill my father and my lifelong friends if I don't resign from the agency and leave him alone. Give me a piece of paper and I will resign right now. Agent Silva can witness it."

Silva signaled B-4 to zip her mouth shut.

"How do you know it was Mr. Castillo who threatened you?" Hall asked.

"That was on the note left in the dead agent's hand."

"Doesn't prove it was Castillo."

"Who else would have done that?"

"Was it signed?" Hall asked.

"Well … no," B-4 said.

Silva's cell phone buzzed. "Excuse me." He left the room.

Hall put the shell down and pushed a piece of paper and a pen in front of B-4. "We can wrap this up quickly."

Silva rushed back in and stood behind B-4. "Don't sign that paper!"

"What?" B-4 said, surprised.

"That was Fireball. He found out that several men carrying large weapon cases just boarded one of Castillo's jets with a flight plan taking them to Elko."

"Castillo is still going after Daddy!"

"How do you know that?" Hall asked. "They might be going on a hunting trip."

"With an arsenal?" Silva said.

"I need to get there right away." B-4 pushed back in her chair and made to stand.

"Agent, you aren't going anywhere," Hall said. "I am arresting you for the murder of Jesus Ramirez this morning and for the murder of several others whose names are too lengthy to list."

"There's no way," Silva said.

"Agent Silva, let me remind you that I am acting with the authority of the attorney general," Hall said.

"This is bullshit!" B-4 slid her chair back further and stood. "I'm out of here."

Agent Klein stood and reached for his weapon.

"Sit, B-4." Ruben put one hand on her arm. "We'll find you a lawyer and clear this whole thing up."

"My daddy needs me."

"So does the detention center! You lose." Hall motioned to Agent Klein.


A private jet flew through the skies above Nevada, high above the clouds. Jose swiveled back and forth in a plush leather chair as he talked on his cell phone. A beautiful female flight attendant appeared with a tray of drinks. "Sir?"

Jose took a glass of red wine.

"I'll take that whiskey," a hired gun said.

Jose covered his cell phone and glared at him. "Keep it down. I'm talking to the boss."

"You heard him. Keep it down." The hired gun said to the others.

Nodding, they all reached for drinks.

Jose continued his conversation. "A little delay at McCarran International. Had to wait for fuel. We're wheels up now. I only have three men."

Inside his luxurious suite, Castillo watched a monitor showing the blackjack tables. He zeroed in on a table with an old woman and a female dealer. "Three?"

"That's all that's left who we can trust, boss."

Castillo leaned back on the white couch. "Let me call some of our customers. I know they're upset at losing some of their brothers and sisters."

"The word might have gotten around that somehow we wasted some of them."

"I'll offer them money and more weapons. The militia always wants more of both … even over some of their friends."

"I have no idea what's waiting for us in Battle Mountain. Better to have an army."

"With those beautiful flags waving."

"Yes, boss. The rookie coming to join the party?"

"They're gonna lock her up, according to the congressman."

"One less big gun. One less fucking female problem."

"Call me when you get to Elko."

Castillo glanced at the monitor, watching the old woman drop a pile of chips on the floor. The female blackjack dealer quickly stepped out from the table and retrieved them for her. As she did, the old woman reached over and grabbed more house chips.

"Sonuvabitch!"

"What boss?"

"Got another fucking female problem to deal with." Castillo reached for a walkie-talkie.


Inside the detention center interrogation room, Silva and Ruben met with B-4. A booking officer opened the door. "Agent Brown, need to get you fingerprinted and booked."

"Give us one more minute," Silva requested.

The booking officer nodded and closed the door.

"I'm going to call some of my friends in Quebec and find out about the shipment that never happened," Ruben said.

"See if it ties back to Castillo," Silva said.

"What about Daddy?"

"We'll call the authorities in Battle Mountain," Silva said. "There's no way we can rustle up enough FBI now, or DEA, or anyone else."

"The local authorities! You mean the Lander County sheriff? Mama would be turning over in her grave if she heard that!"

Inside the Roadkill, Mama was on the telephone as she pulled her shotgun out from under the bar. "Sheriff? This is Mama over at the Roadkill. You need to get your sorry ass over here right now." She glanced at an empty roasting pan inside the kitchen. "I've got a problem."

She listened for a moment. "No, not that kinda problem, you fucking moron. Someone's been stealing rabbits from my freezer."

Mama listened and then cracked her double-barrel shotgun open with one hand. "What the fuck do I pay my taxes for? You get your butt over here now or your Lilly's privileges are revoked."

The Lander County sheriff's SUV pulled up in front of the Roadkill. Sheriff O'Toole, a balding, paunchy man in his forties, jumped out, wiped his lips, and adjusted his glasses. Sweat poured down his forehead. He glanced in the direction of Lilly's and then pulled his belt and revolver up over his protruding belly. He took a deep breath and walked inside.

Mama was in the kitchen doorway, holding her double-barrel shotgun. "'Bout time you showed. What's that shit on your face? Been eating those horrible donkey burgers again?"

"So what's up with the rabbits?"

"Curley, the boys, and Bonnie keep me supplied." Mama pointed at the empty roasting pan. "It's the Roadkill favorite, and I don't want to run out. I come to make a batch today, and the fucking rabbits are gone. All fucking gone!"

"What do you want me to do?"

"You can take fingerprints, can't you? Do a little goddamn detective work. Tell me you learned something at the fucking school the council sent you to."

"Let me have a look."

The sheriff squeezed past Mama. Once inside the kitchen, he opened a large walk-in freezer. Mama watched from the doorway, holding her shotgun high.

"Aren't you gonna use goddamn rubber gloves like they do on television? You might miss something, you blind bastard."

From inside the freezer, he looked at an empty shelf. "There's no rabbits in here."

"That's what I told you, you fucking idiot! They've been stolen. Use your goddamn sheriffing skills. Put out an APB or something."

"I'll go back to the office and see what I can come up with. Never had a case like this before."

"Shit! Hope nothing serious ever comes up like overnight parking or a flat tire on your SUV!"

"I'll get back to you, Mama." The sheriff squeezed past Mama on the way out. "Trust me."

As Sheriff O'Toole left, a young B-4 brushed in past him. "Mama, Mama, they really liked your gift."

"What gift? Who?" Mama put the shotgun back under the bar.

"The Women's Club. They're gonna make rabbit fricassee for the gala."

"Shit! That's right! Forgot we gave them away."

"You OK, Mama? Why was Sheriff O'Toole here?"

"Everything's fine now. Don't mention the gift to anyone. Say, how do you know the sheriff?"

"Came in to speak with us in school."

"What a fool. He was so fucking stupid. He didn't ask any intelligent questions."

"My daddy isn't stupid, is he?"

"Not in the slightest. Smartest thing he ever did was put me on that goddamn bus."

B-4, wearing an oversized orange jumpsuit, sat at a table with Ruben in a small room.

"You're gonna be out quick. Silva's on it. Just not likely by tonight."

"It's almost three o'clock. I've still got time to get on a plane and make it to Battle Mountain."

"Not today."

"I have a pilot friend at Nellis."

"B-4, you're in here for the night."

She surveyed the sparse room. "Locked up while my father is under attack? He'll have no chance against the firepower Castillo's guys will bring. I need to do something, anything."

"I called my contacts in Quebec, and no one has any clue about a shipment of putty to Vegas. My informant set us up real good. What you need to do now is get a great lawyer. You have anybody in mind?"

B-4 glanced around as she checked for security cameras. She leaned in. "Can you look up something on your cell phone?"

Ruben took out his cell.

"JJ Wellington, Mount Vernon. Virginia, I think."

Ruben entered the search. "Who might I ask is this?"

"Apparently a sister."

"You are full of surprises. Wait. Here it is."

"Dial her number, please."

Ruben entered the number. "Yes, is JJ Wellington available? Answering service? Could you please have her call her sister? Right." He glanced at B-4. "Use this number. Thank you."

Ruben's cell buzzed almost immediately. "Hello?"

On the other side of the country, JJ sat on a patio overlooking the Potomac. Her best friend, Jennifer, a brunette woman in her thirties with mesmerizing dark blue eyes, sat with her drinking blue-tinged Bombay. "So who are you? My answering service said my sister called."

Ruben passed his cell to B-4. "Yes, this is Bonnie Brown, Bobby Brown's daughter, the ex-detective from San Francisco. I understand we have something in common."

"Yeah, a very fertile father. He told me about you. Surprise, right?"

"Certainly was for me. Daddy just told me about you. But that's not why I called."

A female guard walked into the room and stepped up to B-4. "You're not allowed to talk on a cell phone."

"Just one minute. Didn't get my one call."

"Rules are rules, miss."

"You guys confiscated my new cell phone."

"This is an emergency. One minute?" Ruben asked.

"Well … you are allowed one call. One minute!"

"What's going on?" JJ asked

B-4 held the cell phone with both hands. "I only have one minute. Agent Ruben will fill you in. He's an ATF agent like me … or I was. Daddy is in grave danger tonight. An underworld boss and his men are going to kill him."

"Where? What?"

"They left Vegas and are headed to Battle Mountain to blow him and my best friends away. I'm a little detained at the moment. Is there any way you can help?"

"I'm four-plus hours away."

"It's nearly four here now. There might be time."

The female guard walked in. "Time to hang up, miss."

"Please?" B-4 handed the cell phone to Ruben, pushed back, stood, and left with the female guard.

"You still there?" Ruben said into the cell.

JJ stood and stared out at the Potomac. "Yeah. Sounds like there's a whole lot more to this story."

"Yep. Right now, though, she needs a great lawyer."

"I have a whole bunch of those at my disposal. But it appears our father needs more than legal minds."

"He does. Castillo has tried to kill B-4 a couple of times since she took out several of his men."

"B-4? Sounds like quite a young bear cat."

"I'd say more like a wolverine with one hell of a big gun. So?"

"I'll see what I can do."

Ruben put down his cell phone and watched B-4 disappear down the hallway. He picked it up again and dialed a number as he walked to an exit. "Silva? Better call Dubby Brown. Castillo's cavalry is on the way to Battle Mountain."

# CHAPTER 26

Agent Silva paced by several office windows inside ATF headquarters as he watched the afternoon sun turn the parking lot pavement into a hot griddle. He had his cell phone to his ear as his call was answered. "Bobby Brown? Agent Silva."

On Highway 80 East, the JJ Posse Express with Bobby at the wheel passed a road sign— "Battle Mountain, 105 Miles"—and pulled into a sixteen-pump Lovelock gas station. The Battle Mountain Boys and Curley stepped down from the truck and headed toward a sign advertising fast-food and slots.

Bobby picked up his cell phone. "Thanks for waiting, Agent Silva. My little girl OK?"

"We had a visit from the FBI. They took her into custody for allegedly killing a civilian at the firing range."

"What? Fucking 'allegedly.' She would never—"

"I agree with you. But the attorney general's ordered the FBI to investigate. They have no choice."

"Is that what really happened, or is Castillo still after her?"

"According to one of the agents who was with your daughter, she picked off a sniper who had just killed another agent at well over two hundred yards, maybe three. An impossible shot. Incredible!"

"That sounds more like it."

"The other agent, one from internal affairs, didn't say anything about a sniper because a rifle wasn't found."

"Shit! Goddamn IA!"

"Castillo's threatened to kill you if she doesn't resign, as you know. Didn't seem to matter when she said she would quit. Castillo's men are on their way there to kill you and your gang anyhow."

"Kill the Battle Mountain Boys? Really on their way, eh? Well, I guess we'll have to get out the welcome wagon."

"Their flight should arrive in Elko at seven."

"I guess the party will start around six."

"Six?"

"I always like a little foreplay."

"I suggest less foreplay. Maybe you and your boys take off and go somewhere out of the way. It'll take several hours for us to bring in the FBI, troops, whatever we can muster."

"No way! I've never backed down from a fight. Not starting now."

Curley walked up. "The boys need some money. They're thinking they're on a hot streak!"

Bobby pulled out a wad of cash, peeled off a few bills, and handed them to Curley.

"Thanks for the information," Bobby said to Silva. "I'm sure you'll hear the fireworks all the way to Vegas. Take care of my baby, please."

"I will. Maybe this should be an exception to your bravado, Mr. Brown. Maybe you should just let it go."

"Never. I did give up once, and that was enough."


In San Francisco's North Beach late at night, Bobby stared at the Gold Spike sign a few feet away with the police captain. Angelo Martinelli's body was covered with a tarp beside a long black stretch limousine. The body of Angelo's wife lay on the sidewalk, also covered with a tarp.

Their teenage daughter, Angelanne, was being consoled by two female officers.

She pointed at Bobby. "I am going to kill you. You murderer!"

The female officers forcibly took her away from the scene as Bobby and the police captain watched. "I'd say you better watch out for her, detective," the captain said. "She's full of fire and vinegar."

"Maybe I've killed my last bad guy, Captain."

"What would you do if you quit? Run a bar?"

"I don't know, but definitely not a bar. Being a cop has been my life ..."

"And you ended the lives of dozens of criminals."

"But never an innocent person, a mother with a young daughter to boot."

"Well, she also has a son. His name's Junior. He might be someone to watch out for too."

"I hear he's left the city."

"Maybe you shouldn't quit right now. We have your back. You go and hide somewhere and you're on your own."

"Somehow I don't think Junior would try. He and his father didn't get along too good. I'd be more worried about that young girl."

"Well, let me know."

Bobby pulled out his badge. "Here's my badge. I'm keeping my gun just in case."

"You're really gonna quit? Means criminals in the city can breathe easy."

"That's the way it's gonna be, Captain. Bobby Brown is finally hanging it up. I've just became eligible for my pension. Time to stay out of harm's way."

"That will never happen. Somewhere, someday …"

"But not today."

In his luxurious casino suite, Castillo sat at the glass-top table, finishing a steak. An scantily clad woman appeared. "Time for your special massage?"

"That'll be dessert, sweetie." Castillo smiled. His cell phone rang. He glanced at the display and quickly answered. "Congressman Jacoby, what a pleasure."

The Washington, DC, skyline glowed as day turned to night. Congressman Jacoby, a slight man with geeky glasses, was on his cell phone in the halls of Congress. "I just stepped out of a criminal justice meeting. Got a text about what's happening. Your men are on the way to do what?"

"Relax, relax." Castillo peeled off his shirt. "Everything's under control. Who texted you?"

"One of my contacts inside the attorney general's office. He said you sent your men to Battle Mountain to kill Bobby Brown and a few others. That's my district! You promised to stay out of my territory."

"Mr. Congressman, no one treats me the way I have been treated, especially a young renegade ATF agent. Just making sure she gets the message to back off."

"I thought we had her locked up." Jacoby started to pace.

"She is, but her father has already been here once and caused some problems." Castillo stepped out of his trousers. "I'm making sure he doesn't come here again, him or anybody protecting the agent."

"What am I supposed to do?" Jacoby stopped pacing and threw up one hand.

"Relax. Keep the money I send you. Go out to one of those fancy DC restaurants and have an expensive meal on me. See one of those beautiful women I provide."

"I also heard there's an army of militia headed there to help your men." Jacoby started to pace again. "This is going to put a black mark on my efforts to keep law and order in Nevada."

"They are angry at the little lady and her father too. Lost a few good soldiers."

"This is too much, Mr. Castillo, way too much."

"Put whatever spin you want on whatever happens tonight in Battle Mountain." Castillo prepared to lay down on the couch. "Then hop on a plane tomorrow and have a constituent's day out here with me. Could be you'll be thanking us and the militia for cleaning up a criminal element in your district."

"That is a real stretch, Castillo.

"A day or two back home could be great for you right now." Castillo lay on his stomach.

"Think you might be right." Jacoby stopped pacing. "Got some pressures on me that have suddenly emerged from God knows where."

"I'll have a special massage waiting for you when you get here." Castillo turned his head to one side so he could continue talking.

"Thank you, Mr. Castillo. See you in Las Vegas."

Castillo dropped his cell phone onto the plush carpet. The almost-naked young lady bent over him.

"I think I'm ready for some sweet young dessert."

Inside ATF headquarters, Silva and Ruben stood near Fireball's cubicle and watched his fingers fly across a keyboard.

The tech whiz paused. "From the internet buzz, there's a few militia groups mobilizing and heading toward the Battle Mountain area."

"Is Castillo's plane still en route to Elko?" Silva asked.

"Yep. Interesting. Elko just received word there's a large private aircraft from Virginia scheduled to arrive in Elko an hour after Castillo's plane."

"Any idea whose plane?" Ruben asked.

"No name, a private company."

"That is very interesting." Silva rubbed his chin.

"Maybe Agent Brown's sister to the rescue?" Ruben surmised.

"Check the military channels, government political channels … See what's going on out there," Silva said. "Could be something big."

"They don't call it Battle Mountain for nothing," Ruben said.

"Shame Bonnie's gonna miss it all," Silva said.

"There's no way the FBI can make any of those charges stick, can they?" Ruben asked.

"Welcome to US politics, Agent Ruben." Silva laid a hand on Ruben's shoulder. "Speaking of which, any way we can check on the congressman's activity? He's in the middle of this somehow."

"He's in a meeting at the Capitol," Fireball said. "Wait, he just left the meeting."

"I'll bet he isn't going to Battle Mountain," Silva said.

"He's booked on a flight to Vegas for tomorrow a.m.," Fireball said.

"Castillo!" Silva pounded the side of his leg.

"Pulling him home to do his political thing," Ruben said.

"After World War III!" Silva said.

# CHAPTER 27

The sun had just set behind the JJ Posse Express as it roared toward Battle Mountain. All five Battle Mountain boys sat in the truck box, checking their shotguns. As Curley drove, he glanced in the rearview mirror and then turned to Bobby in the passenger seat.

"The boys are getting ready, boss. Want me to take an off-ramp and let them take some target practice?"

"Nope. We'll need all the ammunition we got for what's coming."

"You think a bunch of hoods are really flying up here to kill us just because B-4 killed a few of them?"

"It's a possibility. They might try. Always good to be prepared."

"Sounds a little far out to me."

"They got her in jail for nothing, didn't they?" Bobby rested the back of his head against a seat rest. "A bunch of cooked-up charges."

"You know, I liked driving Mama's pickup better than this one."

"You were used to it." Bobby closed his eyes. "This one's got everything and more, except it can't pass a gas station."

"Mama woulda liked it because of the color, bloodred."

"She turned out to be quite a lady." Bobby's eyes were closed.

"Yes, she was, and her namesake chip off the old block is a great one too."

"Yep, she was. Still is in my books." Bobby felt the truck sway slightly. "Keep your eyes on the road. Don't want any roadkill on the way."

"Right boss."

"I gotta make a couple of calls." Bobby opened his eyes, sat up, and took out his cell. He punched in a number and listened. "Rosie, you're still there?"

Rosie was behind the Roadkill bar with Lander County Sheriff O'Toole on the other side. "Yes, Mr. Brown."

"Thought you would be headed to Elko to catch one of JJ's airplanes."

"I called and she told me to wait here."

"Why? The whole world around Battle Mountain will be under siege soon."

"She didn't say."

"That's strange, really strange."

"The sheriff is here, and he wants to talk to you."

"Put him on."

"Mr. Brown? Got called about a bunch of men headed here to kill you, Curley, and the boys?"

"That's the rumor. May be the reality, according to the Las Vegas ATF agents."

"That'll never happen. Too bizarre."

"I'd rather be prepared. Just in case."

"There's no one else on duty. Just me. How much time do you think I have? I need to call in reinforcements."

"We are a half hour out. See if any of our friends might be able to help—"

"Help defend the Roadkill and Lilly's?" the sheriff interrupted. "Good luck. Most of the locals would rather see both burn to the ground."

"Not friends of my establishments?"

"And me, well, I haven't fired a round since certification a year ago."

Rosie poured the perspiring sheriff a shot of tequila. He immediately slugged it back and slammed the glass down.

"You're the law, and these folks will be breaking the law when they attack."

"If they attack." The sheriff motioned to Rosie to pour another shot.

"Well, Sheriff?"

"This is beyond me. My wife and child need me."

"Well, then, leave your badge with the young lady. You've made me the sheriff in your absence."

"I can't do that, Mr. Brown." The sheriff downed the tequila.

"You have the authority to swear me in, don't you?"

"Why, yes … but—"

"You just did. Leave the badge, go home, take a drive out of town with your wife and kid."

"But—"

Rosie slid another shot of tequila in front of the sheriff.

"If I'm still alive after this, if this happens, I will gladly give you back your badge."

"But, but—"

"Bye, O'Toole. Give the phone back to the young lady."

Sheriff O'Toole slugged back the tequila and slammed the shot glass onto the bar. He handed the phone back to Rosie. Then he reached inside his pocket, pulled out his badge, placed it next to the empty shot glass, and left.

"He gave me his badge," Rosie said. "What do I do?"

"Put the badge under the bar. And you, maybe you should get out of there and take a walk."

"Can't. You have a customer playing slots, an old man who keeps asking when you're coming back." Rosie looked at Benneschott in disguise across the floor.

"Old man … graying?"

"How'd you know?"

"He seems to show up now and then. Leave him a bottle and go to the safe room inside Lilly's."

"Yes, Mr. Brown."

"Now!"

Bobby put his cell down and looked at the highway ahead.

"Everything OK?" Curley asked.

"You can call me Sheriff now." Bobby leaned back and rested his head on the seat. His eyes slowly closed.

# CHAPTER 28

The JJ Posse Express pulled up in front of the Roadkill in a cloud of dust and swirls of sand. Bobby, Curley, and the Battle Mountain Boys climbed out.

"It's good to be home," Kermit said.

"Can't wait to eat some good jack," Kevin added.

"Do you think this Rosie person knows how to cook jack?" Karlos asked.

"Boys, if there's jack, I'll cook it," Curley said as they walked toward the saloon doors.

"If there isn't, I'll go and kill us a few," Kareem said. "Just need a flashlight and my shotgun."

Bobby shook his head as they entered the Roadkill. "Well, Curley, guess you just can't take the Roadkill out of the Battle Mountain Boys."

Rosie was behind the bar. She looked up and reached for the shotgun.

"Whoa, Rosie. It's just me, Bobby."

She shook her head. "Sorry, Mr. Brown."

"Meet Curley and the boys."

"Ma'am," Curley and the boys said in unison.

"You sure are big," Kevin said. "You eat yeast or something?"

Rosie smiled as if she'd heard those type of comments many times before.

Curley nudged Kevin to mind his manners.

"Rosie is one of the most valuable people my daughter JJ has at the estate," Bobby said. He nodded at Rosie. "Saved JJ's life once."

"I like her smile," Kareem said.

"Glad to see you all," Rosie said. "I'm all alone."

"The old man?" Bobby said as he looked around for the disguised Benneschott.

"He left just after you and I talked, so I stayed instead of going into Lilly's."

"I guess you're safe with us right now. It's about seven, and the real fun shouldn't start until eight or so. Anybody hungry?"

"Any rabbit left over?" Kermit asked.

"You eat … rabbits?" Rosie said surprised. "When I lived in the park, rabbits were my friends."

"It's pretty much a staple around here," Bobby said. "I have a few steaks, I'm sure."

"The boys probably want to polish off the stew, if there's any left," Curley said. "I'll take one of them steaks …"

"From that mountain lion a few months back," Bobby said.

"Mountain lion? I want one too," Kevin said.

"I'll defrost the stew and the steaks." Bobby walked toward the kitchen. "You guys can have a feast."

"You have a burger and some fries in there?" Rosie asked.

"Check over at Lilly's," Bobby said. "Sometimes the girls send a runner to MacDonald's in between, well, you know. You need to stay in their safe room anyhow. Thanks for watching both places."

Rosie nodded.

"Any word from JJ?"

"Nothing, Mr. Brown. When I call, her phone goes to voice mail. Bye, boys." Rosie walked out.

"I'd like to see her take on that Castillo guy," Curley yelled to Bobby as he watched Rosie disappear.

"Wait until you meet my daughter, JJ. I hear she and Rosie had quite a tussle in jail."

Curley walked toward the kitchen and stood in the doorway. "How we gonna defend ourselves, boss? It's just us … isn't it?"

"You ever read about the Alamo?" Bobby opened the walk-in freezer door.

"Saw it on television. All of them died, including Davey Crockett and Jim Bowie."

"But they gave it their all. It was a glorious stand."

"Maybe I'll eat two of them steaks and some stew." Curley looked back at the boys, who were already playing slots.

The nearly naked young female masseuse served a margarita to Castillo. He finished buttoning his shirt and took a seat on the white couch. "That was some special massage."

"Is that all you want, Mr. Castillo?"

"Give me ten minutes to get my strength back. I need to make a phone call."

"You sure?"

"OK … five." Castillo reached for his cell phone. He pressed speed dial and put the cell to his ear as the young woman sauntered away.

"Hello," Cecilia said. She was alone, sitting on a twin bed inside a cell at the detention center. She was Hispanic, with a long black ponytail and wearing an orange jumpsuit.

"Cecilia?"

"Yes, Uncle?"

"Should be a new woman in there, white, dark hair, large breasts, an ATF agent," Castillo said. "She's the one who murdered Jesus and Raul."

"I saw her. So she's the one?"

"Not only that, she thinks she's the toughest girl in town, if you know what I mean. Can you and some of your friends show her tough? It'll be worth a couple thousand when I get you out."

"Got it, Uncle. It's dinnertime and she just got herself on the menu."

"Your family thanks you." Castillo put his cell phone down. A smile slowly appeared. "Five minutes are up."

The young woman quickly returned.

Silva stared at the phone on his desk as if willing it to ring. Suddenly it did. He jumped backward in his chair. "Jesus, Silva. A little bit frazzled," he mumbled to himself. He picked up and listened to the evening secretary handling calls. "Thanks. Put him on."

FBI Agent Hall, in a hotel room, was on the phone. "Agent Silva, we just got a call from Washington. The director wants us and every available agent in several states to get to Battle Mountain immediately. Apparently, there's an invasion in the works."

"I told you! They're after Agent Brown's father and her friends. Castillo, the casino owner who helped you, this is his doing."

"It's too late for any of us to get there and prevent whatever is going to happen. You have any contacts that can get there from northern Nevada?"

"There's no time. Maybe you should go see Castillo and have him call it off?"

"After you told me what was happening, that was suggested, but the attorney general overrode that idea. He said the congressman will have his job if we go after Castillo."

"You mind if we try?"

"You never heard from me, right, Agent Silva?"

"Got it!" Silva hung up, stood, and walked to Fireball's cubicle. "Any word?"

"The plane from Vegas is about to land. The other plane from Virginia is a half hour out."

"Shit! There's no way we can stop either of them from landing."

"Impossible on the first one ... but maybe the second."

"Get the FAA on the phone." Silva walked past Ruben's cubicle, motioning to him to follow. As they sat down in Silva's office, Silva's phone rang. Silva put it on speaker.

"This is ATF Agent Silva from Las Vegas. Who is this?"

Lights glimmered in the nation's capital. Independence Avenue was packed with vehicles in front of FAA headquarters. Inside, General Jefferson, a distinguished man in his fifties, sat at a polished desk. "This is General Jefferson. What's the problem, Agent Silva?"

"General, there's a plane from Vegas owned by one of our casino operators who is also an alleged gunrunner and explosives dealer. It's about to land in Elko, Nevada. Its cargo is armed men on a mission to kill people in Battle Mountain, about seventy miles away."

"Let me check." Jefferson typed on a keyboard. He entered a query and studied the response. "That plane has top-level clearance, and by the way, it just touched down."

"Is there any way you can have those onboard detained?"

"For that you'll have to contact the FBI."

"They called me. There's no way they can get there."

"Then I'd say you have a little bit of problem, Agent."

"What about the second plane from Virginia. Should be landing anytime now."

"Let me check on that one." The general entered another query. "That plane also has top-level clearance even higher than the Las Vegas plane. Who's on that one?"

"I have no idea. Can you check?"

"Certainly." The general entered another query. "It's been authorized by the president himself. No listing of who's onboard or what its mission is."

"Shit! I do have a problem."

"Want me to alert the FBI?"

"They know, but your call would help too, General."

"Retired."

"Maybe you could omit that part for now and help us."

"Be good to see a bit of action again." The general hung up.

Silva put his phone down and turned to Ruben. "The only solution now is to get Castillo to stop his men."

"On my way, sir." Ruben stood and left Silva's office.


Ruben drove his sedan through heavy traffic on Las Vegas Boulevard and pulled into the valet service area at Castillo's casino. He stepped out, tossed his keys to an attendant, and ran inside. He approached a male security guard and flashed his ATF badge.

"I need to see Mr. Castillo now!"

The male security guard talked into a shoulder mic. "An ATF agent is demanding to see Mr. Castillo." He listened for a moment. "Right. Agent, follow me."

Ruben walked a step behind the male security guard as he crossed the gaming floor and headed toward an elevator. The door magically opened. They stepped inside.

"You know the drill," the male security guard said.

"Yep, short ride," Ruben said.

The door opened, and he followed the security guard into the casino's luxurious suite, where Castillo sat on a white couch.

"Sir?" the male security guard said.

"That's OK," Castillo said to the security guard. "Thank you."

The security guard walked back to the elevator as Castillo studied Ruben. "What is it this time? Your girlfriend left something?"

"You need to stop your men from attacking Battle Mountain."

"My men doing what?"

"The men you sent to kill Agent Brown's father. The airplane you sent to Elko, the men with weapons. Stop them now!"

"I have no idea what you are talking about, Agent Ruben, is it? My men have earned a vacation for working so hard. They are after big game. They have permits. I'm told the bighorn sheep have overpopulated the hills around Elko. They are really on a mission of mercy to save other animals by eliminating a few."

"You and I both know what they are really up to. If they lay one finger on Agent Brown's father or any of her friends—"

"What you going to do? You're from Canada, aren't you? I happen to know one of your federal ministers personally. Want me to call him and mention how you are threatening me? Why don't you calm down, take a few chips on the house, have a drink on me?"

"I don't know how or when, but you, my friend, are going down." Ruben angrily pointed his index finger at Castillo.

"You Canadians and your friends. Well, friend, I will see you later. It's time for my second massage."

Castillo pressed a button, and two barely clad beauties walked in from another room. He nodded to them. "A little 'friendly' advice: maybe you should try a massage yourself. Might help you get rid of all that anger."

Ruben glared at Castillo and then looked at the girls. "I've got something better in mind." He turned and walked to the elevator.

"Good-bye, Agent Ruben."

Castillo stood, walked to the window, and stared out at downtown Las Vegas.

"Little lady, I hope your last supper is going well."

Inside the detention center dining hall, Cecilia sat at a table with three women. They watched B-4 walk from the serving line, carrying a full tray of food. As she passed, Cecilia suddenly elbowed her tray, knocking it to the cement floor. "Watch who you are running into, bitch."

"It was my fault. Sorry." B-4 bent over to scoop the spilled food back onto the tray. "It won't happen again."

Cecilia dumped hot coffee on B-4's back.

B-4 stood, looked at Cecilia, and smiled. "That felt good. Needed something to make my day."

"Who do you fucking think you are, Dirty Harry?"

B-4 extended her hand. "Name's Bonnie Brown. People call me B-4."

"Well, fuck off before I stick my fork in you to feel your insides."

B-4 turned and walked back to the serving line with her tray of spilled food. Hot coffee ran down her back. She emptied the tray into a trash and dropped the tray onto a counter before walking from the dining hall.

On the way, she walked past a middle-aged Hispanic guard.

"It's not time to return to your cell," the woman said.

"I think I need a change of clothes."

"That'll be tomorrow morning after showering."

"Guess it'll be a sticky night then."

"She's trying to pick a fight. Know her?"

"Probably one of Castillo's relatives."

"Oh, like me?"

"Maybe you should tell your relative over there she should never pick a fight she can't win."

"Cecilia? She always wins."

"My Mama didn't raise chickens."

"I will be sure to tell her that too."

As B-4 exited, the female guard mimicked a chicken. Cecilia noticed and ran a finger across her throat.


Curley and the boys ate at the bar while Bobby cleaned his Magnum. Benneschott, disguised as the old man, walked in and approached the slots.

"Anyone want more food?" Bobby asked. "A little stew left and two rabbit legs."

"Kinda like our last supper, boss?" Curley said.

"Never. After we take care of the business that's coming our way, we'll have a feast. Maybe a ham, even a little turkey."

"How about spaghetti the way Mama made it?" Kevin asked.

"With a little Nevada green mixed in," Kermit said. "Better than those chewies for sure."

The phone rang. "Roadkill," Bobby answered.

It was Sherriff O'Toole, calling from the highway in an SUV with his wife and son. "Mr. Brown, we are on our way to Elko, and we just passed a caravan of militia vehicles led by a black Suburban. They're headed your way." The sheriff looked in his rearview mirror and saw the caravan disappear. "A whole fleet of them loaded with men in helmets and fighting gear and lots of weapons."

"How far out?"

"They should be there in thirty or forty."

"How many?"

"Seems like fifty or hundred. I lost count."

"Thanks. Don't panic. Enjoy your evening in Elko. I'll talk to you tomorrow when this is over."

"I sure hope so, Mr. Brown."

"That's Sheriff Brown, for the night."

"Yes, sir. I mean, Sheriff."

Bobby hung up the phone.

"They on their way?" Curley asked.

"Sounds like it. An army invasion." Bobby reached for the Patron and several shot glasses.

"That many?" Curley reached for a glass.

"Apparently." Bobby lined them up.

"Well, maybe we should get into position. Some in here, some in Lilly's," Curley said, pushing his shot glass close to the Patron.

"Not enough of us." Bobby filled Curley's glass.

"What we gonna do? Surrender?"

"You know better than that. You eat one of those damn chewies? Surrender is not in my vocabulary. Shouldn't be in yours either."

Curley nodded. He downed the Patron and pushed his shot glass back toward the bottle.

"Come on, boys." Bobby filled up all the shot glasses. "One for the battle ahead. Bring your guns and all the ammo you got. Let's go for a ride in the JJ Posse Express."

"We gonna make a run for it?" Curley said as the boys hurried to the bar and grabbed their full shot glasses.

"Curley, read my lips." Bobby raised his full shot glass to toast. "No surrendering. No running. We're gonna take them all out into our battlefield, the desert!"

They slugged back the Patron.

"Victory!" Bobby said.


The JJ Posse Express passed thirty-mile waypoint sign for Elko at seventy miles per hour. The old man followed in a Jeep a quarter mile behind them. Bobby drove, and Curley was in the passenger seat. Kevin and Kermit sat behind them. The pass-through window to the truck box was open, and the other three Battle Mountain Boys sat ready to fire.

"When we pass them going the other way, pick off as many as you can," Bobby yelled over the noise of the truck roaring down the highway. "They'll turn and chase us. I'll lead them into the desert. No one can beat us there."

Everyone gave Bobby the thumbs-up.

Bobby glanced at the speedometer, 75 MPH. He punched the accelerator. He watched the speedometer move past 80 MPH and climb as they roared toward Elko in the fast lane.


Inside ATF headquarters, Silva and Ruben approached Fireball as his fingers danced across a keyboard. "Anything?" Silva asked.

"I've pinged Bobby Brown's cell. He seems to be headed toward Elko."

"What about the men in the plane from Vegas?" Silva asked.

"I am using a satellite. There's one heck of a big group. I assume its Castillo's men and the militia headed for Battle Mountain. They seem to be on a collision course with Brown."

"Anything on the plane from Virginia?" Silva asked.

"It landed. Shortly after that, two large older US National Guard attack helicopters took off."

"Carrying?" Silva asked.

"No exact information, sir. But there are definitely people on board."

"Headed for?"

"Moving toward Brown and Castillo's crew."

"And here we sit, unable to do anything," Ruben said.

"The FBI's sending agents from Salt Lake City and Reno by helicopter," Silva said. "They're at least an hour out."

"We were right," Ruben said.

Silva turned around and said, "World War III!"

"And B-4 wishes she was in it," Ruben said.


Lights were out in the detention center's cell area. B-4 lay on a cot, eyes wide open, contemplating what was likely coming. There was a sudden noise, and her cell door was unlocked. She sat up. "What?"

The door was thrown open, and the female guard walked in holding a gun. "My cousin would like to take you up on your offer."

"Anytime, anywhere." B-4 jumped off her cot and walked from the cell.

Several female detainees in orange jumpsuits waited as B-4 was directed toward another door that led into a small gymnasium. It was dimly lit by high windows. As B-4 stepped inside, the door slammed shut behind her, the female detainees, and the guard. Cecilia waited in the middle of the room. "So you don't think Cecilia can beat you, eh, Ms. ATF Agent?"

"No chance." B-4 walked toward Cecilia. "Just like my mama said. You want to fight me, prepare to get your ass whooped."

"My mother said, you fight … leave no prisoners."

"You never met my mama," B-4 said, ready to fight.


Inside the Roadkill, Mama stocked a shelf behind the bar with glasses as three young men walked in. She glanced up. "You boys gotta be checked before you go through the back door to Lilly's."

"Hey there, big tits. We don't need any help from a bitch like you," one of the young men said, and they all laughed.

"Actually, if you don't show me some IDs that say you're fucking old enough, you're gonna go back out the front door."

"Hey, guys," the boy said. "Fatty here thinks we're not old enough. Show her what we got." They start to unbutton their jeans.

"Not your sperm count, you bastards, your fucking IDs." Mama glanced under the bar to confirm her shotgun was nearby. "You know the little plastic cards with your funny pictures on them."

"We're old enough, you—" the boy started.

"Actually, see that sign?" Mama pointed to a placard on the wall. "Owner reserves the right to refuse service. In case you can't read, it says I can refuse to serve anybody at my discretion, and my fucking discretion says you're not fucking old enough. Get your asses and hairless pricks out of my establishment now!"

"And you're gonna make us how?" the boy asked.

Mama reached below the bar for her shotgun. "You don't really want to get into a fight with Mama, do you?"

"Come on. There's plenty of places in this shithole town," a second boy said.

The young men spit on the floor and walked out.

Mama put her shotgun back under the bar and continued to stock a shelf with glasses as young B-4 ran in through the front door.

"Mama, Mama, there's a guy outside beating the pickup with a snow chain while his friends laugh."

"What the fuck?"

"They asked me if the pickup was yours."

"They did, eh?" Mama moved from behind the bar and headed outside. She watched the boy swing a snow chain and hit the pickup's bumper.

"I told you, get the fuck out of here and don't come back."

"And what are you gonna do about it? Go get your shotgun?" the boy said defiantly.

Mama walked toward the young boy. "I don't need no fucking shotgun to take care of a little pissant like you."

The boy turned and swung the chain at Mama. She grabbed it with one hand, yanked on it, and brought the boy nose-to-nose with her.

"Now, Mr. Peach Fuzz, get your fucking ass away from my establishment before I crush you like a cockroach."

She tossed the chain and boy to the ground. "If I see you in Battle Mountain again, I will get my shotgun and you'll get a fucking sex change operation for free."

Wide-eyed, the boy wiped tears from his eyes.

"Now get the fuck out of my town!" Mama stood over him. "I'm counting to three. One …"

The boy stood and motioned to the other young boys. "Yes, ma'am."

"Two ..."

The young men quickly jumped into a Honda with empty snow racks on the roof and started to drive off. The clutch popped. The Honda stalled. It started again and sputtered down the road.

"I'm glad they didn't hurt you, Mama."

"You never get into a fight you can't win, honey." Mama placed one hand on young B-4's shoulder. "Those boys, well, I had them whipped when I saw they weren't even shaving yet."

"The pickup has a few more scratches."

"Yeah, but it still runs." Mama turned to walk inside the Roadkill. "A few more rabbit hunts and it'll have a few more."

"You really know how to win, Mama."

"I definitely fucking do."

# CHAPTER 29

The JJ Posse Express roared east in the fast lane. As they descended a hill, Curley yelled, "Boss! Boss! Look at them headlights. As far as you can see."

"Hmmm!" Bobby studied the string of headlights approaching them on the other side of the freeway. "We might need a different strategy."

Bobby pulled the big red pickup into the slow lane and watched the black Suburban and all the militia vehicles pass in the other direction, heading to Battle Mountain. He took his foot off the gas pedal. The truck slowed. Bobby cranked the wheel hard and quickly crossed the median. He killed the headlights and punched the accelerator to catch up.

"Just like Sergeant York, Sheriff?"

"Love that old black and white." Bobby tried to stay focused on the prize. "One by one from behind. And when the caravan figures it out and slows down, we'll head across the desert to a wash. They'll never know what hit them."

"There's a lot of 'em, Sheriff."

"Like that old African saying about how you eat an elephant. One bite at a time, Curley, one bite at a time."

Benneschott, disguised as the old man, slowed down and pulled off the road. From his place tailing them, he had watched the big red pickup cross the median. He waited, crossed it himself, and followed the parade heading west.

Inside the detention center, Cecilia and B-4 faced off. Cecilia slashed out with her right hand.

B-4 ducked. "Nice nails."

"Ready to carve up your ugly face."

B-4 threw a punch.

Cecilia ducked. "That all you got, Agent?"

B-4 feinted with a left and kicked with her right leg, knocking Cecilia to the mat. "Didn't spend all my time playing with dolls."

Cecilia got up slowly. "Lucky kick." She lunged at B-4, tackled her around the midsection, and fell on top of her.

B-4 rolled over Cecilia and slammed the other woman's head to the mat. Cecilia slashed at B-4 with her nails, cutting her orange jumpsuit to ribbons. B-4 unloaded a vicious right, then a left, then a right.

Cecilia was dazed. She shook her head, went to her knees, and looked up. "That was pretty good for a warmup," she said and then reached into her jumpsuit and pulled out a knife. "Let's see how you do in round two."

The JJ Posse Express moved faster with no lights, coming up quickly behind an old Hummer in the slow lane. It trailed the caravan, lagging behind, American flags flying. Bobby pulled up closer and then moved into the fast lane. "Shoot the tires out. No sense killing them if we don't have to."

Curley and the boys leaned out the windows and off the back. They blew holes in the Hummer's tires, forcing it off the road.

"One down and a whole army to go!" Bobby yelled as the JJ Posse Express sped ahead, chasing the next vehicle.

Inside the detention center, Cecilia circled B-4, looking for an opening. She feinted right and then lunged left, slicing B-4's orange jumpsuit again.

"You know what I'm gonna do?" B-4 said. "I'm going to stick that knife up your ass and fillet you like one of them trout we catch back home."

"You think you're tough? I'm the youngest of eleven from the ghetto. I had to use a knife just to get to the table to eat."

"Got you in here too, I'm guessing." B-4 made a move, circling behind Cecilia. She grabbed the knife away and held it to Cecilia's neck. "You want more?"

The girls in the room moved forward, ready to pounce on B-4.

The JJ Posse Express, lights off, closed in on another old military vehicle. The several men inside saw the truck coming and fired. Bullets smashed the JJ Express's windshield, causing spider web cracks.

Bobby ducked to avoid the bullets. "No mercy on this one, boys. Let 'em have it!" He pulled into the fast lane. Curley and the boys fired their shotguns, killing all the occupants. The vehicle swerved off the road, rolled, and exploded.

A string of taillights turned red on the vehicles ahead. "I guess our Sergeant York strategy has been discovered." Bobby swerved off the freeway, turned on the truck's bright lights, and began plowing through the sage. "Hang on, boys."

Dust and sand swirled into the sky as the truck bounced through the desert. The caravan stopped, turned, and began to follow.

Inside the detention center, B-4 held the knife at Cecilia's throat while the other women moved closer. "Cecilia, call them off while you can still talk."

The guard stepped forward, pointing her revolver at B-4. "Drop it or you're a dead former agent."

B-4 looked at the guard. She pushed the blade harder into Cecilia's throat. The guard checked her revolver for bullets. "Gotta full clip. Really want to do that? You kill her, you'll be seeing your mama tonight."

B-4 hesitated and then dropped the knife.

Cecilia picked it up and started to move toward B-4, but the guard held her off. "No, cousin. It's my turn." The guard put the revolver back into her holster, unstrapped the belt, and let it drop to the floor. "Let's see what you can do with someone who has some real skills." She raised her fists.

The JJ Posse Express fishtailed through the rough desert terrain and over the sage. The caravan was catching up. Bobby wrestled with the steering wheel, fighting with every muscle he had to maintain control. "There's a wash here somewhere. I remember it from one of our rabbit hunts."

"Straight ahead, but it's steep," Curley yelled, holding on for dear life. "The truck will be destroyed!"

"Guess we'll see what a gold card can *really* buy. Hang on, boys!"

B-4 and the guard squared off. The guard swung a trial right and missed as B-4 ducked.

"ATF?" B-4 asked.

"FBI," the guard said.

"Rookie?"

"Never made it. Pregnant."

"Damn trainers."

"Trainee." The female guard's head weaved and bobbed.

"I was academy champ."

"We'll see. Musta been a lot of weak women."

"I was the only female."

The guard lunged at her, clipping B-4's right ear.

"Champ, huh?"

"Yep." B-4 feinted right and then left and then kicked the guard with her right foot, sending her to the floor.

Just as B-4's foot hit the floor, the guard tumbled and grabbed B-4's leg. She rolled and pinned her down. "I saw that move. Gotta think ahead."

"Yes, you do." With a quick move, B-4 slid the guard's arm over her head and used a choke hold. She squeezed tighter and tighter. The guard struggled to breathe. "Just like the academy."


Inside a large gymnasium, nineteen men and B-4 formed a circle on a mat. The instructor, a buff man in his forties, stood in the middle, barking orders.

"This is for the academy championship. Blue team put your best man out. Gold team, do the same. Whoever wins will be the academy champion."

The blue team chanted. "Roger, Roger, Roger."

Ruben was on the gold team. He pushed B-4 out.

The gold team chanted. "B-4, B-4, B-4."

Roger moved to the middle of the mat, displaying a full set of teeth. He was buff and muscular.

B-4 moved to the middle of the mat.

"I'm the Midwest heavyweight Greco champ," Roger said.

"Could've fooled me. Thought you were a braying jackass. That smile was a dead giveaway."

Roger clinched his teeth. "I'll go easy on you."

"I'm Mama's daughter. Easy isn't in my vocabulary."

The fight began. Roger stalked B-4 as he looked for an opening. B-4 retreated in a circle, hands ready. At the same moment, they both put their hands on each other's shoulders.

"Those big things ever have a man grab 'em?"

"Touch them and you're dead."

"Let's see."

Roger dropped one hand to grab one of B-4's breasts. At the same time, B-4 dropped her hands, grabbed Roger by the neck, and threw him to the mat. She followed up with a vicious and strong choke hold. Roger's face turned red as he struggled to get free. He couldn't move her arms. He gasped for air. The instructor stepped in and tapped B-4 arms.

"Enough, enough. We don't want anyone hurt—"

"Or killed," B-4 interrupted.

"Or killed," the instructor said as he tried to peel one of B-4's arms off Roger. "Good job, champ."


The JJ Posse Express crashed into the wash and slid to a stop sideways against a wall.

Bobby jumped out. "Get down! Behind the truck. Here they come."

The upside of the wash was lined with the black Suburban and several militia vehicles, lights on. Men carrying weapons climbed out and began firing, riddling the truck with bullet holes. Bobby, Curley, and the Battle Mountain Boys fired back. A hail of bullets filled the air.

"Just like the OK Corral!" Curley yelled.

"Yeah!" Bobby said as he reloaded his Magnum.


Inside the detention center, the lights in the small gymnasium suddenly turned on. Several guards ran in.

"What is going on here?" a male guard asked.

Cecilia dropped the knife onto the floor and slid it toward B-4 as B-4 loosened her grip on the female guard, who started coughing and rubbing her throat. The male guard approached, and the inmates scattered. B-4 grabbed the knife and shoved it under her orange suit, out of sight.

"What happened?" the male guard asked.

"She was just showing me how to protect myself in case I was attacked," B-4 said.

"Is that true?" he asked the female guard.

"It's very dangerous in here," the female guard said, clearing her throat as she stood up.

"You the ATF agent everyone is talking about?" the male guard asked.

"That'd be me, Bonnie Brown."

"Did she give you the kind of pointers you wanted?"

"Yes, sir. She did."

"Then I'd suggest all of you clear out and get back to your holding cells, assuming they're open. Guards, escort the young ladies please."

B-4 stood and slipped the knife back to Cecilia. "I assume you might need this another time when you get hungry."

Cecilia looked at B-4, took the knife, and slipped it into her suit. B-4 walked by the female guard. "FBI's training has always been for pussies."

The wash was consumed by bullets as both sides returned fire. The JJ Posse Express morphed into a big red piece of Swiss cheese. Suddenly, up from behind the militia and the black Suburban, emerged two helicopters. One landed just behind them, and the other crossed the wash and landed above the bank behind Bobby and the boys. Armed men leaped from both and opened fire on the militia with automatic weapons. Many of the militia were killed before the rest surrendered.

The shooting stopped as the black Suburban took off in a cloud of dust and sand and headed across the desert toward the highway. Behind Bobby and the boys, a female figure in a skin-tight black shiny jumpsuit stepped out, holding a smoking Magnum. Bobby, Curley, and the boys turned and stared up at the figure outlined by bright helicopter lights.

"Father, you've ruined your brand-new pickup," JJ yelled over the rotor noise.

"Curley, boys, meet my other daughter."

At ATF headquarters, Silva and Ruben watched over Fireball's shoulder as his fingers worked the keyboard with lightning speed.

"And ...?" Silva asked.

"Mr. Brown's ping is in the middle of the desert. The convoy of vehicles has stopped. One of the helicopters has reported an incident involving several militias, and it appears an unknown group has thrown in the towel or been obliterated. One vehicle escaped."

Fireball's fingers continued to dance across the keyboard. Then they stopped. "How about that?"

"What?" Silva said.

"The helicopters have been identified. They're part of an emergency search and rescue operation led by a JJ Wellington from DC.

"My God, B-4's sister," Ruben said. "She made it!"

"There's another Brown?" Silva said. "Holy shit!"

Jose was alone in the black Suburban as it sped toward Elko. Blood oozed from a wound in his shoulder. He was talking on a dash speaker.

"Boss. We were ambushed. I'm wounded, and the others are dead."

In his luxury casino suite, Castillo glanced at an unopened box labeled, "Fly Tying Kit." His faced turned red like a thermometer tossed into a fire. He slid up on his couch, reached past the box, picked up a chilled margarita, and gulped it down. He turned his attention back to his phone conversation.

"Ambushed? I thought we had enough men and militia."

"Two helicopters showed up full of armed men and just took over. Many were killed, and the rest were captured."

"Not good."

"Those militia, they're gonna talk, boss."

"Don't sweat it." Castillo tried to refocus and calm down. "No one will believe them. How bad are you hurt?"

"I'll make it back, boss, one way or another."

"Just don't get captured. No one talks. Right?"

"Got it, boss."

"Glad the congressman is here tomorrow." Castillo flipped open the fly-tying book on the table. "He'll make sure nothing touches us."

"How'd everything go with the rookie?"

"I'm waiting to hear, but one thing I know is I can always count on family." Castillo flipped through the pages of the book with his free hand.

"Yes, boss."

B-4 walked across the corridor in the cell area to Cecilia. "You tell your uncle I'm coming for him when I get out. He'd better be ready."

"I'll tell him tomorrow."

"Come on, tell him now. I know you've got a cell phone hidden in there. Tell him even if he leaves town, I'll find him and send him to his ancestors."

"You'll never make that happen, no matter how good you are."

"You'd be surprised how good I am."


The particulates from the firefight had had cleared from the desert air. Emergency and law enforcement vehicles had left with the dead bodies and captured militia men. Four helicopters waited, lights on, two above the wash and two on the ground below.

JJ talked to one man wearing an FBI windbreaker, while Bobby, Curley, and the boys surveyed the big bullet-riddled red pickup and their path of destruction. The FBI agent shook JJ's hand and ran to one of waiting helicopters. The helicopters on the ground immediately fired up, causing a swirl of dust.

JJ made her way down into the wash to Bobby, Curley, and the boys. "Father, you and your guys hop into my chopper. We'll take you back to the Roadkill. I'll pick up Rosie. I've got a hearing before a Senate committee tomorrow. I need to get back ASAP."

"What about the JJ Posse Express?" Curley asked.

"What?"

Bobby nodded toward the red truck riddled with bullet holes.

JJ cracked a smile. "I'll get someone to come out and haul it to the junkyard. I'll have another one delivered first thing in the morning."

"Red?" Curley asked.

"Ruby!" JJ said. "Oh, you can keep the name. Kinda suits you boys."

"Yes!" Curley and the boys cheered, waving their fists in the air. They grabbed their guns and began climbing up the slope to JJ's helicopter.

"So, Father, what's next out here in the middle of nowhere?"

"Next is to get your sister out of jail and back on the job as a special agent."

"I can get her reassigned and back to DC with me," JJ said. "It's obvious from all of this that I do have a few connections."

"There is one connection you can help with."

"Name it."

The congressman, the guy who seems to have started her troubles …"

"Who is he? I mean, I can find out."

"One of Nevada's. There are only a couple."

"Leave him to me."

"I also need help with your sister and her legal issues. I certainly want Bonnie to meet you. Maybe we can be a family."

"I'm taking care of that. She'll have a great lawyer with her tomorrow, my friend Jennifer. And I look forward to meeting another chip off the old block."

"You sent Miss Bombay? The one who almost raped me when I came back after the funeral?"

"Father! She's the best—high, drunk, or sober."

"Viva Las Vegas!"

# CHAPTER 30

An executive jet passed through a layer of cloud lit up by a bright full moon. Inside, Jose, his right arm in a sling, talked on a cell phone. "There was this young lady, tall, strong, using a large pistol. She seemed to be in charge."

"Another fucking broad." The margarita in Castillo's right hand splashed on his white couch as he sat up straight. "Shit." He surveyed the suite for something to wipe off his hand. Seeing nothing within reach, he put the glass down on the table and licked the margarita drops off his fingers.

"Sorry, boss. Guess you won't be going fly-fishing for a while."

Castillo glanced at the open fly-tying kit. "In good time. Canada can wait a little longer."

"Right, boss.

"Glad you made it to the jet." Castillo thumbed through the box. "Tell me all about it when you get back tonight."

"At the compound?"

"Yes. See you there."

Castillo put his cell down, stood, and walked to a huge executive desk. He pulled out a drawer, reached in, and took out a silenced revolver. "No loose ends."

Inside the Detention Center, B-4 lay on a cot, staring at the ceiling. The female guard knocked on her cell. "Yes?" B-4 said. "Another adventure?"

"It seems you have a visitor, Miss Brown."

"Me? At this time of night, or is it the next day?"

"Someone has pulled a lot of strings to see you."

B-4 stood, walked to the open cell door, and held her hands out to be cuffed.

"Just follow me."

B-4 followed the guard into a small conference room. B-4 looked into a mirror, a poor attempt to hide the fact that the room could be watched from the other side. She shook her head as she studied her face.

"What did you expect?" B-4 mumbled to herself.

She looked just like a person who had been roughed up. She was bruised, and the cutup orange jumpsuit sealed it. She saw Ruben waiting at the conference table. He was studying his cell phone as she quietly approached him from behind. Before he knew she was there, she plopped down hard on the wooden chair opposite him.

Ruben pretended she did not surprise him, but the way she looked did. "What in the Sam heck happened to you?"

"Down here it's Sam hell, not heck." She took a deep breath and tried to get comfortable. "A welcoming party set up by Uncle Castillo."

"Uncle Castillo isn't having much luck lately." Ruben clasped his hands on top of the table.

"Daddy?"

"Yep. They were trapped in the desert by several militia and a shitload of men when a rescue party led by your sister arrived in helicopters. They killed a bunch of 'em and arrested the rest. She was definitely in charge."

"Until yesterday I didn't even know I had a sister ... a half sister. My daddy's led an interesting life."

"I guess she has a lot of pull in DC and a whole lot of money."

"Well, right now I just want to get out of here and blow Castillo's head clean off."

"Your sister is sending her top lawyer to do just that, to get you out."

"Tonight?"

Ruben shook his head. "Maybe tomorrow."

"Well ... tomorrow it is."

Ruben nodded and stared into B-4's eyes. "I really tried to stop Castillo from sending his men."

"Thanks for trying." B-4 reached out and touched Ruben's folded hands.

"Get some sleep." Ruben moved one hand on top of B-4's. "We'll worry about Castillo when you're out of here."

"Thanks for filling me in. I'll try to get a bit of sleep …"

"Thirty minutes, right eye, thirty minutes, left eye, maybe?"

"I find forty-five minutes works best, get a little power sleep in. Gotta be on my best game tomorrow."


JJ's large custom Airbus helicopter landed on the street outside the Roadkill. Bobby, Curley, the Battle Mountain Boys, and JJ climbed out. JJ signaled to the pilot to hold tight. She walked with everyone inside. Rosie was tending bar. Curley immediately sat at the bar next to his favorite slot, while the Battle Mountain Boys fought for their usual slots.

"Miss JJ, you want something?" Rosie asked.

"You got some Jack back there, Rosie?"

"Got Jack and jack."

"Jackrabbit is a Roadkill special," Bobby said.

"The other Jack."

Rosie grabbed a bottle of Jack Daniels and poured a shot. JJ took it and slugged it back.

"Another?"

JJ nodded. Rosie poured another. JJ slugged it back and slammed the glass down.

"You ready to leave, Rosie? Those two shots will put me to sleep."

"Yes, Mrs. JJ. It's certainly an interesting place."

"Thanks for watching everything while we were gone," Bobby said.

"I was hiding in the safe room," Rosie said. "An old man watched the place for you until I came out. He left in a real hurry."

"Hmmm."

"This is the famous Roadkill," JJ said as she looked around. "Just like I remembered it."

"Don't forget Lilly's out back," Rosie added.

"Not quite DC, but it's home for now," Bobby said.

"This is where you came after Bonnie's mother was murdered, isn't it?" JJ asked.

"I had nothing better to do."

"Glad you came back after my husband and his father's funeral."

"Glad you found me."

"Do I have any other brothers or sisters out there?"

"I did make the rounds in my youth."

"Jennifer did mention your age had nothing to do with what you could conjure up."

"Never trust anyone who drinks something blue!"

"She does like her curaçao. Rum and Bombay are the garnish. Got hooked when we went to the Caribbean."

JJ glanced at her watch. "Oops, I gotta go."

"Good luck tomorrow, or is it later today?"

"Piece of cake. Senators always like to hear from their largest donor. You and Bonnie have to come east soon, maybe when this is all over. Connie would like to see his grandfather again."

"Maybe someday."

JJ kissed Bobby on the cheek. Rosie shook Bobby's hand and followed JJ out the door.

Curley approached with an empty plate. "Got any more of that stew, boss?"

"It's gonna be breakfast in a few hours," Bobby said.

In the early morning, a black SUV stopped at the isolated desert compound gates. Jose reached out the driver's side window and entered the code. The gates opened, and Jose drove inside and up a circular driveway. With his right arm in a sling, he stepped out of the SUV and walked toward Castillo, who sat in a comfortable poolside chair. Castillo raised his margarita and pointed to a second one. Jose adjusted his sling as he sat down next to him.

"I don't know where those helicopters came from, boss, but the men and this one chick … It was over in minutes. The militia gave up. I had no choice but to run."

"That's too bad. Our plot to get rid of the rookie's father didn't work, and neither did my plan to get rid of her inside the jail."

"Not a good evening, eh, boss?" Jose raised the margarita. "What we gonna try next?" He took a sip of the drink as he waited for his next set of instructions.

"You know I don't like failure or loose ends."

"Don't worry about the militia they caught." Jose took another sip. "They never agree to tell the authorities anything."

"That's not what I am worried about."

"What are we going to do?"

"We?" Castillo took the silenced revolver from his side and shot Jose in the head. Jose rolled off his chair and onto the pool deck.

"There is no 'we' in 'you' and 'I.' I'm going to have to dig deep and find the right person to eliminate the rookie."

Castillo grabbed a cell phone from a table next to his chair and punched in a number. "Mr. Dooley? This is Mr. Castillo from Las Vegas. Is it possible we might talk about a little engagement?"

He listened to Dooley speak and responded. "Five million with three up front? That's doable. Can you be here tomorrow?" Castillo looked at Jose and the blood pooling under his face. "My casino, say at noon?" He picked up Jose's margarita and finished it. "OK. See you then."

Castillo put down his cell and stared at Jose. "That's what I am going to do next."

Bobby stacked empty plates and then wiped the bar down, moving the dishrag around Curley as he slept, his head resting on top of his favorite slot. The Battle Mountain Boys had disappeared. His cell phone rang.

"Who could possibly be calling me this late at night or early in the morning?"

High above the clouds, a nearly full moon shone down brightly. A hint of dawn was visible in the distance. Inside a sleek jet, Jennifer sat in a soft swivel chair, savoring a blue-tinged drink. She was talking on a hand-free device. "It's me, your favorite DC date, hon," she said in her sexy voice.

"Been expecting your call, Jennifer, just not this early."

"Early? Why, hon, it's still evening. Or maybe you really are getting old."

Bobby rested both elbows on the bar, ignoring Jennifer's dig at his age. "I hear you're on the way to deal with Bonnie's dilemma."

"How many daughters do you have anyway?"

"Been asked that a few times lately."

"Guess your Magnum isn't the only big gun you used in your detective days." Jennifer laughed.

"Flattery will get you everywhere. JJ had a successful night defending her old man out here in no-man's-land. She's quite a young lady. Guess you remember that from your soccer days."

"Hon, those broken knees are all in my past. I'm interested in other body parts now."

"Yes, you know how to make an old man cry."

"Hon, the only thing about you that's old is your birth date. As I remember it, you brought me too my knees. I was the one doing the crying."

"Right now, the only thing I have to make sure grows old is Bonnie."

"I understand she was a one-night stand too."

"She's quite a girl, and her Mama, she was quite a young lady herself."

"So what's the FBI up to? The story doesn't quite jive."

"A Nevada congressman has twisted around the facts to support the criminal efforts of a man named Cast—"

"Castillo! The casino owner?"

"Makes more running guns, drugs, explosives—the usual bad guy stuff I dealt with in my younger days."

"And Bonnie tangled with him?"

"She killed a few of his men, one of his cousins, and—"

"A partridge in a pear tree. Not the greatest Christmas ending move of endearment."

"Right. He's determined to destroy her. He tried to threaten her by killing me, but that didn't work. Get her out, and we'll see how long the hood lasts."

"You coming down to Vegas to see me in action?"

"I saw that once and it about killed me."

"Ha! I still say it was the other way around, Grandpa Brown."

"Think I'll stay right here and settle things down in good old Battle Mountain. You take care of Bonnie for me … for us."

"I can always swing by there on my way home, hon."

"Give me a few days to catch my breath and it's a deal. I've got a few things to show you."

"You know me. I'm always ready for your show and I won't tell." Jennifer sat back and sipped her drink as a sexy smile crossed her face.

Bobby put his cell phone down and mused aloud, "I wonder if she likes her rabbit stewed or fricasseed?"

# CHAPTER 31

The clock on the detention center wall read 6:00 a.m. as the female guard rattled her keys in front of B-4's cell. B-4's eyes snapped open. "What the —?"

"Wake up, sleeping beauty." The female guard yawned. "You have another visitor."

"Just got to sleep. Do I have to?"

"Sounds like you're already gonna miss me. It's time for me to go home."

B-4 shook her head as she tried to wipe the cobwebs away. "Guess I'll just have to see you on the outside. Let me know when you want another lesson."

"Fuck you too, silly priss! Get up. It's your big fucking day. Court this morning and then the big house or freedom. Counsel awaits."

B-4 rolled over and sat on the edge of the cot. She rubbed her eyes and ran her tongue over her teeth. Her face soured as she tasted the invisible shit bird's nightly droppings. This morning her mouth tasted worse than the usual shit, likely the blood inside her mouth from the night before.

She stood and followed the female guard. "Who is it this time?"

"Yours is not to reason why ..."

"I know, do or die ... or to use your words, fucking die."

"Better. I'm off for the day. I hope it's freedom for your sake. I saw you pass the shiv to Cousin Cecilia. She was gonna kill you. Sorry she missed."

"Everybody's gonna kill me. It comes with the territory."

"Don't worry. We'll get it back from her once we know what's happening with you."

"I'm already holding my breath."

"It's just between us relatives."

"Fucking relatives. How many does Castillo have?"

"Half of Las Vegas. Better watch out. You can't beat 'em all."

"I'll let them live if they will just leave me alone to do my job."

"Think your job's done here."

"Not until I root out one of their own. He's earned the right to die."

"So have you, little girl."

"Haven't earned it yet. Think I'll choose to live. I want to kill the vermin that infect the earth. Otherwise, live and let fucking live. That's what my mama always said. She knew about the importance of fucking life."

"She musta been some kind of woman."

"You have no idea. No fucking idea."

B-4 entered a small room where Jennifer was waiting. She sat cross-legged at a table, flipping through a thin file. She motioned for B-4 to join her.

"Good luck," the female guard said.

"Thanks. Enjoy your fucking day off. I really mean that."

The female guard nodded and walked off while B-4 walked to Jennifer and slumped in a chair. Jennifer extended her hand. "Good morning, Miss Brown, is it?"

B-4 extended her hand as she tried to shake off all the negativity she had recently experienced. "Yes, and you?"

"I am Jennifer Clemons-Barrows."

"Obviously never heard of you."

"What about the Wellington firm? You heard of them?"

B-4 reflected on the question but was noncommittal.

"JJ?"

"So you speak for her?"

"Don't ever say I speak for JJ." Jennifer chuckled. "I work for your sister's firm, the Wellington firm."

"Only heard about my sister a day ago from Daddy."

"You call him Daddy, and JJ calls him Father. I call him whenever I get a chance, hon."

"Look, I'm tired and not in the mood for frivolity. I'm in here when I should be out there blowing off Castillo's head. What's up?"

"Oh, a right-to-the-point kind of gal."

"Yep."

"Well, first piece of advice I'd give you is to not talk about blowing off Castillo's head."

"Lawyer-client privilege. So what's the drill?"

"You and JJ really are sisters." Jennifer opened the file. "This morning, in a couple of hours, you have a hearing to determine if they're gonna keep you locked up or not. I need a couple of facts from you to get you out of here, and don't—"

"Get me out of here and I'll take care of the rest."

"JJ's working her magic in DC. Let's hope she's successful. Then we can dazzle them in court. What do you say?"

B-4 nodded.

"Good. You have any clean clothes? I mean, you look like shit."

"Just been though a war."

"I believe that."

"Apparently I'll get a fresh jumpsuit this morning after I shower. Is that all?"

"From what I gather, this is about a congressman's complaint, circumstantial evidence, and a few dead guys killed with a nonissue revolver." Jennifer read from the file. "Correct?"

"And there's that cartridge I found near the body of the sniper who killed an agent. I expect I was the target. The agent was shot just as he was leaning into me to tell me to stop firing."

"A sniper? There's no mention of a weapon in the file?"

"Did an area search. Couldn't locate a rifle."

"Sniper without a weapon? Hmmm."

"Are we done? I've got to get a couple of minutes of shut-eye before they get me up again."

"Sleep? Bombay is what keeps me going. Different strokes. You do remind me a lot of JJ. She needs her sleep too. More time for me to party."

"Until court?" B-4 stood up and started to walk toward the door leading back to her cell.

189

Jennifer dialed her cell phone. It was answered immediately. "JJ? She's a pistol. Just like you thought."

JJ was walking into the senate building. "Hope to meet her soon. What's your assessment?"

"Yeah, she'll be fine."

"Great. So …"

"Got some time to kill. You know me, and this is Las Vegas."

"Time for me to kill something else." JJ looked at the double doors leading into conference chambers.

"Gonna find some Bombay and blue curaçao first." Jennifer closed B-4's file. "Then if I have time, maybe a trip to the shooting range. It's early, but the lovely casinos are open all day and night, hon."

In the early morning hours, a taxi arrived at Castillo's compound gates. The driver pressed a button and waited. No one responded, but the gates opened. The taxi moved up a circular driveway and stopped at a walkway that led to the front door. Castillo, wearing silk pajamas and a short robe, stood in the doorway, talking on a cell phone.

"I'll have my new friend take care of business the old fashion way, Cecilia." He waved to the taxi. "I'll get you out of there soon."

Castillo put his cell phone into the pocket of his robe and waited on the walkway for Congressman Jacoby to approach. He had definitely been flying all night. His suit was wrinkled suit, as was his shirt, and his eye hung loose around his neck.

"Congressman, you made it here early."

"Took the midnight flyer. You said you needed me, so here I am."

"Come in. I'm alone, and I make the best huevos rancheros and Bloody Mary in Vegas."

"Let's start with a Mary."

Once inside, Castillo poured a Bloody Mary from a pitcher and handed it to Congressman Jacoby. He motioned for the congressman to take a seat at the kitchen island.

"Some green for your Mary?"

The congressman nodded.

Castillo handed him a piece of celery to use as a stir stick with an olive on the sharpened end. He walked to the stove and began cooking.

"The agent in question will go before a judge this morning. I hope it's one of your appointees."

"Judge Cynthia? Yes, she's mine. At least I recommended her. There should be no problem sending the agent to prison, at least until a trial is scheduled."

"Are you really sure? I don't want any screwups. This young rebel has cost me several men, a cousin, a bunch of customers, and a lot of money. I need her out of the way and a quick return to business as usual."

Jacoby tasted his Bloody Mary and then bit off the end of the celery stick. "Tasty. What could possibly happen? She's killed a lot of people."

"After last night, anything's possible." Castillo sipped his Bloody Mary. "The girl and her old man have more than nine lives."

Jacoby sucked the olive off the end of his stir stick, practically swallowing it whole as he stirred his drink. "Trust me, Mr. Castillo, with these FBI charges, nothing is going to free her." He bit off another piece of celery.

"That's good to hear, but you know me … I've taken out a little insurance."

Jacoby gulped down the rest of his Bloody Mary and slammed the glass down. "Just hope the policy doesn't have collateral damage."

Castillo had a strange look on his face as he poured Jacoby another drink.


Inside the detention center, B-4 wore a towel around her naked body as she walked past a naked Cecilia exiting the shower room. "Enjoy your last shower, Agent," Cecilia said.

"Last?"

"I hear my uncle has a little surprise for you."

"I've got something for him too."

"I bet. Enjoy."

"Me and Johnnson will."

"I call my dildo Dirty Harry."

"Personally, I don't use a dildo."

"Well, you and your Johnnson, whoever it is, will go down."

"Johnnson's deadly. Everyone eventually goes down."

Cecilia smiled to herself as she gave B-4 the middle digit over her shoulder and exited.

Bobby wiped the bar top and nudged Curley with the dishrag. Curley stirred.

"Where are they?" Curley was in a punch-drunk type of stupor as he tried to wake up. "What did they do this time?"

"Time to wake. The war is over, and the roosters have been making noise for an hour."

"And we won." Curley yawned.

"With a little help from one of my daughters."

Bobby's cell phone rang. He looked at the number and answered. "Speak of the devil. Yes, JJ? The congressman?"

Bobby glanced at Curley and shrugged as he continued his phone conversation. "Jacoby? No one ever heard of him, JJ? You think what? Text me his picture. He's the male one from Nevada. I'll get back to you."

Bobby waited for the photo to arrive. *Bing.* A text message appeared. Bobby looked at the photo and then handed it to Curley.

"Take this into Lilly's and see if any of the girls recognize him."

"Then can I have scrambled eggs and rabbit?"

"Yeah. And wake up the boys. They need to restock the freezer."

Ruben stepped out of an unmarked sedan in the ATF parking lot. His shoe immediately sunk into melting tar, and he instantly felt the blistering sun and heat reflecting off the pavement. Sweat ran down his forehead as he walked into Silva's office. He grabbed a tissue off Silva's desk and mopped his face.

"Feels like hell's inferno out there."

"Different kinda hell in here." Silva motioned for Ruben to follow him to Fireball's cubicle. They grabbed chairs and sat beside him.

"There's nothing. The planes are back, one here and one in Virginia. The FBI has been interrogating the captured militia and come up with nothing, and B-4 is still at the county detention center, waiting for the preliminary meeting with the FBI prior to meeting with Judge Cynthia."

"She's another of Castillo's buddies," Silva said as he looked over Fireball's shoulder. "Great! What about Castillo's man, Jose, and his cell?"

"I pinged his cell, and he's back at the compound. The phone hasn't moved. Things in general haven't moved since late last night."

"Agent Ruben, go over to the detention center and see if you can help B-4," Silva said as he stood up.

"I hear she has a lawyer from DC, one of her sister's associates."

"Another Bobby Brown offspring?" Silva asked. "I hope she's a little more tactful than her father."

"And a whole lot richer. I Googled her. She, too, is a real piece of work."

"I hope that means she's good and her associate is a legal genius," Silva said.


Wearing a freshly laundered orange jumpsuit, B-4 sat next to a well-dressed Jennifer in a detention center conference room. Ruben entered.

"And who's this handsome brute?" Jennifer said as she checked Ruben out.

"Agent Ruben from Canada. He's my partner for the moment. His former, now murdered, partner leaked information to Castillo. We were mailed one of his hands."

"Sounds like you've had a lot of fun here." Jennifer remained focused on Ruben.

"Agent Ruben, Mrs. Jennifer Clemons-Barrows," B-4 said to the smiling agent.

"My pleasure. And she should have added 'divorced' in front of my name," Jennifer said.

"Good to meet you, Jennifer."

"Take a seat, partner. Or do you wanna continue the show for my lawyer, on your dime?"

"B-4, how are you doing?" Ruben asked, ignoring her jab.

"Before what?" Jennifer asked.

"My nickname."

Jennifer looked at B-4's boobs and smiled. "Oh, I get it ... Boobs Brown."

"Add big and Bonnie," B-4 said.

"I passed the test?"

"You're a quick study."

"Hon, you have no idea."

Jennifer's cell rang. She stood and walked away, talking in the background.

"Glad to see you made it through the night," Ruben whispered to B-4.

"Barely."

"Better watch the judge you're appearing in front of. Rumor has it she's been handpicked by Castillo."

"I need to get out of here and permanently get rid of that vermin … that cancer."

Jennifer walked back and sat down. "That was certainly interesting information from your newfound sister."

"What?"

The door opened. FBI Agent Hall entered, carrying a briefcase. Agents Shannon and Klein followed. They took seats opposite Jennifer and B-4. Ruben sized up the room and took a seat next to B-4.

"Gentlemen, I'm Jennifer Clemons-Barrows, Miss Brown's attorney. You are …?"

"Agents Hall, Shannon, and Klein," Hall said. "Thank you for meeting with us before we appear in front of Judge Cynthia."

"Anything to wrap up this matter quickly."

"Are you aware of the charges?" Hall asked.

"Yes, but go ahead, hon. I like the way your voice sounds."

"Well, uh, Miss Brown is charged with killing several Nevadans without properly identifying herself as an agent first, killing two citizens in the desert without giving them a chance to surrender, killing a citizen on a hill above a shooting range, and using an unauthorized weapon in the field."

"And you have witnesses, proof, legal justifications?"

"Yes, ma'am. And, under the authority of the Department of Justice, the full legal right to make these charges."

"Miss Brown, you have heard these charges," Jennifer asked. "Any comments?"

"All apparently trumped up at the request of a bought congressman," B-4 said angrily.

"Gentleman, can we take a small break so that I can confer with my client?"

"Sure. Want us to wait outside?"

"No, hon. We'll just step away for a moment."

Jennifer, Ruben, and B-4 got up and walked to one side of the room.

"What's this for?" B-4 asked.

"Shhh." Jennifer held her index finger over her lips. "Just act like we are talking about the charges."

"What?" B-4 whispered.

Jennifer glanced at the agents. She made sure she locked eyes with Agent Hall and politely smiled.

Inside his isolated compound, Castillo stuffed his face with huevos rancheros beside the swimming pool. Congressman Jacoby sat across from him at the glass table.

"You're an excellent chef, Mr. Castillo."

"Never had any complaints." Castillo ate the last of his salsa-covered eggs.

Jacoby's cell rang. "Yes? What? They're going to do what? Stall them. Figure out a way to cover it up." Not liking what he was hearing, Jacoby exchanged a glance with Castillo. "You can't? They want phone records? My God! What can I do?" He put his cell down. His face had turned ashen.

"The stock market took a hit?"

"No. I've been outed. I'm finished. I'm going to have to tell all."

"Tell all?" Castillo sipped on his Bloody Mary. "That'll never happen."

"If I don't, I'll be in prison for a very long time."

Castillo reached into his robe, pulled out his silenced revolver, and shot the congressman in the head. Jacoby fell face-first onto his plate.

"Shame to waste such good huevos." Castillo pushed Jacoby's head off his plate and proceeded to finish the dead man's breakfast.

Inside the detention center conference room, Jennifer, B-4, and Ruben were still huddled in the corner.

"When we get out of here, Bombay on me," Jennifer whispered.

"What?" B-4 said.

Agent Hall's cell rang. He answered and was quickly engaged in a heated discussion.

"Now." Jennifer glanced at Agent Hall. "Back to the table. It's time."

Hall continued to listen and then put his cell phone down. "That was a call from the director. It appears we may have to alter things a bit."

"I was going to discuss our responses to your charges if that's OK," Jennifer said.

"It may not be necessary, except for one." Hall shuffled papers.

"As I suspected," Jennifer said. "You want to enlighten everyone?"

Hall did not respond.

"OK, so let's get on with getting Miss Brown out of here," Jennifer said.

Hall still did not respond.

"So here's the drill," Jennifer said. "Agents do not have to identify themselves when under attack. That's in the manual, article lucky thirteen. Second, when under attack, agents can fire back with deadly force. Finally, Miss Brown did have approval to use her revolver instead of the usual standard issue."

"Correct! All just reinforced by the director," Hall said.

"Finally, there's the matter of the sniper on the hill or the citizen as has been alleged," Jennifer said. "No witness, no rifle."

"Yes." Hall looked up from a sheet of paper.

"I have a little information about that," Jennifer said. "Did you bring the empty cartridge to use as an exhibit with the judge?"

"Yes." Hall pulled a plastic container from his briefcase. "I have it here." He laid the cartridge on the table.

"Was the bullet taken from the dead agent's head?" Jennifer asked.

"Yes, sort of. It's the bullet that passed through the agent's skull."

He pulled another plastic container from his briefcase. "Here."

"Have you completed an analysis of them?" Jennifer asked.

"We intend to give them to our lab."

Jennifer reached into her purse and took out a tape measure. "I can do that for you." She removed the cartridge and bullet from the containers. "So no damage to the cartridge, and the bullet passed through his skull with little damage."

"That appears to be the case. We found the bullet in the sand."

Jennifer put the cartridge and bullet side by side. "You see together these measure 7.62 inches or 5.1 millimeters. Agree?"

Hall, Shannon, and Klein leaned in to study the cartridge, bullet, and the tape measure.

"Yes, approximately," Hall said.

"These shells are used in only one weapon, an M24, a sniper's rifle commonly used in the army," Jennifer said.

"We'll have to have our lab verify that." Hall folded his arms. "There could've easily been a rifle like that on the range."

"Could've been, but there wasn't," Jennifer said confidently. "I went there before I came here to meet with you. They keep very good records of the weapons and ammunition used at the range. Guess what. On the day in question, no such rifle and no such ammunition were used. They also have Bombay and that was used—"

"You're very convincing, Mrs. Clemons-Barrows."

"I know a lot about Bombay."

Hall gave Jennifer a "really" look.

"That's Mrs. without a Mr., for your information. Do you really want me to do this again in front of a judge and completely embarrass the FBI for bringing charges conjured up by a congressman who was acting to protect his largest donor, a noted Vegas underworld figure?"

"No ... well ..."

"Do you have my Johnnson in that briefcase of yours?" B-4 asked.

"You mean this?" Hall struggled to lift the revolver from his briefcase. "Yes."

B-4 took her revolver and looked it over. "Come back to me, baby."

"I believe we are done here," Jennifer said, ready to push back and stand. "Aren't we?"

"I think we are."

"And you will notify the judge, won't you?"

"Yes, ma'am."

"And since there are no charges forthcoming, she gets to keep Johnnson."

Hall looked at the other agents, who shrugged. "Yes, ma'am."

Jennifer, B-4, and Ruben stood.

"See you in DC?" Jennifer said.

"Yes, ma'am."

"Which casino do you recommend?" Jennifer asked as she, B-4, and Ruben walked from the conference room.

"Maybe we should pay Castillo's casino a visit," B-4 answered.

"I think we'll save him for some of your special B-4 treatment later, although mind you, I would love to take his money," Jennifer said.

# CHAPTER 32

Bobby was on the Roadkill bar phone. He listened. A smile appeared. He hung up.

"Well, Curley, that's that. Bonnie has been cleared before she even went in front of the judge."

Curley looked up from his favorite bar top slot. "You think us finding out the congressman was using a phony name at Lilly's all these years helped?"

"I'm sure JJ used that information wisely."

"What now?"

"If I were a certain underworld character and there was a wildcat on the loose, I would get out of town in a hurry. But he's not the type to turn and run like most. I'd still be worried though. You've seen her mad."

"Just like her mama."

Young B-4 ran into the Roadkill and straight to the bar. Mama was busy wiping down the bar top.

"Mama, Mama, there's a bunch of boys beating up Kevin."

"Where's the other idiots? Probably screwing off somewhere."

"They went with Curley to shoot rabbits."

"What's it all about?"

"They called you a whore. Kevin told them to get a life."

"What?"

"What should I do? Your shotgun is too heavy for me."

"Watch me." Mama threw the towel down and headed for the saloon door. "I'll show you."

On the street outside, Mama watched five teenagers taking turns beating on Kevin as he lay on the pavement. She walked toward them.

"There she is, the town whore!" one of the teenagers yelled.

"She's screwed everyone in town at least twice, according to my parents," another teenager said.

"That's why her tits are so big. Everyone plays with them," the third teenager said.

"Take that, you bastard!" the fourth teenager yelled as he kicked Kevin.

Mama walked up and went nose-to-nose with the teenagers.

"What are you gonna do about it?" the first teenager said. "There's five of us."

"After I kick the shit out of you, the rest can line up and see who's next."

"Touch me and I'll have to slug you back," the teenager said.

Mama reached over, grabbed the teenager's nose, and twisted it hard. At the same time, she kicked him in the groin and sent him screaming in pain to the ground. "All right, pricks. Who's next?"

Two teenagers walked closer. Mama grabbed them and slammed their heads together.

"How about you other two? What'll it be? A sore head, black and blue balls, or both? Come get it, 'cause you sonsabitches caught Mama on a good day."

"Thanks, Mama," Kevin said as she helped him off the ground. They watched as the teenagers scrambled away.

"Thank you for defending me. Now go inside, wash up, and get ready for rabbit stew, if your fucking brothers and Curley bring any back."

"Yes, ma'am."

"Is that how you take care of bullies, Mama?" B-4 asked.

"And those who turn on you, the boys or anyone else. There's no taming a wild mama, like your daddy found out long ago."

"You hurt him like that?"

"I was ready to, but he put me on that fucking bus."

"What would he have done to those boys?"

"They'd had his Magnum shoved up their ass and never be seen again."

"Wow!"

Castillo, now dressed in jeans, washed his bloody hands at a sink inside his isolated desert compound. His cell phone rang. He wiped his hands and picked up. "Yes? Judge Cynthia? How long did you put her away for?"

"She's been released."

"What?"

"Released by some higher powers."

Castillo started to throw his cell phone but stopped. "Higher powers from DC? I thought they didn't have any jurisdiction over you. That's why I got you appointed!"

"The FBI withdrew their complaint. Perhaps the congressman could refile."

Castillo looked at the blood in the sink. "No ... probably not."

"Why not?"

"He's indisposed right now."

"This doesn't affect the agreement we discussed, does it?"

"No. I deposited the funds yesterday. Good-bye."

Castillo put his cell phone down. "Only one solution now. Time for good old assassin Dooley to go to work."

He watched the last of the congressman's blood run down the drain.

A sleek private jet landed at McCarran International, on the twenty-seventh longest runway in the world, and taxied to a private hangar. It came to a stop and was secured by an attendant. The stairs unfolded, and Dooley, a man in his thirties with a mustache and goatee and wearing cowboy attire, boots, and a Stetson, walked down the stairs. A black SUV waited nearby. He unloaded a heavy cloth bag and a shiny suitcase from the jet cargo hatch and stuffed the baggage into the back of the SUV. Then he tapped the roof as if signaling he was good to go.

Dooley was alone. He climbed into the driver's seat and sped off. He pulled out a cell phone, looked at an app, and entered a number. "Mr. Castillo? Dooley here," he said in a dripping Texas drawl.

Now at his penthouse, Castillo sat on his white couch. He flicked his fly rod back and forth, testing it for feel and line weight. He set it down and took a sip of his margarita. "Welcome to Las Vegas. Are you on your way to my casino?"

"Yep." Dooley straightened his Stetson. "I see you wired the three mil to my account."

"As requested."

"Where's the target?"

"I have a little job for you before you come to the casino. Then we can talk about her, the target."

"Little add-ons mean more wired into the account."

"No problem. They're at my compound."

"How many problems?"

"Two, in my garage."

"Alive or dead like my last two wives?"

"Dead. They need to disappear."

"A million skins. Now!"

"Done."

"Text me the location."

"After that, come to the casino. There's another add-on when you get here."

"A complication?"

"Nothing you can't handle, according to your references." Castillo put the rod down and started texting.

"Very true. Another little task, another mil in my—"

"Done, as we speak."

"See you soon."

"Lookin' forward to meeting in person." Castillo put his cell phone down, grabbed a remote, and turned on a fly-tying video on a large flat-screen TV. Nearby on the table was an open DVD: *Fly Tying Stress Reliever*.


Silva sat in his office. Fireball walked in and plopped down.

"As you thought, sir. Judge Cynthia called an unknown number that I traced to Castillo. It happened just after the FBI withdrew their complaints against B-4."

"His web is exposed. We'll get them all. Time for a new day in Las Vegas. Speaking of that, any idea where Agents Brown and Ruben are?"

"I can ping Ruben's phone if you want."

"Don't bother. My money's on them coming back here. She'll want her badge."

"The FBI gave her the revolver."

"Figured that." Silva rested both elbows on his desk and placed his head in his hands. "We've just got to keep her from using it. I want Castillo to spend the rest of his days behind bars."

"It's hell above ground here."

"Especially with the heatwave. Prisons are under a financial crunch and curtailing ACs to cut power bills."

They high-five.

After dropping Jennifer at the airport, B-4 walked from Terrible's in slacks, a white blouse, and a short jacket, rolling her suitcase behind. Johnnson was stuck in her belt behind her. Ruben waited next to a sedan as she approached.

"Looks like your first day on the job."

"Almost is."

"You must be starved." Ruben held the trunk open for B-4.

"I'm hungry to have a piece of a certain casino owner." B-4 tossed her roller bag inside the trunk.

"Come on. Food first. Then Castillo."

"We can hit a drive-through."

"Whatever. I'm buying."

After a short ride, they went through a McDonald's. B-4 was on her cell phone. "Daddy?"

Bobby sat at the Roadkill bar, which was empty. "Bonnie. You're cleared, I heard."

"Thanks to JJ and her friend."

"The blue curaçao Bombay lady do all right?"

"Better than all right. She certainly knows her business."

"I'll say she does. She's a great lawyer too."

"Nice, but I ain't got no time for jokes. I'm going to get that sonsabitch and blow his head off."

"You got Johnnson back?"

"Yes, and I'm itching to use him."

"My advice? Castillo will make a mistake. Don't you make one by being overzealous."

"Overzealous? I can't wait."

Jennifer strutted into the Roadkill.

"Gotta go!" Bobby said. "The blue lady just made a house call."

"She's there already?"

"Amazing what a private jet and rental cars can do these days."

"Say hi for me and thank her."

"If I have time."

"Daddy!"

Ruben looked at B-4. "He's right, you know. Castillo will make a mistake."

"You were listening?"

"Best ears in Quebec."

Ruben grabbed their order and passed the bag to B-4 just as his cell phone rang. He answered. "Yes, sir. Today? I'll inform Agent Silva."

Ruben pulled into traffic and continued talking. "Yes. She's out and in the car with me. Yes, she is."

He hung up and stuffed his cell phone back into his breast pocket. "Well, well. According to my Canadian connections, looks like the shipment we were told was coming yesterday is arriving today."

"They musta thought the coast was clear. Want your burger?"

"Let me tell Agent Silva first." Ruben took out his cell phone. With one hand on the steering wheel, he pressed the speed dial with the other. "Sir, that shipment of explosives? It's arriving late this afternoon."

"You gotta a more precise. ETA?" Silva replied.

"In three hours."

"Swing by headquarters."

"On our way."

B-4 was already eating a burger. She pulled out another from the bag and handed it to Ruben. "Never dull, this ATF stuff," she said.

"Never gets old."

# CHAPTER 33

Ruben and B-4 exited their sedan in the ATF parking lot, carrying their takeout. Silva sat at his desk on the phone. He motioned for B-4 and Ruben to enter. They grabbed a couple of chairs and continued eating their burgers.

Silva finished his call.

"Gotta a burger for you, sir."

"Glad you're back, Agent Brown." Silva waved off the burger. "Been pretty dull without you and Johnnson."

"Been keeping the body count as low as I can, sir."

"Detention center time helped," Silva said.

Ruben, with a full mouth, nodded and smiled.

"Time to get back in the game," B-4 said. "How are we going to catch Castillo with his hand in the cookie jar? There's only the two of us and you."

"Now that the desert incident is behind us, I have Agent Schietz on her way back to Vegas. Agents Martin's and Garcia's suspensions have been lifted. With them and you guys, we will confiscate the explosives and arrest Mr. Castillo."

"Want me to check in with CBA?" Ruben asked.

"I already called Canada Border Services in Quebec, and they assured me their information's correct."

"You will leave him to me, won't you?" B-4 asked.

"And what will you do?" Silva said.

"I owe him one for my father, the Battle Mountain Boys, and Agent Smith. And a big one just for me."

"Remember, we catch and contain, not kill," Silva said. "This gangster's gonna spend the rest of his life in prison, right, Brown?"

"I will do my best, sir."

"Your best?" Silva said. "Do better than your best, because your best track record isn't that great."

"Swear I will do better."

"Your future career depends on it. Agent, civilian, or behind bars—it's your choice." Silva tossed B-4's badge in her direction.

The office door opened, and FBI Agents Hall, Shannon, and Klein walked in.

"What did I do this time?"

"Relax, Brown," Hall said. "We have another problem. It seems the congressman has disappeared. You don't know anything about that, do you?"

"She hasn't been out of my sight since we left the detention center," Ruben said.

"We know he left DC late last night and arrived here this morning," Hall said.

"Where did he go when he got here?" Silva asked.

"That we don't know," Hall said. "Our technical people have been unable to track him through his cell. He might have used a burner."

"Maybe he didn't want to be found," B-4 said.

"You don't have the best," Silva said. "We do." He yelled, "Fireball!"

"Who's Fireball?" Hall asked.

"You'll see shortly," Silva said.

"You have something for me?" Fireball peeked his head into Silva's office.

"The FBI can't find Congressman Jacoby," Silva said.

"He doesn't have a cell phone," Hall said.

"Anything else?" Fireball said.

"We've been told he has a pacemaker," Hall said.

"Where's it from?" Fireball asked.

"Renown Hospital up north in Reno," Hall said as he looked in a small notebook.

"Thanks. That's all I need." Fireball left.

"Your father, he went back to Battle Mountain?" Hall asked B-4.

"Your fellow agents can verify that. They found him and his friends in the desert after they were attacked by Castillo's men," Silva said.

"I'll check and make sure he was gone when the congressman arrived," Hall said.

"You don't think he has—" B-4 started.

"Agent Brown, we are checking everything," Hall interrupted. "The congressman is very close to the president. We want to leave no stone unturned."

"What about Castillo?" B-4 asked. "He's got a load of explosives coming into Vegas in a couple of hours. Why don't you help us with that?"

"We have no authorization to deal with Mr. Castillo," Hall said. "Sounds like he's your issue, not ours."

Fireball walked into the office, holding a piece of paper. "There is a faint signal coming from the congressman's pacemaker, sir."

"Got a location?" Silva asked.

"Mr. Castillo's compound, east of here."

"I told you he was the best."

"Thank you." Hall took the piece of paper from Fireball. "Let's go."

"Can I go with you? Representing ATF, of course," B-4 asked.

"You can follow us if you like," Hall said.

"Sir?" B-4 said, looking at Silva.

"Go. We'll still have time to get the explosives." Silva waved her out with the back of his hand.

"Thank you, sir."

"And ...?"

"I know. Catch and contain."

At Castillo's isolated desert compound, Dooley loaded the dead congressman's body into the back of the black SUV. He shut the door and drove out of the compound. Meanwhile, on the freeway heading east, the FBI moved at top speed in an SUV with a flashing red light. They were followed closely by B-4 and Ruben in an unmarked ATF sedan with a flashing portable red light on the roof. They took an off-ramp, still heading east, and accelerated to top speed through the desert.

As they approached Castillo's compound, they turned off their flashing lights, slowed, and entered through the open gates. They pulled their vehicles to a stop inside the compound. The agents jumped out of their vehicles with weapons drawn and began searching the living quarters, a private office, and a casita, walking in tandem, like precision drill teams, from room to room, one agent covering the other as they entered.

"Not a bad place to hang out while your minions do your dirty work," B-4 said to Ruben after the FBI had cleared the place.

"Nothing looks out of place," Ruben said. "Nothing's packed, suggesting he hasn't run."

"Let's check the garage, see what the FBI have found, if anything," B-4 said.

The FBI agents surveyed the large garage with four automatic doors that opened into the courtyard on one side and the desert on the other. Inside were several ATVs, a small boat, and water skis. It smelled of bleach, and there were wet stains all over the floor.

"Something was here, but it's been diluted by a chemical of some sort," Hall said.

Ruben walked to a shelf and took down a half-full container of bleach that was sitting next to two empty ones. He held it up. "Well, if the congressman's body was here, getting a blood sample's gonna be very difficult."

Ruben's cell phone rang. "Fireball?"

Fireball sat in his cubicle, studying his computer monitor. "The congressman's pacemaker is on the move and is now at Lake Mead. It hasn't moved for a few minutes."

"You sure about that?"

"Very. It hasn't budged a microinch."

Hall, Shannon, Klein, and B-4 waited for Ruben to speak. "The congressman's at Lake Mead. Fireball said his signal hasn't moved for a couple of minutes."

"You know the way?" Hall asked.

Ruben nodded.

"You lead. We'll follow."

Both vehicles had their red roof lights flashing as they flew past a sign for Hoover Dam at top speed. As they rolled, B-4 was on her cell phone.

"Fireball, we're heading to Lake Mead."

"Big lake. More than a hundred miles long," Fireball said.

"Heading to the west side, near the houseboats."

"Got it," Fireball said.

The two vehicles ran Boulder City traffic signals as cars pulled aside. They turned onto the road that led to Lake Mead. As they flew down a hill, they unknowingly passed Dooley's black SUV as it headed up the hill.

Almost to the lake, they turned again and headed toward the docked houseboats. They jumped out of their cars and started the search, walking from one boat to the next. B-4 spotted Jose floating face down.

"Over there. We've got a floater."

Klein spotted the congressman's body floating face up. "Got another here."

"That's the congressman," Hall said. "Who's the other guy?"

Agent Shannon and B-4 pulled Jose's body in and turned him over. "He's one of Castillo's henchmen," B-4 said.

"Someone didn't like either one of them," Hall said.

"We'll leave the details to you, Agent Hall," Ruben said. "We've got to get back and stop an explosives delivery."

"And one very bad guy," B-4 said.


Castillo pushed a pair of black framed glasses back up onto the bridge of his nose as he attempted to tie a fly. He looped a fine piece of line around the hook and started to pull it tight. The hook slipped out of the small vice clamped to a table and fell into the plush carpeting of his casino suite.

Castillo sat back on his white couch and stared at the open fly-tying kit on a table. "Stress reliever my ass." He grabbed a full margarita glass off the table and slugged it back. "Now that's what I call a stress reliever."

The suite elevator door opened, and Dooley walked in.

"Mission accomplished?"

"Of course. Two bodies are gone. Did a little garage cleaning for you. No extra charge for the bleach."

"I am beginning to believe you are more than worth your fee."

"Thank you. Maybe I could use you as a reference."

They both chuckled.

"What about the other add-on?" Dooley asked.

"In a bit. There's gonna be a delivery downstairs of some product. Let's just say it needs to get to some friends in groups that don't believe in the government. I need someone to make sure it is received."

"What about your cowboys?"

"Unfortunately, I'm a little short-handed right now due to the work of a damn rookie agent and her father."

"She's the add-on?"

"She's the main target. But first I need you to make sure the delivery is safely inside my casino. Then you are free to go after her."

"And where will I find this little woman?"

"If my intuition is right, she will have heard about the delivery and try to stop it. You'll get to see her up close and personal. She's the real prize."

Castillo grabbed another margarita off the table and gulped it down. "I care about the explosives, but her I need dead like yesterday."

"That's what you are paying me the big bucks for. Think I'll relax a little and try my luck downstairs, unless you want me to show you how to tie one of those little devils. Back home we just use mosquitoes on the end of a fly line."

Castillo got up and walked to a desk. He pulled a drawer open and took out a stack of chips. "Here. Take these On the house. Don't worry about money. With what I have here and at home, I can live anywhere and pay the rest of your fee ten times over. And the fly-fishing … I may take up stamp collecting instead."

Dooley took the stack of $1,000 chips. "Good to know. Maybe I'll put a dent in your savings."

"Take your best shot." Castillo pulled out another stack of chips and handed it to Dooley. "Here. I'll even help you a bit more."

# CHAPTER 34

"They should be here momentarily," Silva said to Ruben and B-4 as they impatiently waited in his office for the FBI agents to arrive.

The door opened, and Schietz, Martin, and Garcia walked in and grabbed chairs.

"B-4! You're out!" Schietz lightly punched B-4's arm. "Hear you've been busy adding notches to your belt."

"Is that what you call it? Missed you too."

"I love San Francisco," Schietz said.

"Where I got my start."

"OK, OK. Old home week is over," Silva said. "The delivery from Canada is due in an hour. We need to get set up. Ruben, Martin, and Garcia, you stake out the delivery dock. Schietz and Brown, go inside and watch security."

"And that bastard Castillo—" B-4 started.

"Agent Brown, for the last time, if you see him, do not shoot him. Keep your powder dry! Got it?"

"I know, I know. Rookie mistakes. But they sure felt good."

"How about making me feel good this time? Or maybe you should stay behind."

"Don't worry. I learned a long time ago about controlling myself. Nothing like a big rattler to teach patience."

Mama and young B-4 were on a day hike in the hills near Battle Mountain. It was just another excursion into the desert, looking for gems and arrowheads.

"If you see anything shiny, pick the fucking thing up and show it to me. If it looks like the head off an arrow, show it to me. Other than that, don't step in any fucking coyote shit."

"Yes, Mama. What about if it rattles?"

"What?" Mama's eyes locked on a big rattlesnake, its tail shaking in the hot breeze. "That's a fucking rattlesnake, a big one. Stop! Don't move and don't be scared. They smell scared."

"Will it hurt me, Mama?" Young B-4 looked at the large rattlesnake mere inches from her right foot.

"Stop talking. Just stay still. Real fucking still. One little move, a goddamn wiggle, and it will strike."

"But—"

"Don't move. It'll figure out you are no threat and just slither on its way after a fucking mouse."

"Yes, Mama. How long?"

"As long as it takes."

"I have to pee bad."

"Goddammit! Stay still."

"I don't think I can hold it."

"Think about riding a fucking horse. Think about when Curley paddled your backside when you broke his favorite slot. Think about—"

The rattlesnake lowered its head and began to slither off.

"Look, Mama. It's moving away. Now can I pee?"

"Yes, and I think I'll join you." Mama quickly unbuttoned her jeans.

Dooley played craps and had been keeping an eye on the casino's front doors when B-4 and Schietz entered. He threw the dice down and motioned to the dealer.

"Can you take care of this for me?" He pushed his chips forward.

"Certainly, sir."

Dooley walked toward the parking garage, took an exit outside, and headed for the delivery dock. He saw Ruben, Martin, and Garcia settling into strategic positions. He quickly disappeared back inside and went over to the elevator. He exited into Castillo's casino suite. Castillo glanced up from his white couch as he savored a margarita. Dooley noticed three partially tied flies strewn across a nearby table.

"It's time to go after some real big fish," Dooley said in his Texas drawl.

"You have everything under control?"

"There are several agents in the casino and in the garage, waiting for the delivery." Dooley picked up one of the flies.

"Maybe I should call off the delivery."

"Is that possible? Do you even have a number?"

"No. My man Jose handled that. Did you see her?"

"Hard to know. Don't think so."

The elevator opened, and a tech rushed in. "Sir. Turn on the television now."

Castillo snapped up a remote and turned on the large flat screen. A news reporter stood in front of several houseboats at Lake Mead.

"This is the tragic end of the long career of one of Nevada's most beloved members of Congress. He was apparently murdered and dumped in Lake Mead. They found his body wedged between a couple of houseboats."

Castillo turned off the television. "You said …" he began but then stopped and motioned for the tech to leave. As the doors closed, Castillo continued, "You dumped them in Lake Mead?"

"Yep. The horse is out of the barn. Maybe it's time for you to exit the casino and Vegas before they bust the delivery."

"Not yet."

"Those agents are more than your men can handle."

"Go down there and deal with them. I heard you can take down a whole platoon."

"I can and have, but I'm thinking of your safety," Dooley picked up one of the half-tied flies and studied it. "Pretty good start. Feather pattern needs a bit of work if you want to catch the big ones."

"Always want to get the big ones."

"I suggest we leave now. We'll get on my private jet and hit Mexico or the Caribbean, someplace warm and far away, someplace you can use these little buggers."

"Maybe we can finish the feather pattern on the flight."

"Exactly what I was thinking. So …?"

"Probably a good idea. But I need to go by the compound first. I have enough money and jewels to buy an island stashed there."

"Come on, cowpoke. Let's get out of here. Now!"

Castillo jumped up and followed Dooley. He stopped and took one last look at the suite. "One second." He walked back to his executive-sized desk and grabbed his silenced revolver from a drawer. "Let's go."

Dooley's eyebrows raised as he glanced at Castillo's pistol. "That the bad boy you used on the congressman?"

"Yep."

"Let me get rid of it so there's no connection." Dooley held out one hand.

"I really don't want to let go of it. It's been my best friend for decades."

"And a connection to the congressman's murder and who knows how many others?"

"You sound like a cop," Castillo said as the elevator moved downward.

"You don't get to live as long as I have in this business without being very careful. Let me have it."

Castillo handed Dooley the silenced revolver just before the elevator door opened. They walked through a side door marked "Casino Employees Only" and into a private parking area. Just as Dooley and Castillo disappeared, Schietz and B-4 entered and walked through the casino.

"Seems like just yesterday we were in the Bellagio," Schietz said.

"It almost was. Time to find my favorite gangster, Mr. Castillo."

"Remember …"

"I know, no killing. But I can break his legs, maybe his fingers one by one."

They walked up to a male security guard.

"We need to talk to the owner, Mr. Castillo," B-4 said.

"Ma'am, he doesn't visit with customers."

"He'll visit with me." B-4 flashed her badge. Schietz followed.

"Let me check."

He turned away from B-4 and talked into his shoulder mic. He turned back to B-4. "Ma'am, I think he's left for the day."

"Any way we can verify that? It's very important."

"Stay here. I'll check."

The security guard disappeared through a door marked "Casino Employees Only." Schietz and B-4 surveyed the casino. The place was humming. Slot bells rang with tunes of big payouts. People jostled for spots as they cheered and crowded around betting tables.

"You miss this?" B-4 asked.

"I was only gone a couple of days," Schietz said. "No. I love Frisco. After this is over, I hope I get reassigned there. What about you?"

"I've lived in Nevada all my life. It kinda grows on you."

"Maybe a change of scenery would be good? San Francisco?"

"After all the stories Daddy has told me about his days there, I'll be run out of town because I'm his daughter."

The door opened and the male security reappeared. "He's nowhere in sight. We checked all the cameras, including his suite."

"Interesting," B-4 said.

The security guard touched his earpiece and listened. "Whoops! Gotta go outside. Something's going down."

"Come on. The delivery," Schietz said as she pulled on B-4's arm.

"You go ahead. I've got to use the ladies room."

"See you outside." Schietz ran toward the garage exit.

B-4 glanced around and then walked quickly out the front door and hailed a cab. One pulled up and she climbed inside.

"Toward Hoover Dam. I'm in a hurry."

The cab flew out of the casino property. B-4 glanced back as she talked to herself. "That's the only place you would go, home, away from the action, and then claim your innocence."

"Ma'am?" the female driver said.

"Nothing. Just drive."

The cab sped down the freeway, past a sign for Boulder City and then another for Hoover Dam minutes later.

"Turn's coming!" B-4 yelled.

As they approached the off-ramp leading to Castillo's compound, B-4 tapped the driver on the shoulder. "Take the ramp and head east."

The cab sped along the road leading to Castillo's compound. As they approached the entrance, B-4 yelled, "Stop over there, near the wall!"

"Don't need a hearing aide," the taxi driver said as she slowed the cab down and brought it to a stop twenty yards from the compound wall.

B-4 tossed a twenty over the seat and jumped out.

The cab driver looked at the twenty-dollar bill sitting on the front seat beside her. "Twenty? Really?"

Inside ATF headquarters, Silva pounded on his desk as he yelled into a cell phone, "She's disappeared? We got the putty, but she's gone? Damn! She's after Castillo! I know it." He looked in the direction of Fireball's cubicle and yelled, "Fireball, where's Brown?"

A rapid series of keyboard clicks sounded from Fireball's cubicle. Then silence. Fireball yelled, "Her phone is at Castillo's compound!"

Silva stared at his cell phone. "Goddammit! Go get her, everyone. Stop her!"

The sun had just set. A saguaro cactus appeared out of place as it cast long fingerlike shadows over the desert between Castillo's isolated compound and the city far away. B-4 took Johnnson from her backside, crouched, and moved slowly toward the tall wall surrounding the compound.

As she moved toward the open gate, she saw a black SUV, lights on and running, parked in a circular driveway. She waited a moment and then moved quickly inside, attempting to remain unseen. She peered through a window and saw Dooley and Castillo at a wall safe.

Castillo pulled bundles of cash from the safe and filled a suitcase held by Dooley. Then Castillo pulled out a tray with piles of diamond necklaces and jewels and dumped the contents on top of the cash.

"Like I said, enough to buy an island."

"Maybe even a city in Texas."

B-4 moved inside and confronted the men. "Agent Brown, ATF. You're both under arrest."

Dooley and Castillo turned slowly to face her. B-4 had Johnnson pointed at them with one hand and flashed her badge with the other.

"You!" Castillo said.

"Yes, me, the rookie. I finally have you exactly where I want you."

"If this is between the two of you …" Dooley drawled.

"Who are you?" B-4 asked.

"Kill her!" Castillo yelled. "That's what I paid you for!"

"It appears she has the drop on us." Dooley nodded at Johnnson. "Clearly a superior weapon. The question is whether she can use it or not."

"That, Mr. Whoever You Are, is something you don't want to find out," B-4 said.

"Kill her!" Castillo yelled again. "Now!"

"I don't think she wants to kill me. It's you she's after. Why not let me just slip away and you can do whatever it is you want to do with him?"

"Looks like you are as dirty as he is… I mean, holding his bag," B-4 said.

Dooley threw the suitcase at B-4, knocking her down, and grabbed Johnnson from her. He pointed it at her.

"Now, now, Miss ATF Agent," Dooley drawled. "You raise your hands."

"Give me my revolver," Castillo said. "I'm gonna do what should have been done already."

"That pea shooter? I threw it out on the way."

"Well, then, give me her revolver so I can get rid of her once and for all, and then we can be on our way." Castillo walked toward Dooley with one hand out.

They heard the sound of approaching sirens in the distance.

"The cops are coming! Do her. Let's go!"

"Actually." Dooley carefully handed Johnnson to B-4. "I think this is hers."

"What?" Castillo stepped back.

"Agent Brown, what would Mama do?" Dooley asked a surprised B-4.

"Mama … my mama?" a shocked B-4 said.

"Yep." Dooley's drawl was gone.

"Why?" B-4 asked still stunned. "She'd never let him live."

Dooley pulled out another revolver from his coat and shot Castillo between the eyes. "That's what I thought. Shall we?"

Shocked, B-4 followed Dooley as he carried the suitcase full of money and jewels out the open front door and toward the garage. "Hurry!"

"Yes, but …" A confused B-4 ran behind him.

Inside the garage, Dooley jumped into an ATV that had keys in the ignition. "Open the door leading into the desert and hop in."

B-4 threw the door open and jumped into the ATV. Dooley fired up the machine and drove them outside into the desert.

As their ATV roared through the sage, away from the compound, the circular driveway filled with police cars and ATF vehicles with lights flashing and sirens blaring.

B-4 held on for dear life as the ATV jumped small humps at full speed and rumbled over top of the tumbleweeds

Ruben and Schietz stood in an open doorway, watching the ATV fade into the distance.

"Her?" Ruben said as he watched them disappear in a cloud of dust and sand.

"Gotta be," Schietz said. "She ain't here."

A uniformed officer walked up to them and said, "The owner has been shot once between the eyes. It looks like his safe was burgled."

"Was the deceased's head still intact?" Ruben asked.

"Why… yes," the officer said, confused by the question.

"Guess she didn't use Johnnson," Ruben said.

"Must've been a burglary gone bad," Schietz said.

"I wonder where B-4 is," Ruben asked.

The only signs of B-4 and Dooley had vanished as the clouds of dust faded.

Across the dark desert, the ATV rumbled toward the Vegas city lights. Dooley, with no drawl, said, "If I drop you off here, you can find your way, can't you?"

"Yes, but … who are you?" B-4 gave Dooley a double-take. "You know my mama?"

Dooley stopped the ATV. "Go on … climb off. Take this suitcase. Donate it to someone in need … maybe in Battle Mountain."

"All right." B-4 took Johnnson out. "Who are you?"

Dooley took off the mustache and the rest of his disguise to become Joseph Benneschott.

"Me? I'm your guardian angel." Benneschott revved the engine. "See you next time. And your mama is my …" The last part of his mumbled sentence was inaudible as he took off.

B-4 watched in stunned silence. She tried to force the words out. "Your what?" B-4 said as she stood off-kilter, holding Johnnson at her side.

Benneschott disappeared over a hill. Suddenly it was eerily quiet.

"Holy shit," B-4 said too herself. "Holy fucking shit!"